Challenge
in the
Golden State

A Dave and Katie Adventure

To Gail,
Enjoy the
adventure!
Kit
Drew

Kit and Drew Coons

Challenge
in the
Golden State

A Dave and Katie Adventure

Kit and Drew Coons

Challenge *in the* Golden State

© 2020 Kit and Drew Coons

ISBN: 978-1-7326256-4-8

Library of Congress Control Number: 2020909708

Illustrations by Julie Sullivan (MerakiLifeDesigns.com)

First Edition

 Printed in the United States

24 23 22 21

20   1 2 3 4 5

To all those who love deeply enough to sacrifice for the good of others. Special dedication to Marnie Rasche, who was always a California girl at heart and loved a good mystery.

Other Books by Kit and Drew Coons

Challenge Series of Novels

Challenge for Two

Challenge Down Under

Challenge in Mobile

Jeremy's Challenge

Science Fiction Novel

The Ambassadors

Life-skills Books

More Than Ordinary Wisdom

More Than Ordinary Faith

More Than Ordinary Choices

More Than Ordinary Challenges

More Than Ordinary Marriage

More Than Ordinary Abundance

Acknowledgments

This novel would not be possible without professional editing and proofreading by Jayna Richardson. The cover and all the artwork is by Julie Sullivan. We also thank our reviewer Leslie Mercer, who read the manuscript and made valuable suggestions. Mary Potuznik provided additional insights.

We had visited California many times, even lived there. Only through attending the weddings of Kit's nieces did we discover the diversity of the lower Russian River area of Sonoma County. There spectacular ocean views, redwoods in profusion, and picturesque wine vineyards co-exist within an easy thirty-minute drive. Combine those with funky and free-spirited unincorporated towns and we found a unique and eclectic setting for Dave and Katie's next adventure. We would like to thank the Baughman family—Eric, Heide, Jane, and Paul—who introduced us to Sonoma County of California and allowed us to stay at their ranch and vineyard while doing research.

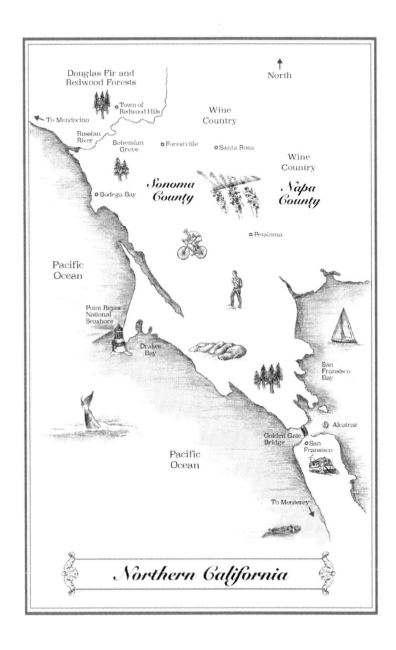

Northern California

Principal Characters

<u>California</u>

Dave and Katie Parker • sixties-aged couple from Mobile, Alabama

Missy Clark • teenager in Redwood Hills

Harley Forbes • associate of Missy

Darla Solsen • Missy's mother

Sheriff Mike Billingsly • sergeant in charge of the local office of Sonoma County

Deputy Devin Conrad • deputy reporting to Billingsly

Tara Grabowski • footloose young woman in Redwood Hills

Jeff Moynihan • widower and bicycle store proprietor in Redwood Hills

Samantha Moynihan (Sam) • Jeff's daughter, age nineteen months

Dr. Peter Lomax • physician in Redwood Hills

Cecil Harbanger • pharmacist in Redwood Hills

Judge Tatum • Sonoma County jurist

Sergeant Gomez Hernandez • California state trooper

<u>Melbourne, Australia</u>

Denyse Larkin Parker • Jeremy's wife and Dave and Katie's daughter-in-law

Katelyn Parker • Denyse and Jeremy's daughter, nearly five years old

Dingo and Beatrice Larkin • Denyse's parents

Trevor Larkin • Denyse's younger brother

Lena Larkin • Trevor's Ukrainian wife

Svetlana Travnikov (Sveta) • Lena's sister, age fifteen

Oleksandra Travnikov (Sandra) • Lena's sister, age seventeen

Vlady Larkin • Trevor and Lena's son, age five

Maria Larkin • Trevor and Lena's daughter, age six months

Hogan • Aussie friend of Dingo's

Honorable Judge Wilma Peabody • inferior court judge in Melbourne

Mobile, Alabama

Jeremy Parker • Dave and Katie's son and Denyse's husband

Anthony Marshall • summer paid intern

Dorothy Goldsmith • secretary/receptionist at Parker and Company Accounting

Old Yeller • Dave and Katie's cat from Minnesota

Ripper • Jeremy's Labrador retriever

Herschel and Candace Johnson • accountant (Herschel) and homemaker (Candace)

Caleb and Jordan Fogle • Dave and Katie's neighbors and a high school principal (Caleb)

Prologue

Missy felt out of place. A throbbing beat of rap music made thinking difficult. The air reeked of tobacco smoke and alcohol. Girls her age and younger were wearing heavy makeup and dressed in provocative, body-highlighting manners.

Why did I come? she asked herself. *Because everybody already thinks you're a grade-grabber. Because you're nearly seventeen now and want more in life than studying and academics. This experience can help prepare you for college life.*

Three women in their early twenties had rented a cabin secluded among second-growth redwoods to live in and host parties. Events there had become infamous among local teenagers. Anybody who expected to be somebody aspired to an invitation. That is, those who waited for an invitation. Most just showed up on Saturday nights. Nearly always a rowdy party greeted them.

Missy meandered through kids trying to affirm their maturity by acting like irresponsible adults. *Mom would freak out if she knew I had come here.* She felt a surge of anger. *All Mom cares about is me getting A's and into Stanford. She should have done that herself if it was so important to her.* Somebody put a can of cold beer in Missy's hand. She smelled a sour odor and tried a sip. The beer tasted worse than it smelled. She set the can aside the first moment she judged others wouldn't notice.

A girl nearby lay on the floor passionately kissing a man—a college student. *That's Beth, the girl who invited me,* Missy realized. *Mom thinks we're at Beth's house making s'mores and having a slumber party. Technically, I guess I am with Beth.*

Missy joined a group of familiar kids from her high school. She saw a girl take a drag on a tightly rolled piece of paper and pass it to the boy beside her. *That's marijuana,* she thought as the joint passed from hand to hand around the circle. When the joint reached Missy, she shook her head and put her hands behind her back.

"What's the matter? Afraid of having some fun?" a slurred male voice asked.

"Beth invited her. Said we needed to include a brain to prove we're open-minded," a girl explained.

The guy extended his hand with the smoldering joint. "Come on. Don't be afraid."

When Missy refused to accept the joint, another voice said, "She thinks our company will corrupt her. She's too goody-

goody to party with us." The circle of kids laughed and walked away, leaving Missy standing alone.

You don't know anything about me, Missy retorted in her head. *Or do they? I can't go home, though. Mom would wonder what happened at Beth's.* She retreated to a corner where she pretended to look at a fashion magazine from a coffee table.

A different male voice startled her. "You'd seem good-looking if you weren't so near to me."

Missy looked up from the magazine to see a guy in his mid-twenties with unkempt shoulder-length black hair and heavy stubble on his chin. He had apparently dressed to exhibit a scruffy persona. She felt relief to have someone paying attention to her. She answered with the only thing she could think of. "So you think you're good-looking?"

The guy shrugged. "Having a good time?"

"Not very," Missy acknowledged.

"Then try this." He extended a small white pill in an open palm. "This is safe. Prescribed by a doctor. No alcohol breath, hangover, or odor of pot." He showed her a prescription bottle with someone's name she didn't know. Missy glanced to where the circle of marijuana tokers had reconvened without her. *I'll show them.* She reached out, took the pill, and swallowed it.

"I'm Harley. What's your name?" her benefactor asked.

Six burly Australians sat on painted steel folding chairs around a wooden oil-stained table. A florescent light fixture hung low, making the table an island of illumination in the dark auto body shop. All the men drank liquor as they played poker. Three also smoked cigars. A tap on the door drew their attention.

Hogan, the largest man and owner of the shop bellowed, "Come in!"

Another knock answered him. "Blimey! Why won't the bugger come in?" Hogan stalked over and jerked open the door. Outside he saw a tall, soft-looking young man with a pale complexion. He had a burn scar under one eye. "Larkin, what are you doin' here?" the big man demanded.

"I've come to pay back the eight hundred fifty-four dollars I took from you several years ago."

"Alright. Let's see it," responded one of the men still at the table.

"No, wait," Hogan ordered. He spoke to the young man. "Some Yanks came asking about you a coupla years ago. Never there was a finer lady than Mrs. Parker. She told us your tricks, planting tells and all."

Hogan turned to address the table. "This is my mate Dingo's boy, Trevor. He's a sharpie, but he didn't cheat us. He just outsmarted and outplayed us."

Hogan faced Trevor again. "We won't take the money back."

Trevor blinked and swallowed. He looked toward the table. "Then do you mind if I sit in on a few hands?"

The men looked at each other. One of them nodded to Hogan. "Mind you, we're onto your tricks," Hogan told Trevor as he held the door wider and stepped back for the young man to enter.

"I know you are," Trevor answered and approached the table.

The men shifted to make room. One of the men pulled up a chair for Trevor to sit. "Deal him in," said Hogan.

The game continued, Trevor folding on most hands. The talk revolved around the worn topics of sports and women. The regular players had nothing new to say. For some variety, Hogan looked at Trevor. "So mate, what have you been up to?"

"I'm just trying to stay out of jail, Hogan."

"The lock up? Just for being a card sharpie?"

Trevor laughed and answered, "I wish." Then he added, "No, I conned the wrong bloke over in New Zealand. He blackmailed me into money laundering and paying off drug mules. Do you remember my sister, Denyse?"

"Yeeah. I went to her wedding. We had a bit of a dust up with your father and his brothers." Hogan indicated the other seated men and showed a clenched fist. A couple of the men chuckled or nodded.

"I heard about that. Anyway, Denyse's in-laws—the Parkers you had mentioned earlier—located my wife Lena in New Zealand and brought her to Oz. Then they found me being forced to work for a gangster."

"Dingo told me a bit about that. Did the Parkers really help arrange a plea bargain parole in return for your cooperation with the coppers?"

"That's right. The Kiwis are letting me serve my parole here in Melbourne. But if I violate probation by doing any hustling or getting arrested for any reason, then my parole is revoked. I go back to New Zealand to serve the full sentence of ten years."

Trevor having a prison sentence hanging over him raised his status among the men with whom he sat. Hogan pointed at Trevor and told the other card players, "Dingo told me this lad and his young wife helped to break up an extortion racket and a human trafficking ring."

Trevor nodded. "Not just Lena and me though. My dad and sister, even my mum, all played a role."

"You blokes ought to read Dingo's book, *The Right Fight*. I'm not much for readin' myself. But it's right entertaining." Hogan looked back at Trevor. "Didn't you help your father write that?"

Trevor smiled and laid his cards face down to fold. "I did. But all the stories are my dad's. I just helped to make them printable." Knowing Dingo, all the men laughed.

Hogan continued, "Dingo used to work for me here at the shop. Now he just talks for a livin'. Trevor 'ere 'as started writin' novels. He's been takin' some uni classes too." Hogan scooped up Trevor's discarded cards. "And the police have been talkin' him up. 'Cause his novels educate people about hustles and con games."

Hogan shuffled the cards, preparing for another deal, and looked directly at Trevor. "I'm not in any of those books, am I now?"

Trevor shook his head but answered, "Sure thing. I made you the handsome detective who gets all the women." All the men roared, Hogan the loudest.

Trevor stood up to leave.

"Where you going, mate? We're enjoying your company," said one of the men.

"You're enjoying taking my money. You guys *have* learned a lot. I'm cleaned out. I'd better go home. I'll be in big trouble with my wife already." The men laughed again.

Trevor waved goodbye and let himself out. Immediately, Hogan asked, "How much did you each take off him?" The men tallied up to count $854. "Booger, the sharpie's tricked us again."

"You made a C?" Missy's mother shouted. "You'll never get into Stanford with C's."

"Mom, it was just a pop quiz. I had that paper on the pros and cons of altruism to finish. That C isn't bad when you consider that I hadn't had time to read the assignment."

"You've got to try harder, Missy. I'm sacrificing everything to help you realize your potential. The least I could expect is a little effort on your part."

Missy's mother left her seated at her textbook-piled desk. Missy despaired, *What does Mom expect? I'm taking two college-credit classes and three college-prep honors classes. She just wants to be able to brag to her friends about me.*

Missy's thoughts went back to the party a week earlier. The white pill offered by Harley had relaxed her, taken away her anxiety. The pill allowed her to enjoy the party, to be happy. *Mom has some pills in the medicine cabinet left over from her broken arm. The doctor wouldn't have prescribed them if they weren't safe. Mom will never miss just one.*

Chapter One

Two years later

* * *

A tall, handsome young mother with a long chocolate-brown ponytail descended the steps of a thirty-foot type C recreational vehicle. She carried an almost five-year-old girl from the rented RV. The mother's stomach showed early third term pregnancy.

"I'm so glad to get out and stretch my legs."

"I should have warned you," agreed her mother-in-law, Katie Parker. "Your husband is just like his father in some respects." She lowered her voice to mimic her husband, Dave, "There's nothing worth seeing in between Alabama and Arizona."

Denyse laughed and put her daughter, Katelyn, down to walk. "You mean you should have warned me before I married your son?"

The child looked up. "What has daddy done wrong?"

Katie took her granddaughter's hand as a car passed. "Jeremy hasn't done anything wrong, honey. It's just that your granddaddy and your father took turns driving nearly 2,000 miles in two days with hardly a stop. Your mom are I are worn out from riding."

Denyse nodded agreement. "At least the RV's air conditioner worked well. July in New Mexico reminded me of the outback during summer back in Australia."

Dave Parker came out of the RV behind them. "You both talk like abused women."

"It's noble of you to admit we've been abused," returned Katie.

Her quip didn't dampen his enthusiasm. "Okay. Is everybody ready to see the Grand Canyon?"

"All I want to see is a toilet that isn't rocking," answered Katie.

Jeremy joined them from the driver's side door of the RV. "Mom, don't forget that Denyse, Katelyn, and I only have eight days of vacation to see Arizona, Nevada, *and* Southern California. After we leave, you and Dad can relax by yourselves."

"We've already spent two days traveling," Dave added. "That leaves only six days to show you three all the sights. Let's go! The Grand Canyon is a national park famous all over the world. Katelyn will always remember being here."

"Aagh! Damn this thing." An athletic-looking woman in her early thirties stepped back from where her bicycle with a flat lay on the ground beside the road. She couldn't get the new tube to fit under the tire. Edges kept protruding to prevent seal of the outer tire to the wheel rim. *I'll never get this right,* she thought. *Maybe that bike shop, Freedom Road, would help me.* She picked up the bicycle—an older mountain bike—and started walking two miles to the center of Redwood Hills, a town nestled in second-growth redwood forest near the lower Russian River of Northern California.

As she hiked down the highway, the woman's aggravation at the troublesome tube opened her mind to rehashing past hurts and difficulties. Uncertainty about her future joined her thoughts. *What are you going to do with the rest of your life? You've never gotten any break,* she assured herself. *You need to keep reminding yourself that you're totally on your own and always will be.*

Cars and pickup trucks with empty beds passed. Unwilling to accept either rejection or help, she refused to extend a thumb asking for a ride. *Just enjoy the moment,* she told herself and lifted her eyes toward lacy green treetops silhouetted against a blue sky. She deeply inhaled alpine-scented fresh air and listened to the tumbling river next to the road. An upsetting thought intruded. *But have you avoided all the good things life might offer? Are you still trying to escape?*

* * *

Katelyn stood with her back to the Grand Canyon, watching a tiny animal beg tourists for food.

"That's a type of western chipmunk, honey," Katie told her. "You've seen eastern chipmunks in Alabama."

"We traveled two thousand miles to admire a little squirrel?" marveled Denyse.

"Well, Katelyn's happy and the men are happy." Katie waved toward the edge of the canyon where Dave pointed out something on the far rim to Jeremy. "Is your family looking forward to your visit in Melbourne?"

"Yeah. And I'm excited about showing Katelyn her place of birth. Three months from now, I'll have the new baby to care for and won't get back to Australia for who knows how long."

"You're still doing okay with the pregnancy?"

"I feel fine. A little tired maybe. But if all goes well, I should be able to resume teaching maths after the Christmas hols."

"You've made a great impact on those kids in Mobile, Denyse."

"I wouldn't have been able to start without your help taking care of Katelyn."

Dave and Jeremy returned from looking over the chasm the Colorado River had created. "Who's ready for Hoover Dam?" Dave asked.

"I'd vote for checking into the campground here at the park," Katie proposed.

"Too bad that's not on the ballot," her husband answered. "We'll need to keep traveling toward California. You'll have plenty of time in campgrounds there."

Jeff Moynihan, owner of the Freedom Road bike shop, was trying to get his eighteen-month-old daughter to eat baby food. More carrot puree ended up on the child's face and on him than in her mouth. *She's ready for more solid food,* he told himself. *If I could afford to hire some help for the shop, I could take better care of her.*

The ringing of the bell over the bicycle shop's door came as a welcome relief. "Stay here a minute, sweetie. I'll be right back," he told the little girl, as if she could escape the highchair and run away.

Leaving the shop's break area that doubled as their kitchen, he entered the display floor. There he saw a tall woman carrying a bicycle. Obviously fit, the thirtyish woman wore a worn athletic top revealing bare arms and shoulders, denim shorts, and a simple backpack. Worn tennis shoes rather than biking shoes covered her feet. "Striking" would describe the woman's bold features rather than delicate or pretty. An unkempt reddish-brown French braid—the color of redwood tree bark—hung down her back. A few squint lines around her eyes and tanned skin indicated a lot of time spent in the sun. Despite himself, the young man noticed the woman's bare ring finger—although in California that didn't prove anything.

She represented the first potential customer through his shop door all day. And lunchtime had already passed. "Can I help you?" he asked.

"All I need is a tube replaced," the woman answered in a husky voice and set the bike down. "I just can't get it to fit." She held out an uninflated tube. "What would mounting this cost?"

The shop owner tried to hide his disappointment. *Some customer,* he thought. *She even brought her own tube.* "Uh, three dollars."

The woman removed her backpack and brought out a cloth coin purse. He saw her pull out a couple of crumpled bills and some change. She looked carefully at her money before answering, "Okay."

Without speaking, the man picked up the bike and put it in the clamps. The woman handed the tube to him. "Mind if I watch?" she asked. "I'd like to learn how to fix a flat."

"The secret is to put a little air into the tube before stretching it over the rim. That shortens the tube and doesn't allow the edges to interfere with the tire seal."

The woman stepped closer to watch. "Thanks." The man detected an athletic odor of dried perspiration from her. The smell reminded him of better days.

Installing and inflating the tube took only a minute. After finishing, the man gave the bike a cursory inspection. "I'm afraid your bearing is going bad." He turned the chain sprocket by hand-revolving the pedals. An unmistakable clicking sound proved the bearing to be near failure. "Have you ridden this much?"

The woman counted out three dollars. "Oh, over to the coast and up to Mendocino. Across the state to Yosemite. All over."

He looked at her again. Those represented distances of hundreds of miles and over significant elevations. She certainly looked fit enough. "Your brakes don't look good either."

"Yeah, I mostly just step off and start running when I need to stop. And the chain keeps jumping sprockets too. But what can you expect for a twenty-five-dollar bike picked up at Goodwill?"

He took the bike out of the clamps. "Over those distances, this bike will strand you sooner rather than later. Maybe hurt you."

"That wouldn't be the first time. But the selection of road bikes at secondhand shops isn't that good." The woman handed him three dollars.

"Well, listen. I've got a rebuilt road bike here that doesn't look like much but should be good for ten thousand or more miles." He walked to a rack of used bikes and pulled out a hearty-looking Schwinn.

The woman had followed him. He saw her look at the $750 price tag and grimace. "New this bike would be two thousand four hundred dollars," he told her.

"Might as well be new. I don't have anything near seven hundred and fifty dollars." The woman gave an appealing wry smile.

"I could let you have it for four hundred fifty." *That would pay the shop rent for another week,* the young man told himself.

Crying started in the rear of the store. "Just a minute," he told the woman. "I'll be right back." In the break room kitchen, the man lifted carrot-smeared Sam from her highchair. After being gently bounced, the little girl quieted.

"Do you live here?" the woman's deep voice startled him. She had followed and stood looking at the makeshift kitchen. A stained sink, portable propane burner, an old refrigerator, a decrepit microwave, a box of mixed utensils, a small toaster oven, and a Formica-topped folding table crowded the kitchen area. He saw her look into the former storeroom. A beat-up couch, second-hand playpen littered with toys for the baby, a dinged-up coffee table, one vinyl-covered chair, and a portable TV with rabbit-ear antennas furnished the sparse living quarters. Farther back, a crib and a single unmade bed plus a pipe for hanging clothes served as a bedroom. A worn rug covered part of the concrete floor.

"Yes, we live behind the shop. This is my daughter, Samantha. I call her Sam."

"Where's Sam's mother?"

"My wife, Megan, died a few hours after delivering Sam. Neither set of her grandparents are in a financial position or healthy enough to take on a baby. It's been tough, the two of us being on our own. I thought about putting Sam up for adoption, but I love my little girl. And I wanted her to know about her mother."

"I'm sorry about your wife."

"Thanks. So what about the bike?"

"I'd love to have that bike. But I don't have seven hundred and fifty dollars, or four hundred and fifty, or even enough for supper, after I gave you the three dollars."

"You know about biking, though, right?"

"Only as a rider. I'm not a racer."

He thought a few seconds before proposing, "Well how about this? Our busiest days are on Saturdays. I've lost business because I can't help customers, watch Sam, and do urgent repairs all at once. But I can't afford to hire anyone either. If you came in on Saturdays and waited on the customers, you could work off the bike in . . . say, about forty hours, in just five Saturdays?"

The woman paused then gave him that same wry smile. "Why not? When do I start?"

"How about this Saturday at nine a.m.? My name is Jeff Moynihan, by the way. What's yours?"

"Glad to meet you, Jeff Moynihan. My name is Tara." She turned to leave.

Carrying Sam, Jeff followed his new employee to the showroom and saw her pushing her old bike toward the front door. He felt concern for her riding the brakeless piece of junk. Another side of him argued, *You don't know this person. She might never come back.* Yet he heard himself saying, "No, you take the rebuilt bike. That thing," he pointed to the older bike, "is dangerous."

She turned, no wry smile this time, only an expression of surprise. "You're sure?"

"Yes. And were you kidding about having no supper?"

"No."

"Then you keep this." Jeff extended the three dollars.

Tara took the money, a mouth-open look of wonder on her face. Without speaking she transferred the saddle bags from her old bike to the new one. "You're kind," she said while pushing her new bike out the door. "See you on Saturday."

Kind or foolish? Jeff asked himself before returning to the kitchen to finish feeding Sam.

Chapter Two

* * *

Five days later all the Parkers felt exhausted from non-stop days visiting the attractions of Southern California—Disneyland, Beverly Hills, the San Diego Zoo, the San Bernardino Mountains, Malibu, and Universal Studios. Jeremy pulled the RV's curtains together to block rays from the setting sun.

"I can't believe we've been camping in the middle of one of the largest cities in the country."

"I was surprised myself when I found their website," Dave answered. "Who would have expected an RV park so near Hollywood? I thought we'd need to drive a hundred miles to park the RV. With California's gas prices, that would have cost more than the sixty-five dollar camping fee."

"I'm enjoying the eucalyptus trees," said Jeremy. "Their sweet smell and the low humidity remind me of Australia."

"California is like if America and Australia had a baby together," said Denyse. She spoke to Dave and Katie, "Thanks for including us on your much-deserved vacation. You two have helped us more than I could ever have imagined, and a lot of other people, too."

"I'm glad we had this time together." Katie put a plate of freshly baked chocolate chip cookies on the RV's little dining table. "This is to celebrate a successful trip."

Katelyn—well accustomed to her grandmother's cookies—reached for one. "I like Grandkate's cookies."

Jeremy pulled his daughter into his lap. "Do you know why Grandkate's cookies are so good?"

The little girl shook her head.

"That's because her grandfather was an elf. That means that you are . . ." Jeremy paused to figure in his head. ". . . one-sixteenth elf yourself."

Denyse couldn't help but smile. Still she admonished him, "Stop telling her those outrageous stories."

Jeremy defended his tale. "Look how short Grandkate is compared to the rest of us."

Katie smiled herself while pouring milk for Katelyn but didn't comment.

Katelyn licked cookie crumbs off her upper lip. "I like Daddy's stories."

"Your grandfather, Dingo, can tell some great stories too, darling," said Denyse.

"Yeah, like bar fights and killing kangaroos for meat," jibed Jeremy.

Denyse gave him a stern look. "Actually, Katelyn looks a bit like my mum. But where did she get being such a sleepyhead in the morning?"

Katie looked at Dave. "I've got an idea about that."

* * *

The next morning the Parkers hugged goodbye outside LA International Airport's security checkpoint. "This is the first time you'll be apart," said Katie to Jeremy and Denyse.

"Batching for a few weeks in Mobile will be fun," said Jeremy.

"I'll be home in Oz only fourteen hours from now," answered Denyse.

Dave and Katie watched while their son, daughter-in-law, and grandchild proceeded through the checkpoint. "That was nice of you to volunteer to take Katelyn to a movie last night leaving Jeremy and Denyse a little alone time in the RV," said Katie while they waited.

"I remember being their age."

"Oh, you do, do you? Tonight we'll see just how well you remember."

* * *

Gripping the steering wheel of the RV, Dave drove north on Interstate 5. He glanced at his petite and pretty wife. Only a few light wrinkles and her salt and pepper shoulder-length hair gave a clue that she'd lived more than sixty years. "I don't deserve a wife like you."

"I don't deserve a husband like you either."

"You could take that comment two different ways."

Katie smiled at her husband of forty-one years. She admired his thin physique, distinguished gray hair, and patrician appearance. "Yes . . . you . . . could."

Dave laughed at Katie's ever-present wit. "I'm just glad to finally get out of the city. We've driven a hundred miles just to leave town."

Katie smiled. "That's an exaggeration."

"Certainly not an exaggeration, if we had started measuring from Disneyland in Orange County."

Katie held up her cell phone. "Well, Katelyn loved Disneyland. I've got a million pictures for proof."

"And Denyse enjoyed seeing Hollywood. Even though we didn't actually see any movie stars."

"What do you think Jeremy liked best?"

"He seemed to enjoy the La Brea Tar Pits. Sabertooths, mammoths, and dirt."

Like father, like son, Katie thought. "It does feel good just the two of us traveling together again. Like we did in New Zealand."

Dave smirked. "I remember that trip as a tribulation. Although having an RV for lodging would have been nice, especially on the South Island."

"That's for sure. But I liked parts of the trip even without an RV. Didn't you enjoy the cabins we rented at mom-and-pop resorts there?"

"Yeah, I did," Dave admitted. "Even though several times I thought I'd freeze. The Kiwis don't use heat in winter like Americans."

"Adventures aren't necessarily fun at the time," Katie reminded him. "I'm glad for a *relaxing* vacation now. For the last year, I've either been getting on an airplane with you or taking care of Katelyn. I love that little dumpling with all my heart, but still I'm glad she'll be starting kindergarten this fall."

"After Denyse resumes teaching, you'll have a baby boy to care for."

"Maybe not all the time. Denyse knows a lot of other young mothers now. They help each other out."

Dave nodded. "I'm tired of working such long hours myself. The firm is doing well, even though my best clients never came back to me. I've got to admit you and I have had some great trips, though."

"Yes . . . we . . . have," answered Katie. "I never thought I'd visit some of those places. Especially the ones in Europe; Budapest, London, Vienna."

"Yeah, who would have thought being a consultant would result in such glamourous trips?"

"Forensic accounting has worked out for more than travel. Remember when you wished that your life could be more than ordinary? Then you solved the disappearance of Mrs. Johnson's husband in Minnesota? Since then your accounting skills have broken more major cases."

"We solved," Dave reminded. "Yes, I do remember. And I do like the challenge and variety of forensic accounting. But right now, I've earned this vacation. A long vacation. Let Jeremy and Herschel run Parker and Company for a while."

Katie complimented her husband, "You've done a great job coaching Jeremy and Herschel. And you gave each of them a stake by making them junior partners."

"Even if he weren't my son, I'd say that Jeremy is a wonderful business manager. And Herschel is an accounting genius."

"Herschel looks up to you like a father, you know?"

"I'd be proud to call him my son. I need a break, though, no airplanes, no jet lag, and no foreign languages. This trip will be a dream."

"Near the end of our trip, Jeremy seemed to be excited to go back to Mobile and run the firm by himself for three weeks while Herschel takes his vacation," said Katie.

"And Denyse certainly acted happy to be headed to Australia with Katelyn."

"Did you notice a little tension between Jeremy and Denyse?"

Dave shook his head. "Nothing serious. I think they were both just looking forward to a break in their routine."

"Aren't we all? I miss Katelyn already, though," Katie admitted.

"You're a good grandmother to her and not a bad wife either."

"I'm not bad?" Katie returned.

"Not bad is good," Dave assured her.

"That's not good enough for me."

"You're saying that you're not a good enough wife?"

Katie looked at her husband, who returned a whimsical grin. "I know a setup when I see one."

"I learned from you," Dave quipped.

Katie looked at the road map. "So where are we headed, besides anywhere away from Southern California?"

"How about Monterey? There's a wonderful aquarium there. And that's the setting of John Steinbeck's classic novel *Cannery Row.*"

Fish and history, Katie thought. *A magnet for Dave.* "I'll bet the waterfront in Monterey has some nice seafood restaurants too."

Arriving home alone felt odd to Jeremy. He and Denyse had purchased a house in a quiet cul-de-sac on the eastern side of Mobile Bay. As a teenager, he'd experienced aloneness in a house plenty of times. But being in south Alabama without his parents, Denyse, or Katelyn disquieted him.

Ripper rejoiced to see his master. Inside Jeremy and Denyse's shady fenced backyard, the black Labrador retriever had been cared for by neighbors. Eight days of limited attention only at mealtimes had been lonely for Ripper. The big dog frisked around and jumped with excitement like a puppy.

Jeremy bent down and roughly pounded Ripper's back. "Hey, boy. Glad to see me? Let's go for a walk." He tossed Ripper an old tennis ball to carry and picked up the ball thrower.

The young man and his delighted dog walked a few blocks to a park on the shoreline of Mobile Bay in the late afternoon. The lush green foliage refreshed Jeremy after the arid southwest scenery they had driven through. Humid air felt like a comforting blanket compared to California's dryness. An asphalt walking path shaded by live oaks and cypress trees covered with Spanish moss paralleled the bay and eventually tied into south Alabama's trail network. Wherever the path passed over water, signs warned, DO NOT FEED THE ALLIGATORS.

As Jeremy and Ripper approached the bay, an armadillo scurried out of their path. A faint odor of decomposing

barnacles and sawgrass roots exposed to air at low tide reassured him. Seagulls stalked along the water's edge. Sailboats slowly returned to their berths as the sun set. In the bay, a school of mullet suddenly jumped. Black-finned backs revealed a pod of dolphins chasing the bait fish. The water in the bay sparkled from reflections of the setting sun.

A mile past his and Denyse's new home, a marina lined both sides of a dredged creek. There Dave kept the cabin cruiser the Parkers had purchased when Jeremy was fourteen. They liked to use the ocean-worthy boat to pass downstream to Mobile Bay and from there access the Gulf of Mexico. Even when not fishing himself, Jeremy loved seeing the boats return to the marina and observing what types of fish had been caught. Brown pelicans always waited on the docks, ready to grab anything dropped into the water. Both Denyse and his mother enjoyed the fresh seafood restaurants nearby.

Jeremy stood on the banks of Mobile Bay at the park. Ripper dropped the tennis ball at his feet and stared at him expectantly. Jeremy looked for alligators lurking nearby before picking the ball up and using the thrower to hurl it a hundred feet into the bay. He didn't want to repeat his boyhood scare with Ruthie—his first dog—and a big gator named Zeek. Ripper whirled and plunged into the water as if retrieving that ball was the most important activity in the universe. Nothing could have distracted the dog from retrieving, the highest calling and greatest joy for any Labrador, especially in water.

Each time Ripper returned the drool-soaked ball, Jeremy picked it up and threw as far as he could into the brown water. Twenty-five throws of the ball took some energy out of the mature but energetic dog. His retrieves in the water became slower and slower. Jeremy started walking home under the streetlights, his canine friend huffing alongside with the ball in his mouth. The sound of humming air conditioners from nearby homes filled the warm, humid evening. A mockingbird sang to express its joy in the twilight somewhere nearby.

"Come on inside, boy," Jeremy invited Ripper into the house. The dog gladly obliged. Jeremy didn't notice the trail of muddy paw prints across the kitchen floor and onto the den carpet. To himself Jeremy said, *Feels good to be home. I'm going to enjoy some time alone while Denyse and Katelyn visit Australia.*

Chapter Three

* * *

Denyse and Katelyn endured a three-hour layover at the Sydney airport prior to catching a connecting flight to Melbourne. After buying Katelyn an ice cream cone, Denyse wandered into W. H. Smith bookstore holding her daughter's hand. First, she looked at the picture books in the limited children's section. Then in the adult section, she found two novels having her brother Trevor's picture on the back cover. A gold seal attached to the front cover of one announced Trevor as a recipient of a public service award for educating people about con games. Denyse also saw her father Dingo's book of colorful bloke stories prominently displayed.

Denyse pointed at Dingo and Beatrice's photo on the jacket cover. "Do you remember your granddad and grandmum?"

The little girl put her finger on the photo. "I want to see them. Will we be there soon?"

"Yes, we'll be home in a few hours. They're excited to see you. After your little brother comes in a few months, we won't have the chance to visit them for a while."

"When will we see Daddy again?"

"In about a month, darling. This is your chance to get to know your home country, Australia."

"I thought I am an American."

"You're both American and Australian because you have an American father and an Aussie mother. But you were born here in Sydney. Your passport is Australian like mine. You're a Parker and a Larkin, too."

All week Jeff wondered if he'd see his new hire, Tara, on Saturday. She had not arrived when he opened the street-front shop at the normal hour of 9:00 a.m.

Fifteen minutes later he'd nearly given up hope of getting a temporary employee or ever seeing the $750 bike again. Then through the shop's front window he saw Tara screech to a halt on the rebuilt bike.

She rushed inside. "Am I late? I don't have an alarm clock, haven't had one in years."

Jeff disguised his relief with a shrug. "Just a few minutes. I knew you'd be here," he lied.

"Well, I nearly wasn't. I haven't had to be anywhere at a certain hour for a long time. And I'm not naturally an early riser. Show me what to do."

The shop's bell rang several times during the first hour. Tara mastered using the register and making out work orders for various bike services. Jeff then left the shop to her care while working on bikes and minding Sam in the back. After a while, things seemed too quiet out front. No bell rings had announced customers entering either. Jeff stepped from the work area to find an empty and unattended shop. He saw the front door open to the sidewalk on Redwood Hills' Main Street. *She's gone,* he thought.

Then through the open door Jeff heard Tara's husky voice: "Good morning. We've got some great deals on bikes today." To a passing jogger she said, "Bicycles give you a great aerobic workout without putting so much stress on your knees." Tara stood out on the sidewalk greeting each passerby. Jeff stole back to the work area, smiling.

All the Larkins met Denyse and Katelyn at the Melbourne airport. Denyse hugged her mum, her dad, her brother Trevor, and his Ukrainian wife Lena in turn. Beatrice scooped up Katelyn and gave her a bear hug. Together she and Dingo admired their granddaughter.

"My, how you've grown, luv," said Beatrice.

Dingo tickled his granddaughter. "How's my little rug rat?"

"She's into dressing up now," Denyse answered for her daughter. "I have her favorite princess costume packed in her suitcase."

Katelyn giggled and squirmed. "She prefers to stand on her own feet," Denyse explained. Turning to Trevor and Dingo, she said, "I saw your books on sale at the Sydney airport."

"Both of them are famous," Lena answered for them.

"Where's Vlady?"

"Likely he's into mischief somewhere," boasted Dingo. "My grandson is growing up right lively."

Lena rolled her eyes a little. "My sisters are taking care of Vlady. Takes two of them to keep track of him. Otherwise he'll get into some sort of trouble. He takes after Dingo in looks and temperament."

"And the baby?" Denyse asked.

"Also with my sisters. She'll be fine, if I can just keep Mama and Poppa from spoiling her so much. Thank goodness they're on the road a lot." She looked at Dingo and Beatrice with a smile. They both simply laughed.

Trevor and Dingo picked up the two suitcases and started toward Beatrice's car. Denyse and Lena walked together while Beatrice led Katelyn behind them.

"How are the Parkers?" Lena asked while Trevor put the luggage in the car's boot. Looking at Dingo she said, "Poppa told us that Mr. Parker and Jeremy are working together."

"That's right. We had worried about them resurrecting Dave's old accounting firm. Dave's still a little sad that almost none of his old clients have returned after his former partners had ruined the firm's reputation. But business has gotten a lot better. They renamed the firm Parker and Company Accounting."

Lena nodded in appreciation. "And you're teaching school in America?"

"Maths is maths. Kids are kids. Like when I taught in Sydney, a lot of my students come from disadvantaged backgrounds. Not much opportunity for them. Maths can help them do something better with their lives. All my calculus students even got uni credit last year."

Denyse turned the questions back to Lena. "How's your childcare business going?"

"We've got some problems," Lena answered. To Denyse's puzzled expression, she added, "I'll tell you about it later."

"Those don't look like otters to me," said Katie. She stood in front of an outdoor pool at the Monterey Aquarium complex.

"Sea otters are a lot bigger than the river otters we occasionally see in Alabama," answered Dave.

"I didn't mean size. They should call these sea loafers." She pointed at six animals floating in the sun on their backs, apparently sound asleep. Each of them used their front paws to shade their eyes. "Have you ever seen a lazy otter before?"

Dave's head shake acknowledged that he hadn't. "Maybe they're more active in the wild."

"They'd have to be. Otherwise they'd starve to death."

"I'm sure the keepers feed them well."

"Maybe a little too well. But weren't the reef exhibits spectacular?"

"Could you believe those jellyfish?" Dave had stood for nearly ten minutes staring at large jellyfish gently undulating in totally transparent water. Back lighting had been arranged to make the jellyfish clearly visible by light refraction through their bodies.

"How about lunch?" Katie suggested as they exited the complex.

Dave sniffed at the odors of low-tide exposed seashore and drying kelp in the bay. "Do you have a place in mind?"

"Any place along the waterfront is certain to be good."

After leaving the aquarium complex, Katie selected a restaurant located in a restored cannery. There smells of seafood and fresh bread replaced the seashore odors. The clear waters of Monterey Bay lapped around pilings on which the original cannery had been built. Large picture windows offered unobstructed views of the harbor.

The maître d' seated them overlooking an outcrop of rocks against which gentle waves splashed. Dave tried to remain calm when looking at the menu. Prices averaged double or more than entrees at Mobile's seafood restaurants. *Don't spoil Katie's joy by worrying about a few dollars,* he told himself.

Katie ordered scallops sautéed in garlic butter. Dave selected a grilled fillet of Pacific cod. Then Dave noticed that a part of the rock seen out the window appeared to move. "Look! There's a seal on that rock."

Katie turned her head to where Dave stared. "That's a sea lion—a male. The males can weigh better than two thousand pounds."

"How do you know about seals and sea lions?"

"Have you forgotten all the years I taught science?"

Suddenly Dave stood up. He pointed. "I see a wild sea otter. He's right next to the pier."

Katie followed his finger. "That's a female."

"How can you tell the sex of a sea otter?"

"Because she's carrying a pup."

Dave looked closer. Indeed, a tiny version of a sea otter rode on its mother's stomach as she floated on her back.

The young man who had taken their order returned with a tray carrying their somewhat skimpy lunches. After serving Dave and Katie, he asked, "Can I get you anything else?"

Dave wanted to say, *Bigger portions.* But instead responded, "You could answer a question for me."

"Certainly."

"Why are sea lions and otters right here in front of us? I thought being wild, they would inhabit remote areas."

The young man smiled. "The city of Monterey has them on a retainer. They're good for tourism."

Dave and Katie both leaned forward in surprise. "What?" they said together.

Their waiter's smile turned into a mischievous grin. "Not really. I'm just joking. Well, sort of joking. People feed the animals. Tourists never get tired of watching them eat. Makes them hungry for seafood themselves. All good for business. You can buy five anchovies for ten dollars several places on the docks. California's wildlife authorities look the other way."

Bait fish for two dollars each? Dave thought. *Seafood is even expensive for the animals in California.*

"Where to next?" he heard Katie ask.

Dave swallowed a bite of cod. "I thought we'd drive up the Northern California coastline. And I'd like to see some redwoods."

"Aren't the trees in Sequoia National Park bigger?"

"Sequoias are a type of redwood that are bigger around the base. The coastal redwoods grow taller."

Chapter Four

* * *

"You sold four bicycles today!" Tara heard Jeff's amazement when he closed the shop at 6:00 p.m. "That's as many as I usually sell in a month."

"Well, you gotta get customers in the door first. Then you chat a bit to find out something they value and relate the bike to that." Tara then thought to herself, *Pulling people into a shop and selling a bike isn't hard when you're used to tricking them into giving you money.*

"Would you like to stay for supper with Sam and me?" Jeff looked hopeful. "Nothing fancy. I put chicken and rice in the Crock-Pot earlier."

Non-instant cooked food? Tara asked herself. *I could take a few minutes to eat.* She gave Jeff the closed-mouth smile she used on gullible marks when soliciting. "Why not?"

In Jeff and Sam's living quarters, Tara felt awkward and impatient waiting with nothing to do. After putting Sam into her highchair, Jeff hurried around the tiny kitchen. The little girl started crying. "She's hungry," Jeff explained and began chopping a piece of chicken thigh into tiny pieces.

"Let me take care of that," Tara offered and held out her hand for the knife.

Jeff handed her the knife. "Thanks! I'll make her a little instant pudding for dessert. Chocolate flavor okay with you, Tara?"

"Of course." Tara finished dicing the piece of chicken on the plate Jeff had selected for Sam. The little girl quieted and stared at Tara. "So, should I try feeding her?" Tara asked.

"Check to make sure the chunks aren't too hot. Then just put a few on her tray. We can let Sam use her hands."

After spreading some chicken before the child, Tara watched as Sam reached to take a piece and fist it into her little mouth. She admired the toddler's soft brown curls, chubby cheeks, and blue eyes. Sam turned her eyes to stare at Tara and then smiled. Tara was surprised by her own internal reaction of joy. *She's adorable.*

"The plates are in the dish drainer," said Jeff while beating the pudding mix. "Help yourself to the Crock-Pot. If it's cool enough, put a little rice in front of Sam."

Tara felt the warm rice and then put a little before Sam. She found a variety of plastic plates in the drainer along with mismatched stainless utensils. She served both Jeff and herself and put both plates on the portable Formica table. "All ready."

"What would you like to drink?" asked Jeff after putting the pudding into the old refrigerator to congeal. "Actually, all I have is Sam's milk and tap water."

Tara shrugged. "Water will be fine."

"Then please sit."

Jeff sat himself after filling two plastic cups with tap water. "Sam, are you ready to give thanks?"

Once the little girl closed her eyes, Jeff quickly prayed with his eyes open. "God, we thank you for this food. Amen."

He smiled and explained to Tara, "When you have a young child, it's best to pray with your eyes open." Tara saw Sam resume eating from the tray and getting most of the chicken and rice into her mouth. Jeff visibly relaxed.

Tara took a bite of the rice. She tasted the chicken's flavor along with some garlic, a little salt, and a dash of black pepper. "This is really good, Jeff."

"Thanks. Sam's mother used to start this cooking before we went out to train."

"Train for what?"

"We are, were, both competitive cyclists. That's how we met." Jeff chewed and swallowed before continuing. "Both of us tried to make a career of professional racing. Neither of us ever won enough money to live on. Married and sharing expenses, we could barely survive. We lived in a small camper towed behind the car. But we had a lot of fun traveling and participating in the races."

Jeff resumed eating and watching Sam. Tara took that opportunity to examine him. About the same height and age as herself, his thin physique gave credibility to his days of bike racing. He had dark hair cut into an uneven crew-cut and a four-day stubble of facial hair. Tara suspected that the necessity of caring for a shop and a child rather than stylishness had created the overgrown look. His thin face looked masculine rather than handsome. *I wouldn't have minded traveling with him, before I gave up on men and roosted here*, she thought.

"Do you have family nearby?" Jeff asked.

"No. I grew up on a communal farm in Wisconsin. That's where a midwife helped my mother give birth. My mother and father were genuine hippie dropouts in the sixties and seventies."

"Hippies?"

Tara smiled. "Yeah. I'm the seedling of two flower children. I took my mother's last name, Grabowski. The man my mother has lived with since I can remember is Gnarly Harkness. He might be my biological father. Now they both work at a dry cleaner in Madison, get stoned, and watch TV all night." Tara didn't often feel comfortable sharing about her unconventional upbringing, but she felt strangely at ease with Jeff. And she didn't feel a compulsion to eat and leave. She took a sip of water and wondered what he would think of her if he knew her whole story.

* * *

"Katelyn, meet your cousin Vlady," Denyse told her daughter.

"G'day," said the stocky five-year-old boy facing her. "Would you like to see my room? I've got a kangaroo rug. Come on," he invited and ran down the hall without waiting.

Katelyn chased her rambunctious cousin down the hall into a bedroom filled with toys and sports equipment. Denyse and Lena followed their children. Trevor disappeared to someplace without any comment.

"This used to be my room," said Denyse. "Sure does look different now."

"Boys' rooms always look different than girls'," Lena answered. "I stayed in here when your room still looked the way you'd left it. Your room was lovely, Denise."

"I'm glad you and Trevor kept Mum and Dad's house when they moved. I can hardly wait to see their new home. I still can't believe they're able to afford a brand-new house, and so close to the southern coastline and Melbourne Bay."

Leaving the two children playing, Lena led the way farther down the hall. "This is where my two sisters sleep," she pointed into Trevor's boyhood room. "We gave them his room because of the bunk beds. Trevor and I sleep in your parents' old bedroom."

"And here are my two sisters making lunch for us," said Lena when they entered the kitchen. "This is Oleksandra and Svetlana." She pointed at them in turn. "You can call them

Sandra and Sveta. This is Trevor's older sister, Denyse," she told the two girls. "She sent the Parkers looking for Trevor where they found me. Later Denyse and I together helped stop a ring of human traffickers in New Zealand."

Denyse saw two teenagers—undeniably related to Lena—and yet significantly different. The smaller girl had the same blond hair and light blue eyes as Lena but rounded, less delicate features. Sandra stepped forward to clasp Denyse's hand. "Welcome home." Her accent sounded just like Lena's.

The second sister had Lena's beautiful face, perhaps eight additional inches of height, and a shapelier figure. Her eyes tended gray rather than blue. "G'day," said Sveta. Denyse heard that a little Aussie intonation had already crept into Sveta's voice.

Presuming the taller girl to be the oldest, Denyse asked, "Sveta, you're in the fifth form this year, right?"

"Blimey, no. I'm in third form."

"I'm in fifth form this year," volunteered Sandra.

"Sorry, I got you reversed," Denyse apologized.

"Everybody does that. I'm seventeen. Sveta's fifteen," Sandra elaborated.

"Sveta is fifteen going on twenty-one," Lena commented.

"You're just jealous," Sveta returned.

"*Bud'vezhliv*," Lena responded in a terse voice.

Sveta sneered. "Speak English. I won't speak Russian anymore."

"I told her to be polite," Lena told Denyse.

"Where's the baby?" Denyse asked to divert the awkward moment.

"She's having a nap. I'll get her up," Sandra volunteered and left the kitchen. A few minutes later she returned carrying a six-month-old. She looked at Denyse. "This is Maria. Lena named her after our mother."

Denyse held out her arms to receive the infant. The baby stared at her face. "How precious. Maria looks a little like all of you."

"Lunch is ready," announced Sveta.

"I'll tell Trevor," Sandra volunteered again.

"How long have you had the shop, Jeff?" Tara asked as she forked the last bit of chicken on her plate.

"Well . . . because Megan and I couldn't afford a bike mechanic, I maintained both of our bikes. Then I started taking care of other people's bikes at biking events. Soon I realized that I could make a lot more money serving as a mechanic on chase teams for the best riders than I could by my own winnings. About that time, Megan became pregnant with Sam.

"We couldn't raise a child the footloose way we lived. A child needs a more stable environment. So two years ago we rented this shop to give us a base and a place to stay with a baby. When a chase team offered me a job—usually for a weekend, occasionally for a week—Megan could stay here and mind the business. Between the two of us, we made good money at first and even saved to buy a house. Then Megan died of a one-in-a-million internal hemorrhage after the delivery. I didn't know anything about taking care of a baby and needed to travel to earn money. That's when I thought about offering Sam for adoption so she could have a normal family. She's my greatest joy, my life now. I'm glad I didn't. But making ends meet financially here by myself and not able to take work on chase teams has been tough. The money Megan and I had saved for the baby and a home is all gone. Those bikes you sold today will be a big help."

Jeff shook himself. "Sorry for rattling on. I don't get a chance to talk to adults much these days. What about you, Tara?"

"Oh, I've traveled around. I like being outdoors. I've been a long-distance backpacker in the Appalachians, Rockies, and Sierras."

Jeff raised his eyebrows at that. "Bicycling?"

"Started biking to get around. But it's outdoors too. I discovered that I like riding."

"Get around? Don't you drive?"

"I can drive. Don't have a vehicle anymore."

Jeff took both his and Tara's plates and served more rice and chicken. "What brought you to Redwood Hills?"

"I just kind of landed here. But it's a good place. Lots of parks close to the coast and redwood forests. Rides through the vineyards to the east are beautiful." She looked at Jeff to find him paying close attention. "I really like to spend time outside. The weather here is usually perfect for that."

"Where do you live?"

"I live in a tiny trailer at a campground. They let me stay there for cleaning the communal areas."

"Don't you have a regular job?"

Tara shrugged. "No, when the weather is good, I want the freedom to hang loose outdoors." When Jeff nodded understanding, Tara answered his unasked question. "I do all sorts of odd jobs to get a little money. When I get desperate for a few dollars, I collect aluminum cans and plastic bottles along the road for the five-cent deposit. At least that's working outside." She didn't mention that "odd jobs" had included raiding fountains for coins and asking strangers for money in parking lots.

Jeff laughed. "I've thought about collecting cans and plastic bottles myself. I'd make more money than many days at the shop."

Tara smiled in sympathy and feigned a teaching voice. "If you ever do try it, avoid the glass bottles. Glass is heavy to carry. And they don't take alcohol bottles at the recycling center." Sam turned her head to watch as Jeff and Tara both laughed out loud.

"Good advice. Let's see if the chocolate pudding is ready. Sam's little hands won't work for this. I need to warn you that spoon feeding her will get a little messy. Pudding is likely to go everywhere."

Tara found herself in no hurry to leave Jeff and Sam. She started clearing the table.

Chapter Five

* * *

"Mom, I'd like to hang out with some girls from school. Would you drop me at the shopping center?" asked Missy.

"Okay, but you promise not to leave the shopping center, right?"

"Mom, I'm over eighteen. I can go where I want."

"Not when you're living under my roof and before you demonstrate some responsible behavior."

Missy crossed her arms and scowled. "If you insist."

"I'll be back to pick you up at four."

"Sheeese!"

Missy remained silent during the ride to the shopping center. Her mother pulled up to the curb. "Remember four o'clock, right—" Missy exited the passenger side and slammed the car door, cutting off her mother's words.

Locating Harley didn't take long. "Hello, sunshine," he greeted her.

"Your text came. Whataya got?" Missy's voice was curt.

Harley smiled lasciviously. "All your favorites. I'm flush today. But it'll cost you."

"The usual?"

"Of course."

Missy grimaced. "Where?"

"In my car. We'll go someplace."

* * *

Having piloted the RV over San Francisco's Golden Gate Bridge, Katie drove north on Highway 1 along California's northern coastline. "This is a lot like the southern coast of Australia."

"Yes, it is. Except that here fog blows off the ocean nearly all morning, and the surf is less violent. I do like California's relatively calm beaches where a valley creases the hillsides."

From the driver's seat Katie twisted her neck, looking at the vistas. "What beautiful views. California has done an amazing job of non-commercializing this road. And compared to a lot of tourist destinations, hardly anyone is here."

Dave saw a sign promoting The Center for Spiritual Studies decorated with new age symbols. "This is amazing and *totally* different from south Alabama. But occasionally look at the road while you're driving, okay?"

"Very funny," said Katie, but she did watch the winding two-lane road more closely. When the road offered a turnout, she pulled in for both her and Dave to gaze at the spectacular scenery.

Outside the RV, she and Dave stood on a cliff overlooking the lower Russian River emptying into the Pacific Ocean. A sandbar created a freshwater lagoon and a nozzle-like gap that funneled the clear river water into a plume extending like a tongue into the blue ocean. On the sandbar between the freshwater lagoon and the salty ocean, thirty or more sea lions and seals lay basking in the warm sun. Several pups played at the water's edge. Katie shook her head in amazement. "The adults look as lazy as sea otters."

"Food must be easy to find," Dave speculated.

"I'm looking forward to reaching Mendocino," said Katie as they returned to the RV.

"Let me guess. You're hoping to find seafood restaurants there."

"Ha ha. Maybe we could park the RV and spend one night in a Victorian bed and breakfast."

"Didn't our adventure in Minnesota give you enough experience in a Victorian mansion?"

"I'm curious about how different a West Coast mansion might be."

"Well, okay. But would you be willing to make a short excursion first?" asked Dave.

"Where to?"

Dave looked at a map he had picked up. "There's a grove of old-growth forest only about half an hour inland from the coast highway. It's near a town called Redwood Hills. I'd like to see the coastal redwoods. I've heard they have a grandeur completely different from the woods in south Alabama."

"Of course. The seafood restaurants in Mendocino will wait."

"I'm glad we're on our own relaxing timetable now."

"Me too."

The route to Dingo and Beatrice's new home passed through several charming bay-side villages on the ninety-minute drive south of Melbourne. Denyse toured Dingo and Beatrice's new home on the Mornington Peninsula with eagerness.

"Mum! Dad! This is lovely." Denyse admired the high ceilings with crown molding, polished granite countertops, and sparkling new appliances.

"This will be your room, luv." Beatrice directed her daughter to a spacious bedroom with a queen-sized bed. "Katelyn can sleep over there." She indicated another bedroom containing twin beds across the hall.

"Thank you, Mum. We'll be fine here."

"We'll let you get settled in now. Tomorrow I'll show you the path to the ocean, right through those trees," Dingo added.

Denyse could hear distant surf pounding on the rocks. "Brilliant! Katelyn will love that."

"Just you be careful of her," Beatrice insisted as she led the way back to the living room. "You know our ocean isn't like the peaceful Gulf of Mexico."

"I'll keep her out of the water. Winter is too cold for getting wet anyway."

Dingo sat down in an easy chair nearby letting Katelyn trace the tattoos on his forearm with her finger. "Yeeah, we're expecting a frost tonight. The wind off the ocean gets a might nippy in mid-winter."

"Mobile is hot and humid right now. We run the air conditioners all day and night."

"I remember that," said Beatrice. "Our hot is more dry than Mobile even though we're by the ocean. How about I just make us some fresh tea?" she offered. "What about Katelyn?" She pointed at her granddaughter.

"You probably remember Dave and Katie are tea drinkers too. We let Katelyn have tea with about half milk," Denyse explained.

Beatrice leaned over to speak to her granddaughter. "I'll bet you'd like an Anzac biscuit too, wouldn't you, luv?"

"What's an Anzac biscuit?" Katelyn answered.

"That's a big, sweet cookie, darling. You'll like it," Denyse told her.

"Okay."

Dingo reacted to Katelyn's reply. "You've let my granddaughter start speakin' American."

Denyse smiled at her father. "Just don't you be teaching her any Aussie insults, talking to yourself, and all."

"Talkin' to myself's the best conversation I can get round here, since you left," he answered before standing and sauntering off.

Beatrice enjoyed her daughter and husband bantering while she brewed the tea in her favorite teapot.

From the patio the sound of barking attracted Katelyn's attention. "Can we let in the dogs?" she asked.

"Of course, luv. Mind you they don't jump up and knock you over." Beatrice opened the door.

Katelyn eliminated the knock-over threat by sitting on the floor. Two corgis crowded around her, licking any exposed skin. The little girl giggled as she tried to fend off Beatrice's fur babies.

"Do Lena and her family come here often?" asked Denyse.

Beatrice poured the tea. "Lena and Trevor sometimes do with Vlady, especially in the summer. They like the breezes off the ocean. Vlady loves exploring the tidal pools down by the sea. Tea's ready, Dingo," she called before continuing her answer to Denyse. "Lena's sisters hardly come at all, though. Mornington is too far from the city."

"They like the city?" Denyse asked as she added milk to Katelyn's teacup. "I thought they grew up on a farm in the countryside."

Dingo returned to the kitchen in time to hear Denyse's last comment. "Maybe that's why the girls like the city. Farms can be a right hard place to live. Sandra and Sveta wouldn't even consider going back when their mother returned to Ukraine."

Denyse added a spoonful of sugar to Katelyn's milk and tea. "Maria married again, I understand."

Dingo nodded in response to Denyse. "Yeeah. After the Russians murdered Lena's father and forced the Travnikovs off their farm, they walked more than a hundred kilometers to a refugee camp in western Ukraine. There a kindly farmer and part-time Baptist pastor and his wife tried to help all the refugees as much as they could. Nearly a year ago, the farmer/pastor contacted Maria in Australia with a proposal. His wife had died unexpectedly, leaving him with three children. Lena's mother traveled back to Ukraine and married him. That's the life she knows."

"The girls are giving Lena some trouble," Beatrice confided.

Denyse stirred her own tea and milk. "What sort of trouble?"

Beatrice poured tea for herself and Dingo. "They're trying to become Australian all at once, especially the tall one. She's always cheeky. Worse, she makes Lena's management of her daycare extra hard by arguing and spending time text messaging her new friends."

"Sveta is the most trouble?"

"That's right, luv. She looks a lot older than she actually is. The men notice her right away."

Dingo picked up his teacup. "That one is on the prowl," he added. "I know the look of a sheila."

Denyse gave her father a harsh look for that mildly course description. "What about Sandra?"

"The older girl is sweet and looks younger than her sister. But she's got her own problems adjusting to Australian culture. And she's jealous of Sveta."

"How is Lena dealing with her sisters?"

"She's trying to be their mum. The girls don't like that."

Dingo broke in, "Lena's answer to every problem is to go to church. She attends an old-fashioned Ukrainian Baptist church alone."

"Trevor doesn't go with her?"

"Not hardly. You know how Trevor is with authorities. That church is all about authority and full of don'ts. Plus, all of the services are conducted in Russian." Dingo sipped his tea and took an Anzac biscuit. He looked at Beatrice. "I'm happier being married to your mum than ever in my life. But I can still tell when a woman is on the make. That Sveta is."

Chapter Six

* * *

Katie parked the RV away from most of the cars in the unpaved overflow section of a parking lot at a California state park. Signs pointed the way to a trail through a protected glen of redwoods.

Dave started lacing up his hiking boots. Katie put water bottles, their cell phone, and Chapstick into a day pack and stepped down from the RV.

Warm, dry air and a clear blue sky made the day seem perfect for a hike. A slight breeze smelled alpine fresh with a hint of cedar. Wildflowers bloomed beside the beckoning trail. Dave locked the RV behind them. His steps bounced with eagerness; his eyes lifted toward the towering trees ahead.

Following Dave, Katie walked with her eyes lowered. She didn't want to trip and fall before even reaching the trail. A late-model compact car sat idle and isolated near where she had parked the RV. As they passed the car, Katie noticed a young man and woman in the front seats. They appeared to be sleeping.

Closer examination revealed the man's head tilted to the side, his mouth open, and eyes cracked. Katie called her husband back. "Dave, look at this. Something doesn't seem right."

Dave paused in his hurry to see the redwoods. He stopped and partially turned. "Looks like somebody is taking a nap."

"In a parking lot? That seems an unusual place for a nap. And with all the windows rolled up on such a lovely day?"

Dave took a few steps back. Katie leaned over to look inside the car. The woman had slumped forward, her forehead touching the dashboard. Katie tapped on the passenger side window. "Hello! Are you okay?"

Silence answered her, but it was an eerie silence—not the silent grandeur of the redwood trees that surrounded them. Dave stood by the driver's side window. "Look at this guy. He looks like he's in a trance rather than taking a nap."

"Dave, something is wrong here."

"You're right." Dave rapped on the window next to the man. "Hey! Wake up!"

Still no response.

"We've got to help them, Dave," Katie pleaded.

Dave tried to open each of the car's doors and found them all locked. His eyes searched the ground. He picked up a softball-sized rock near their feet. As Katie watched, he hit the driver's side window. Cracks appeared in the glass. Three more blows shattered the window enough for him to insert his arm and unlock both doors using the electric switch. "Check the woman," he told Katie and put his hand on the man's neck. "I'm not feeling a pulse here."

Katie opened the other door then smelled stale cigarette smoke. She leaned the woman back and noticed how young she was, just a teenager. The girl mumbled a bit but didn't wake up.

Dave had put his hand under the man's arms and pulled him outside the car. The body felt heavy and stiff. He laid the man on the ground and his hand on the man's chest. "I don't think he's breathing."

Katie had her hand on the girl's neck. "I do have a pulse here. She's barely breathing, though. Help me get her out of the seat."

A few hikers, hearing the nearby commotion, had gathered around the car. "I'm a nurse," one woman volunteered. "Lay her on the ground."

After Dave complied, the nurse started CPR.

Katie took the cell phone out of her day pack and called 911. "What is your emergency?" a voice answered.

"We've found two people unconscious in a car. We can't wake them up."

"Where are you?"

Katie reported their location as the parking lot at the state's redwood grove. "We think the woman is near death."

"Do you know a cause?"

"A cause?" Katie said out loud. She looked to where Dave pointed. A plastic ziplock bag on the front seat contained several pills. A liquor bottle lay on the floorboard near the gas pedal. "Maybe a drug overdose."

The nurse spoke to Dave, "Can you do CPR?" When he nodded, she ordered, "Take over here," and indicated the young woman.

Dave started alternating pushing on her chest and blowing into her mouth. The nurse moved to check the man. "This one is *already* dead."

By reflex, Katie stepped back from the body.

"Start CPR on the woman," the 911 voice ordered. "Assistance is on the way."

Within a few minutes a patrol car from the Sonoma County sheriff's department rolled up, lights flashing and siren wailing. A young deputy jumped out. The nurse told him, "This looks like an overdose. The male is already dead."

After Dave showed him the pills in the car, the deputy went to the squad car and returned with a first-aid kit. He administered an injection of naloxone to the girl. "This combines with and binds the opioid," he explained. "She should breathe easier in a couple of minutes, if it's not already too late."

The deputy, nurse, and Dave alternated administering CPR until the young woman's breathing became deeper and more regular. Because of the closeness of the park, the emergency workers arrived only eight minutes after Katie's call.

The paramedics asked simple, direct questions to find out what had happened. They looked at the injection of naloxone the deputy had used. Then they checked the girl's vital signs, gave her oxygen, and placed her on a stretcher. A female paramedic pointed to the girl's male companion. "This man is beyond our help."

Another police car arrived. The nurse spoke in a low voice to Dave and Katie. "That's Sheriff Billingsly. The elected sheriff of Sonoma County is based in Santa Rosa. Billingsly is actually the sergeant in charge of the local office. But he's been here as long as most people can remember, so everybody calls him sheriff."

A man who appeared about seventy years old with chevrons on his police uniform stepped out. Short in stature, he stood about five feet five and weighed probably two hundred pounds. He wore a cowboy hat. Deep creases furrowed his no-nonsense face. The ambulance carrying the woman screamed away.

Sheriff Billingsly checked the male overdose victim and ordered the deputy, "Radio the funeral home and the coroner." He took off his cowboy hat to investigate the car and picked up the plastic bag with pills by a corner. Dave and Katie saw he had a balding head with gray hair combed over.

The sheriff stood a few seconds, grimly shaking his head. Then, after placing the pills into an evidence bag, he looked around and asked, "Who found the victims?"

Dave stepped forward. "My wife and I did." He pointed to the broken car window. "I had to break the window to get them out."

The sheriff nodded. "Can you two show me some ID?" Dave and Katie produced their drivers' licenses. "Alabama, huh?" The sheriff pulled a spiral notebook from his shirt pocket and jotted down the Parkers' names, address, and license numbers.

"Do either of you know the victims?" He handed the Parkers back their IDs.

"No, we're in California on vacation," Dave answered for both. "My wife noticed the man and woman in the car as we started to hike the grove." Dave waved in the direction of the trail.

"I know the girl," the young deputy volunteered. "She's Melissa Clark, called Missy. I went to high school in Forestville with her."

Sheriff Billingsly recorded the girl's name before returning his attention to Dave and Katie. "Where are you two staying?"

Dave pointed at the RV without speaking.

A hearse pulled up, followed by the part-time county coroner in an SUV.

"We haven't touched the body," the sheriff told the coroner. "Mr . . ." he consulted his notes, ". . . Parker pulled him out of the car before he had been judged deceased."

The coroner checked the man's pulse for himself and shook his head. "I'd guess he's been dead an hour, or more."

"See if he's carrying any ID," the sheriff told him. The coroner checked the man's back pocket, produced a wallet, and took out a driver's license. "Harley Tanase. Address says Alder Drive. Picture matches the deceased." He then pulled a girl's backpack from the car's front seat. An ID card inside gave a local phone number.

"Okay, Conrad," the sheriff addressed the deputy. "You go over to Alder Drive and see if anyone else lives at the deceased's address. If anyone is there, you'll have to break the news. If they're not next of kin, ask who is. I'll check over the vehicle and notify Ms. Clark's family that she's been taken to the hospital."

Deputy Conrad got into the patrol car and departed. The sheriff started rummaging through the vehicle where Katie had found Missy and Harley. He brought a digital camera from his patrol car to photograph the drugs and alcohol he found.

The sheriff noticed Dave and Katie still waiting "Oh, you two. Thanks for your attentiveness. You likely saved Ms. Clark's life. How about you stay local for a day or two, in case we have any more questions?"

Katie answered, "Okay."

The sheriff glanced at the RV. "I'll speak to the park manager. He'll let you park a couple of days here at the picnic area. That way, I can find you if I need to."

"Alright. Can we go now?"

"I don't see why not. I'll notify you in a day or two when you can leave town." The sheriff extended a business card. "Here's my number in case you need to contact me."

Dave took the sheriff's card and looked at Katie. He tilted his head toward the RV. Without a word they returned to their vehicle residence. Neither Dave nor Katie felt like hiking after their discovery. And the afternoon shadows had grown long. After parking in the bare-bones picnic area, they ate canned stew for dinner in silence. The seafood dinner Katie had expected in Mendocino never came to mind.

Chapter Seven

* * *

Jeremy drove his pickup truck to the offices of Parker and Company Accounting early on Monday morning. At 6:00 a.m., the empty office space felt less odd than the house without Denyse and Katelyn. He walked alone around the firm. Large prints of sailing ships and English foxhunts decorated the walls. The conference room walls displayed photos and diplomas. He dragged his fingers across the highly polished surface of the long mahogany table. He could detect a slight papery odor from the orderly bound sets of regulations and file cabinets for the records of major clients. In the break room, he remembered celebrating the influx of new tax clients that had saved the firm nearly three years earlier.

Unlike the atmosphere that would follow during the coming workday, at this early hour the firm's offices did not overflow with the quiet energy of professional work. *This place is the result of Dad's life of diligence.* The thought of carrying on the work his father had begun made Jeremy feel hopeful. He entered his office eager to begin the day. A hand-written note waited on his desk. Herschel, Jeremy's former classmate at Auburn and fellow junior partner at the firm, had written:

Hi, Jeremy. Welcome home. I hope you enjoyed your trip to California. Candice and the boys are so excited about our vacation at Disney World. Each of them made a list of different areas they want to visit first. I'm not sure how I'm going to keep everyone happy at the "happiest place on earth."

A typed and detailed summary of the status of various projects followed. Two CPAs were working on four audits, one CPA who supervised three bookkeepers would be managing accounts of various local businesses, another CPA and a bookkeeper had started vacation themselves, and their paid summer intern, Anthony Marshall, would continue to help the bookkeepers.

The summary concluded, *No problems. Good luck with your class on taxes for businessmen week after next. Call if you need me.*

Jeremy turned on his computer and started catching up on three weeks of emails.

Anthony reported for work just before 8:00 a.m. and paused by the entrance to Jeremy's office. "You're back. Have a nice vacation?"

Jeremy looked away from his computer screen to see the African American teenager standing in his doorway. "We did. Traveling in Mom and Dad's rental RV with the whole family makes home seem quiet. Are you ready to start at Auburn next fall?" He waved for Anthony to enter and take a seat.

Anthony sat in one of the chairs facing Jeremy's desk. "I hope so. My mother is over-the-top excited about me getting accepted there and the partial scholarship they gave me. I'm just nervous about not letting everybody down."

"You'll do fine, if you discipline yourself and don't let all the on-campus activities distract you too much from your studies. You should study every day rather than wait to cram before a test." Jeremy paused as he thought about his own days at Auburn. "How are things at Herschel's house?"

"Nice. House sitting is a new experience for me. Thanks again for taking us all fishing before you left. Herschel's boys couldn't stop talking about the fish they caught."

"We got into some crappies, didn't we?"

"We sure did." Anthony thought a few seconds then added, "I hope I have kids someday to take fishing."

"I hope you do, too. What's our registration look like for the seminar week after next?"

"Fifteen. We signed up three more businessmen last Friday."

Jeremy winced a little. "That'll make the conference room crowded. I had expected only eight to ten of our clients."

"Oh, these aren't all clients. Six who heard about the seminar from others phoned asking to attend. Herschel approved them based on our Golden Rule policy."

"Sure. Everybody's welcome."

"What's the seminar about?" asked Anthony.

"Minimizing taxes. A lot of business owners don't keep the records they need to declare complete deductions to the IRS or state revenue department."

"Can I sit in?"

"Of course. You can also help me get ready for our guests."

An energetic Katelyn woke Denyse the following morning by climbing on the queen bed and bouncing up and down. "Grandmum says you need to get up. Breakfast is ready."

Denyse struggled to wake up, having just fallen asleep after suffering jet lag through much of the night. She looked at the clock. *This is past my bedtime in Mobile.* "Aren't you sleepy?" she asked her daughter.

Katelyn shook her head, slipped off the bed, and yanked on Denyse's arm. "Come on."

Denyse swung her feet to the floor and stood up. A bathrobe Beatrice had left on the bedpost offered her comfort against the midwinter chill. The aroma of frying sausages and coffee encouraged her to allow Katelyn to pull her into the kitchen. There she found Dingo sitting down to a traditional English breakfast: eggs, sausage, mushrooms, beans, a cooked tomato, and toast with jam. Beatrice had placed three laden plates on the table.

"Where's your plate, Grandmum?" asked Katelyn.

Beatrice smiled at the little girl. "I'll just have tea and a piece of toast, luv."

Denyse sipped the coffee her mother had made and watched Katelyn sampling all the foods before her.

Dingo pushed a jar of brown paste toward his granddaughter. "Try this, ankle biter."

"No, Dad! Not *Vegemite,*" Denyse objected.

"Vlady loves it," Dingo retorted.

Katelyn, eager to try everything, looked with curiosity at the unfamiliar food. "What is it?" She saw Dingo spread a thick layer on a piece of toast and take a big bite. He smiled at her while chewing.

"That's a paste made from brewer's yeast, darling." Denyse picked up a triangular piece of toast, scraped a thin layer of the spread on one corner, and handed it to her daughter. "Remember, no spitting out food you don't like. Just swallow it."

A sour expression covered Katelyn's face as she tasted the bitter Vegemite. She chewed and swallowed the bite, though. Then she reached for her orange juice to take away the taste.

"Good on ya, Katelyn. Try things and decide for yourself," Dingo encouraged her. "She's like you were at her age," he said to Denyse.

Denyse looked at her daughter with joy. "Yes, she is."

Immediately after breakfast, Katelyn started falling asleep. Although the bed beckoned to Denyse also, she realized, *This is the middle of the night back in Mobile. We both need to stay awake so we can sleep tonight.* "Dad, will you take us to the ocean like you offered last night?"

"Love to."

Denyse and Katelyn followed Dingo to the ocean south of Port Phillip Bay. There they found a rugged coastline with bits of secluded beach hidden among huge rocks. Tidal pools—each one like a fancy saltwater aquarium with star fish, sea urchins, sea cucumbers, and brightly colored little fish—collected where waves splashed over the rocks. An octopus darted away, leaving a smear of black ink.

Dingo urged them on, "Listen carefully and you can sometimes hear seals barking. And penguins come ashore near here. Just remember that the water has riptides that can pull you offshore before you realize, and box jellyfish can kill a person in a few minutes."

After those comments, Denyse collected Katelyn in her arms and requested a ride to tranquil Port Phillip Bay on the other side of Mornington Peninsula. There Denyse watched Katelyn wade in crystal-clear shallow water with a beige-colored sandy bottom. She remembered Mobile Bay's murky brown waters. A ship slowly departed Melbourne's harbor under a cloudless blue sky. *It's good to be home,* she thought. *I'll enjoy a few weeks away.*

After working all day at Parker and Company, Jeremy drove by his parents' home near Fairhope. They had downsized from the big house where Jeremy had grown up in the Spring Hill area of Mobile. Live oaks draped with Spanish moss spread branches horizontally across the streets in their eastern-shore neighborhood. Dave and Katie's house seemed cooler than the sweltering south-Alabama heat outside. As soon as Jeremy opened the front door, a short-haired, orange-striped cat trotted up to him.

"Hello, Old Yeller. Are you doing okay? Looks like the Fogles took good care of you before they left for their vacation."

The cat rubbed against Jeremy's leg. *Rrrow.*

Jeremy checked the cat's food and water. Old Yeller followed him, seeking attention. He rolled on his back inviting a belly rub. Jeremy petted the cat some more before checking the inside thermometer. It read 83 degrees. "You're enjoying the warmth, aren't you, boy?"

No complaints came from the cat.

After some more cat petting, Jeremy started to leave. Old Yeller followed him to the door. "I've got to go home now."

Jeremy then promised, "But I'll come by to see you again tomorrow and take really good care of you until my parents get home. You're safe with me."

Rrrow, rrrow, rrrow.

Chapter Eight

* * *

The morning after their gruesome discovery, Katie found herself alone in the queen-sized bed at the rear of the RV. She found normally late-sleeping Dave sitting at the tiny dining table behind the driver's seat adjacent to the cooking area. She put water into the teakettle then put it on the propane stovetop.

"What would you like for breakfast?" Katie asked.

Dave rubbed his face. "Tea is enough. I don't feel like eating much this morning."

"I feel the same way. Finding a dead body is the last thing I expected on this trip. The experience is much creepier than they portray on TV. I'm glad Katelyn wasn't with us. Or Denyse and Jeremy either."

"I lay awake thinking about the death of that young man. And who knows what's happened to the girl?"

"Don't I know about your restlessness last night? When you're awake, I'm awake. A fish would flop less than you." Katie took two cups out of the overhead cabinet and poured hot water onto teabags. She took milk and lemon juice from the small refrigerator by the sink. "Plus, I couldn't stop thinking about them either."

Dave added lemon juice and artificial sweetener to his tea. "How do you think the girl is?"

Katie poured milk into her tea. "Well, they took her to the hospital in Santa Rosa. That's only about twenty miles away. We could drop by there and try to see her. We're not supposed to leave the vicinity anyway."

"That sounds like an old detective show." Dave imitated the rough voice of a no-nonsense detective stereotype. "And don't leave town."

Katie shrugged and sipped her tea. "You heard the sheriff. They only want us around in case a question comes up."

"Do you remember the girl's name?"

"Sure. Melissa, Missy Clark. All night my mind rehearsed the whole scene."

"Let's look around the nearby town a little in the RV first, have lunch, then drive to the hospital."

"This is United Kingdom's traditional roast dinner, luv," Beatrice explained to Katelyn as she served well-baked beef plus peeled oven-roasted potatoes.

"This is wonderful, Mum," said Denyse.

"Will you have room for pudding?" Beatrice asked after the roast dinner. Without waiting for an answer, she brought out a meringue dish with a crisp crust and soft, light filling topped with fruit and whipped cream and set it before Katelyn. "This is a pavlova, luv. It's a part of Australia's national cuisine."

Katelyn asked, "Is it all for me?"

"No, luv. It's like a birthday cake. The special guest, you, shares it with everyone."

After enjoying the dessert, called "pudding" Down Under, Denyse started preparing Katelyn for bed. Beatrice interrupted them. "I've got something you might like to see first." Beatrice led Katelyn to a dark window. "Now watch this." She turned on a spotlight to reveal several raccoon-sized animals. "These are brushtail possums," she explained. "I put out bread slices for them."

Katelyn saw yellowish-brown animals with soft fur, bright eyes, and long furry tails. One mother possum carried a baby that looked a bit like a flying squirrel on her back. The little girl couldn't stop watching. "Better than a chipmunk, huh, darling?" said Denyse.

* * *

The Parkers found the town of Redwood Hills to be a juxtaposition of two cultures. Gleaming upscale clothing shops, real estate agencies, and gourmet restaurants catered to tourists, vineyard owners, and part-time residents. Both vineyards and luxurious lodge-like cabins in the forested hills served as second homes to wealthy owners from San Francisco and Silicon Valley.

A lot of the year-round residents seemed to be less affluent, get-away-from-it-all types. A variety of unpretentious establishments—a hardware store, an older grocery store, sandwich shop, a 1940s Rexall drug store with an old-fashioned soda fountain, a second-hand store, a shoe repair shop, and other practical businesses—mixed with the shops for more affluent patrons on Redwood Hills' main street. A single-story bicycle shop looked like it didn't know in which group of shops it belonged. An ice-cream shop advertising a lavender-honey flavor with chunks of honeycomb attracted both types of patrons. Posters advertised avant-garde concerts and modern art studios. Freedom of expression in dress and grooming gave Redwoods Hills a funky vibe.

An earthquake warning had been posted on many of the older, albeit still occupied, buildings. Dave read aloud, "This is an unreinforced masonry building. You may not be safe inside or near unreinforced masonry buildings during an earthquake." He examined the older building. "That's a surprise. I thought that masonry made strong walls."

84

"Vertically, yes. But an earthquake shakes side-to-side. And the San Andreas Fault is just a few miles west of here. It created Tomales Bay."

Dave winced. "So, if part of California sank into the Pacific Ocean, we'd be on the dry side?"

"Our campground might end up right on the waterfront." Katie studied her travel guide. "The lumber industry—logging massive redwood trees—brought workers into the area and resulted in the town. They also discovered and mined quicksilver, or mercury, nearby. Like many of the towns along the lower Russian River, Redwood Hills remains unincorporated. That is, the town doesn't have a municipal government."

"That would explain why Sheriff Billingsly and his deputies are an extension of the Sonoma County Sheriff's Office." Dave looked down the street at somewhat rundown buildings. "This makes me think of an Old West town inhabited by free spirits. I like it."

Sensing Dave's improved spirit since the gloomy beginning of their day, Katie suggested, "I noticed a seafood restaurant near the ocean yesterday. Maybe we could have lunch there?"

"Why is that not a surprise?"

Thirty minutes before quitting time on Tuesday afternoon, a young African American girl appeared at the reception desk of Parker and Company Accounting.

The receptionist, a well-dressed lady wearing wide glasses with a lanyard and a string of pearls, smiled. Dorothy Goldstein had been with the firm since before Jeremy was born. "Can I help you?" she asked the girl.

"I'm Sherri Thompson, one of Denyse Parker's math students. Anthony Marshall is taking me to a movie. It starts at 5:30. I thought I could save us time by meeting him here."

"Oh, well, Anthony is certainly one of our valued employees. Why don't you follow me?" Dorothy led her to Anthony's cubicle, where he sat at a computer doggedly tallying and re-checking sales figures in order to pay a client's sales taxes.

"Hello, Anthony," said Sherri.

Anthony turned in surprise and smiled broadly. "Hi, Sherri." Then he looked sorrowful. "I'm not off work until 5:00."

Beverly, Parker and Company's newest CPA and Anthony's supervisor, heard the voices and joined them. "You can finish those figures tomorrow, Anthony. Why don't you give Sherri a tour of our firm?" She and Dorothy exchanged little smiles as Anthony showed Sherri the offices with obvious pride.

Sherri paid rapt attention as Anthony explained various aspects of the accounting firm. "Everything has to be done perfectly for our clients. No room for *any* mistakes."

Jeremy stepped out of his office when he heard Anthony's voice in the hallway. He shook Sherri's hand and said, "Anthony has been doing a great job helping me organize a seminar for businessmen."

"I know about that. My father is going," answered Sherri. "You're Ms. Parker's husband, aren't you?"

"Yes. Denyse has spoken of your thoughtfulness, Sherri. You warned us before the big demonstration blocked the highways in Mobile a few years ago. We got home to our daughter because of you."

Sherri seemed surprised that Jeremy would know of her. She said the only thing she could think of. "I'm not good in math, but I took geometry last year just to be in Ms. Parker's class. I'm going to be a nurse."

"That's great. Nursing is a wonderful vocation. Did I overhear that you two are going to a movie and it starts at 5:30? Let me drive you there."

"Lena's brothers are in their early twenties now and still happy in New Zealand," Denyse told Jeremy over the phone. "You remember your parents met a farming family, the Fergusons, there? They helped Lena's family transition from Ukraine. The Travnikov brothers are still working for wages at the Fergusons' but have bought a hundred acres to start raising sheep themselves. Working and starting their farm keeps them busy. Both boys are apparently sweet on the Fergusons' daughter, Holly."

"What does Holly think about them?" asked Jeremy.

"Lena visited her brothers not long ago. She says Holly enjoys the attention. But she's getting ready for a year-long working holiday in Canada. A lot of Down-Under kids take a year or two for an OE, overseas experience."

"I remember that," Jeremy responded. "I'm hoping you won't consider Mobile your OE and stay in Australia."

"No worries, as long as you're in Mobile."

Jeremy laughed in appreciation before asking, "Well, what about Lena's mother?"

"Lena's mother is a typical Ukrainian farmer's wife with no English skills. She got desperately homesick Down Under. Lena said that both New Zealand and Australia were strange worlds to her. Maria returned to Ukraine and married a widowed farmer. She had wanted to take her teenage daughters with her. But having experienced Australia, the girls wanted no more of farm life in Ukraine and stayed with Lena. They're using Trevor's old bedroom with the bunk beds and attending college where Trevor and I both did."

"Farm life is what Lena's mother knew and felt comfortable with," commented Jeremy.

"Exactly. And Lena's sisters knew they didn't want farm life. I hear from my mum and dad that they're having some adjustment problems here."

"What sort of problems?"

"I don't know the whole story yet. I'll try to find out."

"Well then, how is Katelyn enjoying Australia?"

"The whole world here is new to her. She likes everything. We're staying in Mornington with Mum and Dad and walk down to the ocean every day. Mum has already trained some possums to come to the house for food. The corgis are nearer

Katelyn's size than Ripper. And Mum and Dad compete trying to spoil her. Your daughter is having a wonderful time."

"Your trip Down Under counts as Katelyn's OE, right?"

"I doubt that. She loves everything she sees and wants to try everything. Our girl is likely to see a lot of the world by the time she's our age."

Chapter Nine

* * *

Dave grimaced again when he saw the seafood restaurant's menu prices but didn't comment.

"What is a cioppino?" Katie wondered aloud. She waved over the waiter who had lingered nearby allowing them privacy to make their selections.

"Cioppino is just a fancy name for whatever we have on hand for seafood stew," the waiter explained. "There's always some sort of mussels in the shells, Pacific Ocean fish, and maybe some shrimp or squid. Our chef adds tomatoes and a little red wine. The cioppino comes with freshly baked bread and melted butter."

"The cioppino sounds amazing. I'll try that. Plus, I'm intrigued by this photo of the shrimp tostada. Is that slices of avocado?"

"Yes, ma'am. California avocados."

"That too, then."

The young man turned to Dave. "And for you, sir?"

"Why don't you try the Dungeness crab?" Katie suggested.

Dave looked at the waiter. "I don't suppose you have fried catfish."

"No sir, sorry."

"Then I'll have the crab and a bowl of clam chowder."

"One cioppino, one shrimp tostada, a crab cluster, and clam chowder. The crab also comes with bread." The young waiter hurried away.

"Catfish?" Katie looked at her husband like he was a stranger.

"I was kidding." After a moment's reflection, Dave reconsidered. "Actually some catfish would be good right now."

Katie rolled her eyes.

"Maybe you should turn me in for a new husband," Dave suggested.

"I would, but you're past the expiration date." As Dave laughed, Katie challenged her husband. "I'll bet you don't know why California is called 'The Golden State.'" She held up a California travel guide from her purse to authenticate her source.

Dave gazed at his wife in admiration. "I'll bet it has something to do with the California Gold Rush that started in the 1840s at Sutter's Mill near Sacramento."

Katie nodded appreciatively of Dave as an amateur historian. "1848 to be exact. But there's another reason, too."

"Because things are so expensive here?"

"No, because California is covered with golden poppies each spring."

Dave remembered the beige hillsides of dried mid-summer grasses they had passed. "Too bad we can't see them. What else have you got in that guide?"

"Well, California used to be called the 'Grizzly Bear State' because the settlers found so many here. A bear is even on their state flag. And despite a reputation for Hollywood, oil reserves, tourism, and the biggest trees in the world, California is by far the richest state in agriculture. If California were a country, it would have the fifth largest economy in the world."

Their lunches arrived. Six eighteen-inch crab legs made the Dungeness cluster. They came with a sheller that looked a lot like a pecan cracker. After enjoying a California seafood lunch, the Parkers returned to the RV with the leftovers in a Styrofoam box. On her cell phone, Katie searched for and found the directions to the hospital in Santa Rosa. "Part of me dreads what we might find," she volunteered.

"Let's hope for good news," Dave returned.

Anthony came to Jeremy's office again on Wednesday morning. "We've got seven more businessmen asking to attend your seminar on taxes."

"Seven more? Are they our clients?"

"Only one of them is a current client. Should I tell them we're full?"

Dave shook his head. "No, no. But we'll need to find a bigger place to meet. Do you have any ideas?"

Anthony thought a few seconds. "We could meet at my church, Calvary Baptist."

"Do you think they'd allow us?"

"My preacher is always looking for any way to get people into church."

"Your pastor would understand that we're not asking him to preach to them?"

"Of course. Pastor Graves says that hospitality is sermon enough."

"Okay. Would you ask your pastor on behalf of Parker and Company, Anthony? I'll phone him after you've made the initial contact. And if the church agrees, can you notify all the businessmen of the new location?"

"Glad to."

Dave and Katie's drive to the hospital in Santa Rosa paralleled the lower Russian River. Modest 1950s vintage motels calling themselves resorts lined the river's banks. Redwood trees had been planted around many of the establishments. Wherever the river provided a deep hole, vacationing families played in the clear, cool water.

Dave parked the RV in the lot for visitors. After entering the modern facility, the Parkers experienced a familiar smell of disinfectant. The odor reminded Katie of her chemo treatments seven years earlier and her surgery two years previously. She pushed down an involuntary surge of fear.

"Can you tell us where to find Melissa Clark?" Dave asked the front desk receptionist.

A taciturn middle-aged woman looked at her records on her computer screen before answering. "Ms. Melissa Clark is in room 218."

After taking an elevator and walking down a linoleum-floored hallway, Dave and Katie stopped in front of a door left slightly ajar. They heard voices inside.

"I don't know what to do with you, Missy. We've paid for your rehab twice already," a mature female voice stated with intensity. "Your father has taken your little brother and sister with him to Sacramento to remove them from the situation you've created."

"Henry isn't my father," a younger female answered with an emotionless, robotic voice. "And you don't have to do anything with me."

"Do you want me to let you just die? That's the direction you're headed."

"Suit yourself," the emotionless voice returned.

Katie looked at Dave, who puffed out his cheeks then exhaled. He reached out and knocked on the door.

A handsome, well-coiffured, mid-fortyish woman opened the door. "Yes?"

"My name is Dave Parker." Dave gestured at Katie. "And this is my wife, Katie. We dropped by to check on Missy Clark."

The woman forced a smile, but suspicion tinged her voice. "And how do you know Missy?"

"We don't really know her," Katie answered. "We discovered her unconscious in a car yesterday."

"Oh, you're that couple. Thank you so much." She opened the door wide and stepped back, using a gracious gesture to invite them to enter. "Please come in."

Inside the hospital room, Dave and Katie found a thin girl lying on her back, staring at the ceiling.

"I'm Darla Solsen, Missy's mother," the woman explained. To the girl on the bed, she said, "Missy, these are the Parkers—the people who saved your life."

"I heard," the girl responded without any inflection.

Dave and Katie stood by the bed. Dave, not knowing what to say, made eye contact with Katie. He tilted his head in Missy's direction.

Unseen by the Parkers, two figures approached the partially open hospital room door. Rather than knocking, the figures loitered, listening.

Katie shrugged a little, then began, "We just wanted to see if you're okay, Missy."

Suddenly, the girl seemed to come alive. She sat up and used her hands to push back shoulder-length blond hair. Her lips spread into a broad smile.

She spoke with the chirpy voice of an affluent California teenager. "I'm happy to meet you, Mr. and Mrs. Parker. I'm so glad you happened by just in time yesterday. I don't know how it happened. I'm totally embarrassed."

"That's okay, honey. We're glad you're feeling better." Katie noticed that Missy was an exceptionally pretty girl with delicate features and blue eyes, albeit painfully gaunt.

Missy shook her head and continued, "Thank you so much for what you did. Like, how can I ever repay you?"

"You don't need to," Dave answered. "We're just relieved that you're okay." Katie noticed a look of disgust on Darla's face.

Another knock sounded at the door. A uniformed nurse said, "Mrs. Solsen, can you come to our accounts department? There's a problem with your insurance."

"Of course." Darla gave a stern look at Missy. "I'll be right back," she promised Dave and Katie.

As soon as her mother had departed, Missy spoke with a sense of urgency. "Do you have anything that could make me feel better?"

"What do you mean?" asked Katie.

"You're older people. You must have some sort of painkillers on you."

"I'm sorry, we don't. But we could ring the nurse for you." Dave moved toward the nurse call button.

"Forget that Nazi woman. She doesn't care how much I suffer."

Katie shook her head. "We don't have any drugs, Missy. And even if we did, we wouldn't give them to you without approval from the hospital."

"Are you two Nazis too?" Missy pouted a minute before asking, "How about just some Tylenol then?"

Dave shook his head.

"Then you can both go to hell," finished Missy with malice and fell back onto the bed from her sitting position.

Dave and Katie stood stunned at Missy's venom. Fortunately for them, Darla reappeared. "They say our insurance doesn't cover treatment for self-inflicted drug abuse. Then my credit card was declined. I don't know what to do now." Darla seemed on the verge of despair.

"I'm feeling better, Mom," Missy said sweetly as she sat back up, composed and smiling. "We can check out and go home."

"Well, we better get going then," said Dave. Katie nodded affirmation.

Both Dave and Katie felt confused and embarrassed to have witnessed a family's internal trauma. They hurried out of the hospital room away from Missy and Darla. In the hallway, they nearly collided with Sheriff Billingsly and young Deputy Conrad. Already stressed by Missy's inappropriate plea, Dave demanded, "Have you two been eavesdropping?"

Chapter Ten

✱ ✱ ✱

The sheriff gave a sheepish grin and a shrug to Dave's accusation of eavesdropping. "Sometimes you can learn more by quietly listening than you can by questioning. I've talked to Missy before. With me, she's as tight as a clam."

Dave softened his tone. "I'm sorry for reacting."

The sheriff nodded acceptance of Dave's words. "I'm at my wit's end about the rash of overdoses we're experiencing. I've got people getting higher than a redwood all over. I'll try any trick to save some kids' lives. Otherwise, I'm afraid we'll be visiting Missy at the morgue next time."

Partly to make amends for his abruptness but more from curiosity, Dave offered, "Let me buy you both a cup of coffee, tea, or a coke."

"That would be nice. Thank you, Mr. Parker."

Seated around a table in the hospital cafeteria, Sheriff Billingsly and Deputy Conrad watched with interest how Dave made tea with lemon. Then Dave asked about the overdose crisis. "This crisis seems worse than drug abuse during previous decades."

"We're in northern California. Cannabis is as common as high prices here. But prescription drugs are how most victims get hooked on opioids, especially upper-middle-class kids, like Missy. They think if a pill is medicine, it can't hurt them. That leads to heroin and even worse." The sheriff took a deep swallow of coffee. "I don't know what to do."

Katie leaned forward. "How do the kids get the prescription drugs?"

"That's what I'd like to know. But in Redwood Hills we're just a small-town police department. Only me and a few deputies. We mostly give traffic tickets and assist at accidents. Deal with a few domestic disturbances. The state troopers don't have enough resources to help us. I just wish I could figure out how so many legal prescription drugs are available here."

"Have you tried to follow the money?" Dave asked. "Somebody must be benefitting financially. The money can frequently lead you to the criminals."

Sheriff Billingsly looked carefully at Dave and Katie. "What? Are you two like those amateur detectives on TV who frustrate the police by solving mysteries before the authorities?"

Katie intervened, "No. No. We're just an ordinary couple from Alabama trying to enjoy a vacation and see California."

Billingsly sighed. "Well, that's too bad."

Sheriff Billingsly's disappointment surprised Dave. "Huh?"

The sheriff explained, "I'd be happy to have someone to swoop in and find some leads, solve the whole case, and make us cops look incompetent. Anything to save some kids. Without some help, I'm like a duck in a desert." He sighed more deeply. "Too bad you're just ordinary tourists."

"Well, I *am* a forensic accountant," returned Dave.

"What do forensic accountants do?"

"We investigate illegalities by examining financial records. That's like turning over a big rock. All sorts of slugs and crawly creatures are exposed."

"How do you do that?"

"You start by finding some probable cause, subpoena or confiscate the records with a warrant, and then follow the money trail in the paperwork. The money and benefiter always show how things really work."

The sheriff leaned forward in anticipation. "Could you do that for Redwood Hills? You'd probably save some kids' lives."

"Sorry, I'm on vacation to get *away* from work."

Katie had become sympathetic while listening. She remembered the distress Missy had exhibited and thought of the kids she had taught, of Jeremy as a teenager, or Denyse, or Katelyn. She spoke to Dave, "Can't we help them a little?"

Dave stared at his wife. "Help them?"

She reached out to put her hand on his arm. "Dave, you're an expert. You could give them a day or two of pro-bono consulting. You might save a few lives." She paused a second before adding, "Remember, drugs may have contributed to your brother Chuck's death."

"What? How did you know about that?"

"Your mother told me."

Dave leaned back and shook his head. But his mouth said, "Sure. Okay. For a few days."

Sheriff Billingsly's demeanor instantly became cheerful. "That's great! We can't afford your big forensic accountant fees. But Holiday Home Park Campground is a nice, quiet place and the owner owes us a favor. You can stay in a prime spot without charge. And I'll get you a loaner car from a used car dealer, so you won't have to drive your RV everywhere. Deputy Conrad here will help you get settled at the campground. Just keep me in the loop. Got to go now. I'm supposed to be at a meeting with local businessmen about the new traffic light already. Help 'em out, Conrad."

Katelyn will be fine with Mum, Denyse thought as she drove Beatrice's car to her former home in Melbourne. She parked in the same driveway spot Beatrice had for many years. Ringing the doorbell to her childhood home felt awkward. No matter. Nobody answered the door even though Denyse could hear loud female voices inside. Finding the door unlocked, she let herself in.

"*Vam nuzhno idti v tserkov.*" Lena's tone sounded harsh compared to the demure young woman Denyse had known.

The voices came from the kitchen. Sveta answered Lena with her own harsh words. "Speak English. I've told you I won't speak in Russian anymore."

Denyse lingered in the dark hallway, hating to eavesdrop but not wanting to intrude either. Light came through the partially open doorway to the kitchen. Denyse's heart cringed at the angry words of inner-family conflict she heard.

Lena spoke again. "You know that I said, 'You need to go to church.' Have you forgotten your Russian?"

"I'm trying to forget that language and our old life in Ukraine. We have a new life now in Australia. Maybe I *could* forget Russian if you'd stop using it."

"Your new Australian life is going to lead you into trouble."

"Oh? How can that trouble be any worse than having your father murdered, fleeing on foot from your home, and living in a refugee camp tent? When winter came, we stayed in an old warehouse along with hundreds of other miserable people."

Denyse felt tightness in her chest at Sveta's description of the dilemma the girls had endured.

Lena's voice softened. "That *was* bad, Sveta. We all had it hard."

"Then you left us there!" Sveta shouted. "How would you know how hard it was?"

Lena's voice rose again. "You know that I went to find a good place for all of us."

"A place so good that Mama returned to Ukraine."

"I lived outdoors in the woods without the tent or warehouse you had," Lena shouted in return.

"You did that until you met a man to protect and take care of you. That's what I'm trying to do, too."

"I met a *good* man. You're going to find a bad man the way you're going. Or one will find you. A man who won't let you live as a Christian."

"Living as Christians didn't help us in Ukraine, did it?"

Denyse found herself holding her breath and forced herself to breathe.

Lena tried a different approach. "You say you're looking for a man. You could find a decent man in church. Make a good marriage."

"Is that how you met your husband? Trevor doesn't go to church even now."

"Our parents went to church. They had a good marriage," Lena insisted.

"A good marriage to our parents meant planting potatoes together in the fields. Is that the kind of marriage Sandra and I would find in your church?" Sveta returned.

Lena had no answer. Sveta stormed out of the kitchen and passed Denyse in the hallway without acknowledging her. Sandra hadn't spoken in the argument but followed her younger sister.

"Where are you going?" Lena shouted after them.

"Anywhere but here. And you're not our mother!" Sveta shouted back.

Although exhausted, Jeremy kept his promise to visit Old Yeller that afternoon. After a long day at the office, he wanted dinner, and Ripper would be expecting a walk to the bay. *A promise is a promise,* Jeremy told himself. *Even to a cat.*

Hearing the door open, Old Yeller came running to meet Jeremy again. Obviously lonely, the cat acted desperate for attention.

Rrrow. Rrrow. Rrrow.

"I've got an idea, boy. Why don't you come home with me?"

When the cat didn't object, Jeremy looked in his parents' storage room until he found their cat carrier. Old Yeller resisted being stuffed into any enclosure, even if he *was* lonely. But Jeremy didn't allow him any options. He collected Old Yeller's litter pan, a fresh bag of litter, and a bag of cat food from his parents' utility room.

This is a great idea, Jeremy thought as he drove while Old Yeller rode beside him in the carrier on the pickup's bench seat.

Rrrow. Rrrow. Rrrow.

"Settle down, boy. You'll enjoy visiting my house. You know and like Ripper. Well, he likes you, anyway."

Once home, Jeremy took the carrier inside. He opened the carrier door to let Old Yeller exit on his own when ready. The cat waited a few minutes then emerged, looking all around and sniffing with curiosity.

"Come on in, Ripper," Jeremy invited. The big Labrador bounded in and frisked around in his joy to see Jeremy. Old Yeller, unnerved by such energetic enthusiasm from an animal ten times his size, arched his back, burred up, and then retreated behind the couch.

"Let's go for a walk, Ripper. Let Old Yeller settle in," Jeremy said to his dog. They headed out the door toward the bay, Ripper carrying the tennis ball.

As he walked, Jeremy acknowledged to himself, *I'm totally bushed. I wish I had returned from California a day or two earlier to get some rest before returning to work. And without the family here, all the chores fall on me.*

Returning to the house after many tennis ball throws, Jeremy found Old Yeller out from behind the couch investigating his surroundings. Ripper, subdued by expending a lot of energy fetching, approached the cat. Old Yeller rubbed against the dog's legs and received a pink tongue lick of welcome on his face. The cat continued to explore without complaint.

Jeremy put a frozen pizza in the oven. While the pizza baked, he put a bowl of dry cat food, fresh water, and the litter box in the laundry room. He opened a can of Denyse's tuna and put it on a saucer.

"Kitty, kitty, kitty," he called. The cat came to the call and the odor of tuna, a special treat. When Ripper showed interest in stealing Old Yeller's food, Jeremy put him in the backyard. Then he noticed Old Yeller sitting beside the front door after eating the tuna.

He wants out. Mom and Dad let him go outside, Jeremy reasoned. He got up and opened the front door cat width. Indeed, Old Yeller darted out.

Jeremy returned to the pizza and TV. He found a baseball game. With the drone of the ball game, he soon fell asleep.

After a couple of hours, his aching neck woke him. *I need some rest. Should go to bed early tonight.* Then Jeremy remembered Old Yeller outside. *I'd better let the cat in before I go to bed.*

He opened the front door and called, "Old Yeller, come on in." No cat.

He opened the door wider. "Kitty, kitty, kitty." No cat.

Feeling a touch of alarm, Jeremy shouted, "Old Yeller, Old Yeller!" No cat.

Jeremy got out a flashlight and circled the house, pointing the beam under the azaleas and camellias. He shined the light every place that could conceal a cat, hoping for the gleam of green eyes in the dark. No cat. Jeremy walked up and down the street at 11:00 p.m. shining the light and calling. No cat. Old Yeller had disappeared.

Chapter Eleven

* * *

With care, Denyse entered the kitchen where the confrontation between Lena and Sveta had occurred. Baby Maria sat fussing in a highchair. Lena looked up, her cheeks streaked with tears.

"Oh, Denyse. I didn't know you were here."

"I let myself in. I hope you don't mind."

Lena noticed Maria's distress and picked her up. "Of course I don't mind," she answered Denyse. "You should always consider this as your home, too." Lena rocked Maria in her arms until the infant quieted. She looked at Denyse standing awkwardly. "Did you hear us arguing?"

"Yes, I'm sorry for eavesdropping."

Lena shrugged. "You heard nothing that doesn't go on here all the time."

Denyse sat down in a kitchen chair. "Apparently your sisters are having some adjustment challenges."

Lena put Maria back into the highchair. "Would you feed her? I'll make us some tea."

"Sure. What do you want Maria to have?"

"Try the flavored yogurt. She likes that. The spoons are where Beatrice always kept them." Lena put on the teakettle. "My life was as hard as my sisters', harder. Holding onto the church and my values is what saw me through to a better life."

Denyse extended a tiny spoon of mango-flavored yogurt to Maria, who accepted it eagerly and smiled. "Your faith and courage also made life better for your brothers and have given your sisters a chance at a good future."

"I wish Sveta and Sandra appreciated that."

"That's the eternal lament of mothers. And you're trying to be a mother to your sisters."

More tears rolled down Lena's cheeks. "Our real mother abandoned us."

"I suspect all the challenges simply overwhelmed your mother. And she knew how strong of character you are, Lena. Your mother knew that you are the only real hope for her daughters. She couldn't have possibly dealt with the circumstances here."

Lena nodded as she poured tea for herself and Denyse. She brought out milk for Denyse and put lemon and sugar in her own tea.

"Dave uses lemon in his tea," said Denyse, trying to lighten the mood.

"Everybody in Ukraine does, too. All the people in Russian-speaking countries use lemon in tea."

"How is Trevor dealing with your circumstances?"

Lena sighed. "Trevor is a good man. But he doesn't know how to deal with my sisters either. He just closes himself into the little place he made for himself and writes, except for the days he takes classes at the university. I think he takes walks alone when my sisters are at school. I'm usually at the childcare center with Vlady and Maria then."

"How is the childcare business going?"

"We make plenty of money. I started the childcare center to give my mother and sisters a place to work and earn money. Now my mother is gone. Sandra and Sveta are in school and don't help much even when they could. The center takes nearly twelve hours of my time every weekday. That, and two children, and my sisters, don't leave me much time for Trevor."

"Has he complained?"

"No, but he used to ask me to go places with him, to do things like we did at first. I never had time to join him. Now Trevor has stopped asking."

"Could you close down the childcare business?"

"That would allow me a lot more time. But Trevor doesn't earn much money writing yet. Australia has a small population compared to America or the United Kingdom. His books aren't popular outside of this country and some in New Zealand. We need the money from the childcare business for the children and my sisters."

"Would a loan help? Maybe a family loan?"

"No, if we took a loan and closed the childcare business, then we couldn't pay the loan back. When the loan ran out, we'd have no childcare business and no money. The Parkers have already spent a fortune rescuing me and Trevor. Then Dingo gave us half the advance he got for his book. Now we need to keep making a living on our own and find a way to have some free time."

"Maybe your sisters could help out more when not in school."

"I'm just trying to keep Sveta and Sandra from running away and being homeless like I was. Bad things would happen to them." Lena sighed and sipped her tea. She looked back at Denyse. "Would you try talking to my sisters?"

"Me? What would I say?"

"You could encourage them to go to church. If I knew anything better, I'd have already told them."

Lena finished her tea then took Maria to bathe before putting her down for a nap. Denyse sat alone in the kitchen for a few minutes then went looking for Trevor. She couldn't locate him in any room of the house. Then she put her ear to the closed door of the closet where Beatrice and Dingo had kept tools and household supplies. She heard music playing inside and knocked.

The door swung outwards. Denyse saw Trevor sitting in a cramped five-by-six-foot space. He had just enough room for a swivel chair and a computer console. Loaded bookshelves lined the wall above the computer. A few empty Pepsi cans lay around. A vent fan brought air into the windowless cubby. Trevor looked away from the computer, smiled, and reached to turn down the music. "Hi, sis. How do you like my office?"

"It's nicely . . . cozy. This is where you work?"

"The very place. I'd ask you to sit down . . . but . . ." Trevor lifted his hands to indicate the lack of space.

"I'll be right back." Denyse collected a chair from the kitchen to allow her to sit in Trevor's doorway.

"I have everything I need to work in here," explained Trevor. "The internet lets me research anything I want to know from this chair. Where's my charming niece, Katelyn?"

"Mum has taken her to a bayside beach. She loves playing in the sand."

"Your daughter is really special. And I hear you're expecting again."

"We are. This time we've asked the doctor about the baby's sex. We're having a boy. We're going to name him Jeremy Graham Parker. The middle name honors dad."

"A few years ago I'd never have said this, but our father has earned the honor."

Despite her surprise at her brother's respectful demeanor, Denyse had to smile. "So how's life, little brother?"

"I'm soldiering on. Things could be worse."

"What things are less than good?"

Trevor slumped to gesture weariness. "Well, I'm tired of being stuck in Melbourne."

"Your writing is going well."

"Yeah. But we're not making enough money from my novels yet. I'll need to become known outside Down Under to generate major sales. That's hard when I'm stuck here in Melbourne. And I sure could use a vacation or something.

Dad's book and then three novels in just four years was a lot of work. And I'm starting on another story now. Do you have any idea how much effort is involved in creating eighty thousand interesting and readable words?"

"I can hardly imagine." Denyse leaned forward. "Why don't you and Lena take a vacation? Mum could take care of Vlady and Maria. Lena's sisters could run the childcare center."

"A vacation? Where? If I leave Melbourne, I get sent to prison in New Zealand. I'm required to get special permission from my parole officer just to visit Mum and Dad on the Mornington Peninsula."

"You might try a staycation. You and Lena could just lie around for a week or so, maybe at Mum and Dad's while they're on a trip."

"Fat chance. Lena is consumed with Vlady and Maria, her daycare center demands attention, and now her sisters are acting out. Lena wouldn't trust Sveta and Sandra unsupervised to keep the plants watered, much less take care of a bunch of kids all day."

"What do you mean?"

"The girls are getting involved with some pretty rough types. They can't read Australian cues of personality and sexuality."

"Lena thinks I might be able to help them."

"You're welcome to try. But I doubt you can change those girls. Sveta is a natural flirt. And you've seen how she looks. She doesn't understand how Australian men interpret her words and gestures, or the danger she's putting herself in. So I don't think you can help, sis. We've got nobody to depend on but ourselves."

Denyse detected a hard edge and underlying anger in Trevor's voice. She realized, *Lena wants to depend on the church. Trevor insists on complete self-reliance. They are growing further apart every day.*

* * *

Dave and Katie followed Deputy Conrad's squad car to Holiday Home Park Campground. The sheriff had already phoned the proprietor.

"Drive around the loop. Pick any empty spot you like," the middle-aged woman at the campground's office told them. "You can use the communal toilet and shower, if you wish. We also have a wastewater dump behind this office for sewage you collect in the RV. Here's the Wi-Fi password."

The Parkers found the campground to be a bit run-down but located in a charming setting. The parking spots had been nestled into a second-growth stand of redwoods and Douglas firs. Trees six to eight feet in diameter towered a hundred feet and more above them. A ten-foot-wide stream—a tributary to the Russian River—with crystal-clear water splashed over rocks along one side of the campground. Dave and Katie selected a shady campsite with a concrete parking pad, water and electrical hookups, a cable TV connection, an outdoor grill and fire pit, and a redwood picnic table. Cool, damp air and the smell of firs surrounded them as they exited the RV.

"Now this isn't so bad," said Katie. "I was tired of spending so much time driving and riding in the RV everyday anyway. I'll enjoy being in this lovely spot a few days."

Dave stared at an enormous black bird stalking around the campsites. "That's the biggest crow I've ever seen."

"That's a raven," Katie answered. The bird began a low drawn-out croak quite different from the caw of a crow. "They're related to crows, though."

A teenage boy pulled up in a gray pre-owned car—a compact. "This is your loaner car," Deputy Conrad told them. "I'll return the driver to the car lot. Call us if you need anything." He handed Dave a business card and departed with the deliveryman.

Dave looked at the sun low in the western sky. "Are you hungry?"

"Sure. Would you like to drive to Mendocino for dinner?"

"Not today. How about we take the car to a local burger joint instead?"

"Alright for tonight. But not tomorrow."

✳ ✳ ✳

An old-fashioned diner with tile floors, an original jukebox, and vinyl-covered booths welcomed the Parkers.

"I don't think they're trying for a retro motif," Katie whispered. "I'll bet this place simply hasn't changed since they opened."

Dave pointed to the menu. "Well, one thing has likely changed. I'll bet the 1950s restaurant didn't feature Mex."

In addition to hearty burgers and chicken-fried steak, the diner offered quesadillas, burritos, and tacos. A perky Hispanic girl approached the table. "My name is Camila. I'll be serving you. What can I get you to drink?"

After Dave enjoyed a burger and Katie a quesadilla, the Parkers returned to the campground. While Dave piddled with the RV's TV, Katie opened her laptop and connected to the Wi-Fi. She googled "opioid epidemic" and started sharing with Dave.

"Opioids can be useful as sedatives and painkillers. Morphine occurs naturally in poppy plants and has been used as a painkiller and as a recreational drug."

"I guess opium was an early form of addiction," suggested Dave.

"Yes, cultivation of poppies for drug use dates to the earliest years of human agriculture. Opium use was well known in ancient Mesopotamia and Greece. Heroin, a refined form of morphine, was first synthesized for medical use before physicians realized its potent addictive properties."

Dave turned off the TV. "What makes it such a killer?"

"All opioids act by stimulating dopamine release in the body. In human physiology, dopamine is related to the pleasure center of the brain. That's why people are tempted to use opioids for recreation. Others may seek a sedative to deal with an emotional pain. Regardless of why people use opioids, the sedative aspect also affects the part of the brain that regulates breathing. That's how opioids kill. Deaths occur when the respiratory center is severely depressed."

"Then Harley died of respiratory failure."

"So it would seem. After periodic use, anybody can get addicted to prescription painkillers and experience severe symptoms of withdrawal. When the prescription drugs are unavailable or the user wants a stronger effect, many seek out heroin. Fentanyl is another very strong opioid used primarily as an anesthetic. Only two milligrams of fentanyl can kill a person. Deaths from drug overdose have increased dramatically in the last decade. The leading cause of death of Americans under fifty is now drug overdose."

Chapter Twelve

* * *

At dawn, Jeremy got up to search the neighborhood for Old Yeller. He found no cat, nor anyone who had seen him.

Jeremy knew Dorothy and her husband liked cats and kept several. When she arrived for work, he told her about Old Yeller's disappearance. "I thought he would mostly sleep all day like at Mom and Dad's. Then he'd occasionally go outside and come back in—the same as at their house."

Dorothy looked at Jeremy in exasperation. "You let Old Yeller go outside in a strange place?"

"Mom and Dad let him go outside."

"Your parents' house and yard are his home. Dave and Katie are his family. Now he's trying to find his home and family."

Jeremy looked hopeful. "So I should go to their house to get him?"

"You think Old Yeller is a homing pigeon? He doesn't know the way to your parents' house. But he's risking everything trying to find them. He thinks he has to take himself home."

"Cats can think?"

Dorothy nodded. "Sure, cats can think. But they think like a cat. That means *rescue your own self.*"

"What should I do? Mom and Dad love that cat. Old Yeller alerted them when the gunmen invaded the mansion in Minnesota."

"You'll have to find him. I'll help you," Dorothy offered.

"You'd walk the streets calling for him?"

"That won't work. Your parents are his family, not you or me. Even if he heard one of us calling his name, he would likely expect us to find him rather than come running. He's not a dog." Dorothy thought a second. "The first thing we'll need is a photo."

"A picture of Old Yeller?"

"Who else? Maybe somebody will recognize him. And we need to get the picture distributed quickly. The more time that passes, the farther he'll travel, hoping to stumble across your parents' house."

Jeremy immediately left the office and drove to his parents' house. There he spent most of the morning looking for a photo of Old Yeller. Not having lived in their downsized house, he didn't know where his parents kept their photo albums. He finally found the albums in a bedroom closet and Old Yeller's image among the Christmas photos. After emailing the photo to Dorothy, he spent the afternoon making a LOST CAT notice with Old Yeller's photo and the promise of a reward. Then he made a hundred copies and posted them in his neighborhood wherever people might notice.

* * *

Denyse sat facing Sandra and Sveta at a café. A pot of tea and a plate of scones she had purchased waited between them.

"Thank you for meeting with me. We're all family now. Lena thought I, as a native Australian, might have some advice for you."

"What sort of advice could you have for us?" Sveta asked in a petulant tone.

"Well, Australia is a new place for you. I might have advice about fitting in."

Sandra squeezed juice from a slice of lemon into her tea. "We're doing alright. We've made a lot of Australian friends." She then bit into a pastry.

"Not everyone who acts like your friend, is a friend. You need to be careful about the friends you make."

Sveta crossed her arms. "Show us the friends Trevor has made."

"Well, Trevor is a special case. He always preferred being alone. Until he met your sister."

"He still spends all his time alone, even though he has our sister. Even now he's locked away in a closet. That's not the type of man I want to be with."

"Trevor is trying to support his family by writing."

"So?"

"That's honorable at least. A lot of Australian men aren't honorable in their intentions."

"What good is being honorable? Our father was honorable. He refused to fight for the Russians because he didn't want to get killed and not be able to support his family. That got him murdered anyway. Then we fled to a refugee camp. Men there took advantage of girls who had no home. Even Lena had to accept their help even though she mistrusted them."

Denyse started to feel some exasperation at Sveta's cheekiness. "Lena took a desperate chance trying to rescue you from that camp. It nearly backfired on her. Holding onto her values is what ultimately got you out of that camp. She remained true to the things the church had taught her."

Sveta leaned forward. Her face curled in malice. "How about you? Did you hold onto your values?"

Denyse rocked back in her chair. "What do you mean?"

"At first, Dingo tried to be a father figure to us. He told us not to do what you did."

Denyse sat dumfounded.

Sveta's look of malice turned into a sneer. "I am counting Katelyn's age against your wedding date. Didn't you get pregnant before you were married? And where did you meet your husband?"

Denyse felt stunned by the personal accusation.

"Lena told us that you met Jeremy in church." Sveta rose to leave.

"Wait a minute, Sveta," Denyse demanded. To her surprise the girl stopped and stood waiting. "Jeremy and I made a mistake. But we were already engaged to get married. A permanent marriage and joining of two lives. Don't throw away the chance you have for that."

Sveta shrugged and walked away. Denyse felt an immense burden of failure. She could hardly look up from the table. Once she did look up, she saw Sandra sitting watching her. "Sandra, I'm sorry for forgetting you."

"That's alright. I'm easy to forget when Sveta is around."

"I didn't mean that. I should have said—"

Sandra interrupted her. "I know you are trying to help us, Denyse. Sveta knows that too somewhere inside of her. She's just too angry and afraid to show any weakness." Sandra reached out and took another scone off the plate between them. "These are good. Sveta didn't touch her tea. Do you mind if I drink it?"

"Certainly I don't mind, honey." *I can't believe I called her honey. Katie is rubbing off on me.*

Sandra talked without looking at Denyse while she prepared her second cup of tea. "Sveta is the youngest of our family. The baby in any family naturally gets more attention, especially when the baby is as cute as Sveta. Our father doted on Sveta and called her his 'littlest girl.' His death was terrible for all of us, but especially for Sveta. Afterwards our mother had lost all her joy. Mama dealt with our situation by grimly doing day-to-day things. Sveta, who had been adored, suddenly became just another hungry kid."

Denyse watched Sandra munch the scones and sip her lemon-flavored tea. "You said Sveta was afraid. What does she fear, Sandra?"

Sandra spoke with her eyes unfocused. "In the camp, after Lena left, we didn't have enough food or warm winter clothes. Most of us got sick and we didn't have any money for medicine. Sveta is so beautiful. Men came and tried to buy her. Our mother said 'No.' But some desperate families did sell daughters to save their other children. Sveta knew how much we needed money. She even talked about her duty to allow herself to be sold to save the family. But even without paying, sometimes rough men would steal girls like her. You don't get over a fear like that easily."

Denyse felt her mouth go dry in horror. "What about you, Sandra?"

"I'm not so pretty like Sveta or Lena." Sandra glanced at Denyse for an instant. "You're beautiful too, Denyse." She looked away again. "Men also offered money for me. But only a small amount compared to Sveta. I felt safe as long as our mother wouldn't take the money for Sveta."

Denyse felt overwhelmed at Sandra's story. She forced herself to speak. "Sveta is looking for a man to protect and take care of her. How about you, Sandra? What would you like for your life?"

"Our father died trying to take care of us. He was a good man and he loved our mother, all of us. I'd like to marry a man like him, except not a poor peasant farmer. And I'd like to find a way to get a good job to take care of myself until then. If something happened to my husband, I would have the job to take care of our children."

"You're in fifth form. Have you thought about going to uni next year? That could help you to get a good job."

Sandra shook her head. "I don't have money for a university. Nobody in our family has ever gone to a university."

"I was the first in my family to go. I found a way to pay for my uni. You can, too."

Sandra shrugged without emotion or belief. "Denyse, there's something else I would like to learn."

"What's that, honey?" *I called her honey again.*

"Lena told us about what a good man is your husband, Jeremy. Trevor admires Jeremy, too. Can you teach me how to get a good man like yours? But maybe not as handsome a man as Jeremy, because I'm not pretty like you."

"Well, a good man is a lot better to marry than a handsome man. You first start by becoming a woman a good man would want to marry. Shall we order another pot of tea while we talk, Sandra? How about a sandwich or some pumpkin soup?"

Sandra looked Denyse in the eyes for the first time and smiled. "Yes. Thank you."

That afternoon Anthony came to Jeremy's office again. "I typed the sections you had underlined in the **IRS** code and from those textbooks. Then I inserted them into the places you indicated in the PowerPoint."

"Thanks. Footnote the sources then email me the files. I'll look over them."

"Got it."

"The seminar is in just a week. Have you got the binders, dividers, and name tags ready?"

"I have them all laid out in the conference room."

"Okay. When I send the files back to you, print the pages and assemble the handouts."

"I'm ready," Anthony assured Jeremy. "Have you heard anything about Mr. and Mrs. Parker's cat?"

"Not yet. We're hoping for a phone call from the bulletins I posted yesterday. Dorothy has placed several online notices and is scouring the internet for possible sightings. She's found nothing so far. But Old Yeller's only been gone two days."

Anthony nodded in sympathy and turned to leave. "How many do we have registered for the seminar now?" Jeremy called after him.

"Thirty-nine."

"Better make sixty handouts."

Chapter Thirteen

* * *

Jeremy opened the front door to his and Denyse's home after a long day at the office. He imagined the joy he would experience to see Old Yeller coming out to rub against his leg. No cat greeted him, though. He knew that Ripper in the backyard would be raring for a walk together. *I'm just too tired tonight,* he told himself and left the dog alone.

Jeremy's cell phone rang. He fumbled the phone trying to answer quickly. *Please, let this be somebody calling about Old Yeller.* "Hello."

"Hi, lover," greeted Denyse.

"Oh, it's you."

"You don't sound happy to hear from your wife. Who did you expect to call?" Denyse demanded.

"Of course I'm happy to hear from you. I was just hoping for someone else to call."

"Someone you want to hear from more than your wife?"

"No, of course not, sweetheart. It's just that I have a big problem here."

"Whatever your problem is, it'll get bigger by taking me for granted."

"Yeah, you're right about that," Jeremy answered with resignation. "I'm sorry."

"Fair dinkum. So what's the rub?"

"I've lost Mom and Dad's cat, Old Yeller. I'm trying everything to find him. The call I'm hoping to get is from someone, anyone, who's seen him."

"Oh, bummer. Your parents love that cat. So does Katelyn."

"Yeah, they do. So does Katelyn still like Oz?"

"She's doing fine. We petted a koala today at the Healesville Sanctuary."

"I love how sanctuaries in Australia let you get so close to the animals. Is your family enjoying seeing Katelyn?"

"Of course. Mum and Dad are still spoiling her. Letting her eat pav every day."

Jeremy sighed. "I miss pavlova—all that fruit, meringue, and cream."

"I've picked up an easy pav recipe here. Don't worry, I'll make you one when we get home," Denyse promised. "Katelyn adores Mum's corgis. I think she'll be an animal lover."

"How about Trevor's family?"

"That's where I've got problems."

"Problems?"

"Trevor and Lena have very different values. They know how to work together in a crisis but not when life's normal. They don't know how to communicate."

"We're still learning how to communicate ourselves."

"Yes, and it's hard work." Denyse sighed before continuing. "Then Lena's sisters are acting out. They're making bad choices trying to fit into Aussie culture."

"What sort of bad choices?"

"Making the wrong friends. Misunderstanding the intentions of men. They won't listen to Lena. Trevor has simply withdrawn from everything. Mum and Dad tried some to influence the girls. But my parents hardly have a history of good choices themselves."

"Hey, you and I have something in common! How do you feel about having dysfunctional in-laws?" teased Jeremy.

"Very funny," Denyse returned without any humor in her voice. Then she added with a teasing tone of her own, "Aren't you the one who lost Dave and Katie's cat? Better dysfunctional in-laws than a dysfunctional son."

"Maybe so," Jeremy admitted. "Well then, what are you going to do about Lena's sisters?"

"I thought I'd call your mother and ask her what to do about the girls."

"A good idea. Remember Mom doesn't know about Old Yeller. Maybe I can locate him before she and Dad find out."

"No worries. I won't breathe a word of the cat crisis. And I'll ask Lena and the others to pray for you to find Old Yeller."

* * *

Since the dump drain was behind the campground's office, Dave would have to disconnect all the hookups and move the RV to empty the waste tank. To reduce that inconvenience, Dave and Katie decided to use the communal campground toilet and shower. The abundance of hot water—all that mattered to Dave—affirmed that decision for them.

Katie sniffed the strong odor of Pine-Sol. *Clean but hardly welcoming,* she rated the facility. Returning to the RV by herself from a shower in the early evening, she walked past a tall thirtyish woman headed there.

"Do I know you?" Katie heard from a husky female voice behind her. Katie turned to see the young woman looking at her with a wry smile. "You look familiar," the woman said.

Anybody could tell from her tanned skin and the light tips of her reddish-brown hair that the young woman spent a lot of time outdoors. A taut physique and stocky legs identified her as an athlete, maybe a triathlon competitor. Katie shook her head. "I doubt you know me. I'm not from California. You're probably confusing me with someone else."

The woman persisted. "And you have an accent. You're from down South."

"That's right. My husband and I are from Mobile, Alabama. We're on vacation."

"Mobile. Mobile." The young woman puzzled. "I got stranded there once." Then her eyes widened. "I know you!"

Katie waited.

"You're Jeremy's mother. Jeremy Parker."

Katie politely replied, "Yes, that's right. Sorry, I don't remember you."

"I'm Tara. I was Jeremy's date to his senior prom."

Katie's mouth gaped open. The woman in front of her didn't look like the woman she and Dave had met—the woman Jeremy had nearly absconded with.

Recognizing Katie's confusion, Tara continued, "Have you got just a minute? There's my camper." She pointed to a twelve-foot, single-person unit sitting on the ground with two flat tires. "Wait right here. I'll be back in just a minute."

Katie watched the woman run to her camper, listening as her flip-flops flapped a rhythmic beat. In literally a minute, the young woman had returned with an older-model laptop. Cradling the device with her left arm, she made a few taps with her right hand. She turned the screen toward Katie. The picture Dave had taken before Jeremy's senior prom filled the screen. Katie recognized the staircase in the Mobile home where she and Dave had raised Jeremy. But the provocatively dressed and made-up girl in the photo hardly resembled the outdoorsy young woman who stood before her. Katie looked back and forth between the photo and the woman holding the laptop. Yes, the face was the same.

Tara smiled. "Your name is Katie, right? Katie Parker. And your husband's name is Dave."

Katie didn't know how to respond other than, "You look different."

Tara looked at the photo on the laptop herself. "Oh, that. I had just decked out to impress Jeremy's school friends for him." She looked at the picture again. "Wow, I guess I really did put it on thick. This is the real me." She gestured, waving from her head to her feet.

"What are you doing here, . . ." Katie couldn't remember the young woman's name.

"Tara."

"Yes, Tara," Katie slowly repeated.

"I live here for now." Tara pointed to her tiny camper again. "I might move on after I work off a new bike at a shop downtown."

"Oh, right." Katie—still trying to visualize the woman before her as Jeremy's date—couldn't think clearly. And being damp from the shower, she shivered in the evening air. The warmth of their RV beckoned her home. "Well, Tara, it was nice meeting you again." Katie turned to go.

"Say hi to Dave for me."

"I'll do that."

* * *

Back in the RV, Katie suffered from surprise bordering on shock. "You'll never believe who I just met," she said to Dave while snuggling up to him to get warm.

"Amelia Earhart?"

"That would be more likely."

"Really? Well, likely I won't be able to guess. Who then?"

"Tara."

"Tara? The ice skater?"

"Tara, Jeremy's senior prom date."

Dave leaned forward and turned to look at Katie. "You must be kidding!" Dave thought for a few seconds. "Let's see if I can remember her: tall; long hair and legs; skimpy, tight red dress; dramatic make-up; a bold and confident demeanor. No, I don't think I remember," he said and squeezed his wife.

"I'm not kidding. And very funny."

* * *

Dave perked up slowly the following morning—normal for him. Katie had tea waiting when he struggled out of the RV's bedroom.

"From all the sleep music I heard last night, I think you got more rest last night than the night before," Katie said.

Dave recognized a complaint about his snoring. "Why didn't you nudge me?"

"You needed sleep. I was afraid you might lie awake afterwards."

"Thanks, sweetheart." Dave sipped the tea Katie had prepared. Together he and Katie commiserated about a new and unpaid case to tackle. "This won't be like our pursuit of Trevor. Two weeks at the most, I'm home," Dave asserted.

"I'm with you on that," Katie agreed. "Then, where should we start?"

"Let's talk with Missy again." Dave used Katie's cell phone to contact Sheriff Billingsly for Missy's address.

The sheriff agreed. "Devin knows Missy from high school. You'll need a deputy to accompany you to her home. I'll send Deputy Conrad," he promised. "I'll also call Darla Solsen to ask her permission for you to visit her daughter," he offered.

Dave put down the phone. "Deputy Conrad is on his way to take us to Missy."

Katie smiled. "Shall we try our wise and loving adult routine on her?"

"How about a two-by-four to her noggin instead?" Dave suggested. "Can you believe how she acted when she wanted something illicit from us?"

"I'm just pulling your dinosaur tail," Katie explained.

Dave finished the dregs of his tea. "Pull Old Yeller's tail and you're likely to get scratched."

"I miss our cat," said Katie. "I'm sorry the Fogles aren't there right now to take care of him."

"I'm sure Old Yeller's been lonely. But Jeremy will be checking on him every day. He'll be okay."

Jeremy had posted another hundred fliers at convenience stores, on telephone poles, bus stops—anyplace a notice could be posted where people might see it, recognize the cat, and call. Dorothy sent Old Yeller's photo to shelters, posted it on a lost-pet internet site, and took out a newspaper ad. Despite Dorothy's warning that the cat wouldn't respond to his voice, Jeremy spent evenings walking streets calling in desperation.

Nobody reported a cat of Old Yeller's description.

* * *

Devin Conrad met the Parkers at the campground. Before leading them to meet Missy, he gave them a little background.

"Missy Clark was popular, motivated, on a success trajectory, a straight-A student up until our senior year. She had already been accepted to pre-med at Stanford. Then she fell in with the wrong people somehow. I think maybe her mother put too much pressure on her."

"Did you ever date her?" Katie asked.

Devin laughed. "Missy was way out of my league."

Dave and Katie drove the loaner car Sheriff Billingsly had arranged, following Devin's squad car to a neighborhood of fashionable homes. The houses reflected a rustic exterior reminding Dave of ski chalets. Each home blended into the woodsy setting, giving an impression of ecological elegance.

A real estate agency's FOR SALE sign had been positioned in front of the Solsen home. Darla waited inside and emerged from the house when she saw the Parkers and Devin park on the street. She met them in the driveway. "Thank you for coming. Missy seemed to like you yesterday at the hospital."

Dave remembered how Missy's demeanor had changed with Darla's absence and thought, *Uh-huh* to himself. He made eye contact with Katie, who merely shrugged.

Darla went on, "I wasted my potential getting married too early to the wrong man. I just wanted Missy to have the success in life I squandered. Maybe I pushed her too hard." She waved toward the FOR SALE sign. "Drug rehabilitation is expensive. My husband, Henry—Missy's stepfather—already paid for two rehabs. Missy bailed out of each near the end. She's legally an adult and can't be confined without her assent. Then Henry said, 'No more money.' I had to give him a legal agreement that the house value would be my settlement in our pending divorce. I'm selling the house to pay for another treatment center."

Darla added with some bitterness, "Henry will likely use my homelessness to argue for full custody of the two younger kids we have together. They're staying with him now in Sacramento while I try to deal with Missy."

"What about Missy's biological father? Can he help pay for rehab?" Katie asked as they followed Darla to the front door.

Darla shook her head. "Brandon Clark? I couldn't even get consistent child support from my first husband. Now that Missy is an adult, fat chance. Brandon had an addictive personality himself. Alcohol in his case. Maybe he passed a gene or something on to Missy."

Inside the house, Dave and Katie found a luxurious interior that belied the house's rustic exterior. An oil painting of an exceptionally pretty girl hung over a wide stone fireplace. The girl in the picture smiled broadly and tilted her head in a playful gesture. Katie pointed at the painting. "Is that Missy?"

"Yes, Henry commissioned a local artist when she fifteen. He gave the painting to me for Christmas that year. That seems like a different life now."

Dave spoke to Darla, "Mrs. Solsen, Missy will probably be more open if you let us talk to her alone."

Darla reluctantly agreed. "If you think so." She ushered Dave and Katie into the den where Missy was watching TV and announced, "You have guests, Missy. Remember the Parkers from the hospital?" Darla ignored Devin, who had followed them. She departed and closed the door to the den.

Chapter Fourteen

* * *

Nobody would have recognized the girl Dave and Katie saw in the den as the happy one in the painting. She looked unwell with sunken eyes and unkempt hair.

"How do you feel today?" started Katie.

"Crappy." Despite the presence of the deputy, Missy asked, "Did you bring me anything?"

Dave sat down without being invited. "We don't have anything, Missy. And we couldn't give any pharmaceuticals to you, even if we did."

Missy glared back in anger. "Then what good are you?"

Dave spoke carefully, "We're here trying to help."

Katie joined Dave sitting and tried resorting to reason. "Missy, do you realize that your addiction is affecting everyone who loves you, as well as yourself? The rehabs and counseling have nearly bankrupted your family and driven your mother away from her husband. Your younger brother and sister are living away from their mother."

Missy remained silent for a minute, then nodded. Her voice took on a more plaintive tone. "I started each rehab meaning to break the addiction. But when I began to get better, I realized how badly I had ruined my life. That depressed me. Getting away from myself drove me back to the pills both times."

Dave leaned forward and spoke softly, "Where did you get the pills, Missy?"

Missy remained unresponsive. Katie started again, "I've had surgery for cancer twice, honey. The doctors prescribed all the painkillers I wanted. Drugs dulled the pain, but they also gave me the feeling that everything would be alright. The pills took away my fear, until they wore off. Soon I looked forward to taking the next one. Dave took the painkillers away after a week to protect me. But I can see how they would become a powerful temptation."

Missy spoke to Katie, "Pills don't make me feel good anymore. They just make me feel normal. Without them, I feel terrible. At first it was fun. Like getting away with something, being a secret agent maybe. Now, I feel like I'm in hell."

"What is it like, feeling you're in hell?"

"My arms and legs are sore and my back aches. I lie awake all night and am tired all day. My nose runs all the time. I feel cold and at the same time sweat like a pig. Sometimes my stomach cramps. Nothing is enjoyable for me anymore without being high. I think a lot about just killing myself. Everybody would be better off if I were dead."

"I'm sorry Missy." Katie then appealed. Do you want other girls or boys to get in the same trouble you're in? If not, tell us how you got the pills."

Missy shook her head. "No, I don't want other girls to be like me. Hell, I might as well tell you. I won't get any more pills from him anyway. Harley was my supplier."

"The young man we found with you?"

Missy nodded. "Harley had been drinking before he picked me up. Then he brought out the pills. I don't like alcohol."

"Staying away from the alcohol may have saved your life," interjected Dave.

Katie pressed forward. "Where did Harley get the pills?"

"I don't know."

"Then, how did you know Harley?"

"He gave me the first pill I tried at a party. My mother thought I was on a sleepover at a friend's."

Katie gave Missy time. After a few minutes of silence, Missy spoke again.

"Harley bought the pills from kids. 'Just take a couple from your grandparents' medicine cabinet. They'll never know,' he told them. Harley paid twenty dollars per pill. He sold them to others for fifty. He only occasionally used them himself. He wasn't hooked. Said pills kept him from getting hard. He drank a lot, though."

"How did you pay Harley for the pills?"

"With money at first. Then after I ran out, Harley started calling me his girlfriend. He gave me pills after I was nice to him." Missy left the details unsaid.

Dave and Katie looked at each other. Dave tilted his head a bit for Katie to continue.

"Then how did Harley overdose, if he wasn't hooked himself?"

"More kids wanted more pills. Harley couldn't keep up with the demand by getting kids to pilfer them. So he found some guys. Got a steady supply. Eventually pills weren't enough high for some kids. Harley said he'd gotten something stronger from his source. He wanted to try the new stuff once before selling it, make sure it worked like his supplier promised."

"Jeremy, a Ms. Austin is here asking to see you," Dorothy reported over the office intercom.

"A potential client?"

"Probably not. But she says you know her."

"I'll be right out." At the reception desk, Jeremy saw a beautiful and svelte woman his age with long blond hair. She was stylishly dressed and tastefully made up. He noticed her sparkling blue eyes.

She approached and kissed him on the cheek. "Jeremy, you're looking good!"

"Uh, you too, Giselle." The musky smell of her perfume took him back to the Georgia lake where he had first fallen into love.

Jeremy noticed Dorothy arching her eyebrows in an unverbalized question. "Giselle and I used to go to church together," he told her. By the look of Dorothy's eyebrows, she still had a lot of questions.

Giselle turned to stand side by side with Jeremy and put her hand under his arm. "OMG. We were just kids then," she gushed while tightly squeezing Jeremy's arm.

"How can we help you, Giselle?" he responded as he loosened her grip on his arm.

"I've gotten some money. I need your advice and all. Could we talk, you know, in private?"

"Ah, okay. Let's go to my office." Jeremy saw Dorothy staring at him. He pointed down the hall. "This way." As Giselle turned and sashayed toward his office, Jeremy shrugged to answer Dorothy's stare.

Jeremy left the door to his office open. "Please sit down." He waved at the chairs in front of his desk. "You have money questions, Giselle?"

"Sort of. I got a lump-sum settlement of nearly a million dollars from my divorce after the legal fees and taxes. What should I do with it?"

"I didn't know you and Brody had divorced."

"Oh, not Brody. We never got married. He had lots of girlfriends interested in marrying a professional football player. Too much competition for me, I suppose. Brody transferred from the University of Alabama when they tried to make him into a tight end rather than quarterback. He played quarterback at SMU. The NFL Lions drafted him in the eleventh round. They cut him during the preseason. After that he joined the army. I heard Brody got discharged for abusing some prisoners. I think he sells insurance now."

"So who did you marry?"

"Someone you probably don't know, Matt Austin. He had inherited a huge car distributorship over in Pensacola. Like, he was nearly sixty when I married him. I'm his fourth wife. By then he'd learned to insist on a prenup agreement before getting hitched. But I got a lot of money anyway."

"Oh, sorry."

"It's cool. And I got to be on TV making ads for his dealership."

"Kids?"

"No, Matt didn't want to mess up his family's already-confused inheritance. He had three sons and a daughter from his other marriages. A couple of others also claimed his genes."

"Well, Giselle, I recommend you invest your settlement in a balanced low-fee index fund. Don't spend it unless you absolutely must. You'll really need it someday."

"Yeah, that's pretty much what my lawyer said, too." Giselle looked around Jeremy's office for the first time. She glanced at but didn't ask any questions about the pictures of Denyse and Katelyn on his desk. "You're a partner in Parker and Company now, right?"

"I'm a junior partner in my father's firm."

"Whatever. You'll be in charge soon. And the Parkers are well known all over Mobile. I saw those online videos from Australia. Even when we were in high school that was true."

"My Mom and Dad are well known and respected," Jeremy admitted.

"Sure." Giselle paused for a moment then continued. "The other day when I heard you had made partner, I thought about the last time I saw you. That was at your high school prom. Remember I was there with Brody? That woman you brought looked red hot. Everybody was looking at you two and talking. Who was she?"

"You mean Tara? She was a friend of mine back then."

"I'll bet. Well, maybe you and I should go out to dinner together. You know, talk about investing my money, old times, and all."

* * *

After a few more questions, Dave and Katie couldn't pry any more information out of Missy. The girl had returned to sullen silence. As they prepared to leave, Deputy Conrad called Darla back in and spoke quietly to her.

"Why did you call her mother back?" Dave asked once outside.

"You've got to keep an eye on those withdrawing. You heard Missy say that she would be better off dead. Some addicts decide that suicide is their only way out."

Katie looked at Dave. She recognized a flash of sadness in his face. She knew he was thinking about his older brother, Chuck. Then she saw his jaw tightening in determination.

Devin continued, "I can confirm parts of Missy's story, though. She had prescription oxycodone in her blood. A serious narcotic, but not as strong as fentanyl. Harley had fentanyl in his blood. That's derived from an opioid, and it's a lot more powerful than most painkillers. Fentanyl is only supposed to be used for terminal cases and in hospitals."

"How did Sheriff Billingsly get the results so quickly?"

Devin grinned. "Somebody in the hospital's lab probably owed him a favor."

"Sheriff Billingsly calls in a lot of favors, it seems," said Dave.

"You've seen our town. Most people don't make much money to pay taxes on. Those who have money, come here to avoid paying taxes. Sheriff Billingsly gets whoever he can to help us."

Katie asked, "Even strangers?"

"Those who can help us."

"What made Sheriff Billingsly think we could help?" asked Dave.

"He had me run the plates on your RV after you found Missy and Harley. And he had your names and address from your driver's licenses. Then he made some phone calls back East. Apparently, he found something he liked because he had me discretely watching for you. When I saw you passing through town a few hours later, I followed far enough to guess you could be headed toward the hospital. I radioed Sheriff Billingsly and he came right away."

Dave and Katie looked at each other. Katie laughed first. "I think we've been had."

"I think we need to meet Harley's family next. Can you find out about the funeral arrangements?" Dave asked Devin.

"Sure."

Chapter Fifteen

* * *

The doorbell ringing early on Saturday morning awakened Jeremy. He struggled out of bed and stumbled to the front door. There he found Anthony and Sherri on the doorstep.

"Good morning," he managed. "Come on in."

"Thank you," the teenagers answered.

As she entered, Sherri's eyes scanned the home Jeremy and Denyse shared with Katelyn. "And this is where Ms. Parker lives? It's very nice."

"Yes, we bought the house after we moved here from Australia. Denyse and Katelyn are visiting their Aussie family in Melbourne now."

"Sherri's dad loaned us his car and encouraged us to come over to help you look for Mr. and Mrs. Parker's cat," Anthony explained.

"Oh, thanks. I was just about to begin." Jeremy waved toward the kitchen. "Would you like some coffee before we get started?"

"Sure," answered Sherri. As Jeremy made three cups of coffee, Sherri looked at a picture of Dave, Katie, Jeremy, Denyse, and Katelyn. "My daddy thinks your parents are wonderful. I once heard him tell Mama that they had saved his business. But when I asked him about it, he only said that your parents got some bad people in Mobile arrested. Do you know any more about that?"

She's referring to the protection racket targeting African Americans, Jeremy realized. *There are still some thugs out there. Anthony and I need to protect Mom and Dad's identity.* "Sorry, Sherri. As accountants, we can't talk about the private affairs of a businessman, even if he is your father." He gave Anthony a meaningful look warning him not to elaborate.

Anthony took the hint. "So what do we do to find the cat?"

"Just walk the streets looking for him. Show his picture to those you meet and ask if they've seen him. I'll give you a section of blocks to cover after we've finished our coffee. Cream? Sugar?"

A chilly fog obscured the morning in Redwood Hills. Carrying an umbrella to ward off drips falling from the trees, Katie sidestepped water-filled potholes to make her way to Tara's camper. There a cinder block served as a doorstep. Katie tapped at the door. From inside the camper she heard a bump, as though somebody had swung their feet onto the floor. The door opened to reveal Tara wrapped in a sleeping bag. Her hand held a book about Alaskan adventures.

"Hello, Katie," she said.

"Tara, I'm glad you're home."

"Come on in out of the damp."

Katie stepped up into the tiny camper. "Thanks."

Inside, Katie saw a living space befitting the older twelve-foot camper. No plumbing; just a bunk to sleep on, a tiny built-in table, and two electrical outlets. Katie saw a propane camp stove, paperback novels, inexpensive add-hot-water foods, an older microwave, a simple CD player, and books on nature.

Tara noticed Katie looking around. "The camper keeps me dry. Good thing the campground has a toilet and shower, huh?" Tara moved some stuff and motioned for Katie to sit on a stool, the only seat.

"I dropped by to apologize for being so rude the other night. You caught me by surprise," said Katie.

Tara sat down on the camper's bunk. "No problem."

"Thanks. And Dave and I would like to invite you to have supper with us in our RV tonight. I'm making a Cajun dish, jambalaya."

"Really? You want me to come to supper with you and Dave?"

"Why does that surprise you?"

"Well for starters, I tried to steal your son."

Katie acknowledged the truth of Tara's reminder with a nod and a smile before replying, "But you didn't, when you could have."

To that, Tara had to agree. "Yes, I could have."

"So, will you be our guest?"

"Let me see. I could have plain ramen noodles for the fourth time this week, alone, in a cold camper. Or I could have a spicy Southern dish with two—judging by their son—nice people." Tara pretended to be considering. "Why not?"

Katie had to smile. "Okay, we usually have supper at six. Is that a good time for you?"

Tara smiled, then nodded. "I'm always ready to eat."

"Alright. See you at six. We'll be glad to have your company."

"Shall I bring my computer to show Dave the picture from Jeremy's prom?"

"No, he seemed to remember you just fine."

Jeremy unlocked the door to enter his home after taking Ripper for an evening walk. He heard the house phone ringing. He ran to pick it up.

"Hello."

A gruff male asked, "Are you the one looking for a cat?"

Jeremy couldn't conceal his excitement. "You've found Old Yeller?"

"Maybe. But you'll have to identify him first," the caller demanded.

"He's an orange male with stripes. He holds his tail erect when walking."

"Yep. That's him alright," the gruff voice confirmed.

"I'll come get him. Where are you?"

"Wait a minute. Your newspaper ad offered a reward."

"No problem. I'll give you a check for two hundred dollars when I pick him up," Jeremy promised.

"We were thinking a thousand dollars."

"A thousand dollars?"

"Yeah. He's hurt from a dog or maybe a car. We had to pay vet bills."

"Who is this?"

"Doesn't matter. You just send the money to our bank account and you'll get the cat."

Jeremy recognized a scam and hung up.

Tara thought about her impression of Dave and Katie and their home in Mobile as being like a 1960s TV show. She felt apprehensive about being alone with people whom even Jeremy had called "fossils." *Will I commit some faux pas? Will they criticize me for what I tried to do years ago?* she wondered. Just in case her hosts became blameful, Tara had thought through her defense.

Dave opened the door when she knocked at six. "Please come in, Tara. Good to see you again." Inside, he shook her hand. Tara smelled the aroma of garlic, spicy tomato sauce, and sausage prepared in true Cajun fashion. She saw a pot of white rice simmering.

"I'll be just one minute more," Katie called from the RV's cooking area. "you can both sit down."

Dave gestured toward a card-table-sized dining area. Tara slid into the booth. Dave sat down himself. "Tara, we never had the opportunity to thank you for the positive influence you had on our son. He's happily married and has a daughter now."

"I had a positive influence on Jeremy?"

"Sure. Before you came, Jeremy had no idea what he wanted to do with himself. You helped bring him to his senses."

Are they playing games with me? Tara thought. Not knowing what else to say, she launched into her defense. "At the time, I really thought Jeremy going on the road with me would be good for him. I tried to share the wit-living lifestyle I knew and loved. If I had just told Jeremy that I loved him, he would have come with me." She smiled as she remembered more. "And he would have brought thirty thousand dollars in cash with him."

Katie answered as she served the jambalaya. "We know all this, honey. Jeremy told us. Thank you, Tara, for your honesty to him about how you felt." She placed a glass of iced tea before each of their places.

Dave spoke up. "You *did* have a big effect on Jeremy, though. He figured out that part of your allure was that you had decided for yourself who you wanted to be. He followed your example by deciding who he wanted to be. Then he followed his decision as you had yours. Apparently, you complimented him on being a good man. And that's what he decided to be. All the details were secondary to that decision."

Tara looked back and forth between Dave and Katie. "You're not mad at me?"

"Certainly not, honey," answered Katie and slid into the seat herself. "Dave, would you say grace?"

After Dave prayed, Tara sat stunned for a long minute. *That's twice in a week somebody has thanked God. Jeff, now the Parkers. And she called me 'honey.' This is too weird to even be a TV show.*

Katie noticed Tara's inactivity. "Is anything wrong, honey?"

Tara heard her own voice say, "No, ma'am." She tasted the jambalaya. Flavors burst in her mouth. Shrimp, sausage, celery, garlic, and peppers. Above all, hot pepper. Tara reached for the iced tea.

"It's too spicy for her, sweetheart," Dave said to Katie.

"No, no, I like spicy foods. I just didn't expect Southern food to have so much punch," Tara insisted.

"Actually, this is Cajun food," Katie explained. "Most Southern foods *are* mild. I've got unseasoned rice left over. Let me mix in some more with your food to cut the heat a little." In a few seconds, Katie returned with Tara's plate.

Tara tasted again. "This *is* delicious. I really like it."

While eating and listening to Dave and Katie talk about the nuances of Cajun food, Tara didn't feel like closing the Jeremy story. "About Jeremy," she began. Dave and Katie both gave her their undivided attention. "I never understood about the effect of my honesty on Jeremy. I've lied to people from one corner of this country to the next. But I just couldn't treat Jeremy that way. Jeremy reminded me of a baby seal."

Both Dave and Katie laughed at the baby seal comparison. "He was pretty naive," said Dave. "Still is in some ways."

Tara smiled and continued, "Telling Jeremy the truth may be the most decent thing I've ever done. Sometimes I've thought I made a mistake letting Jeremy get away. Although I knew then what I wanted and who I wanted to be, living from day to day has gotten old. Now I think maybe I want to be someone different. Not totally different, of course."

"Who do you want to be now?" asked Dave.

Chapter Sixteen

* * *

Before Tara could respond to Dave's question of who she wanted to be, Katie said, "We'll have cookies for dessert. Would you like coffee or hot tea with the cookies, Tara?"

Dave broke in, "Not tea like you gave Jeremy, though." His smile proved him to be teasing Tara.

"OMG! I had forgotten that I gave Jeremy marijuana tea. That's who I was then. Sorry."

"So, coffee or tea?" Katie reminded.

"Coffee, please." Tara reflected on the memory Dave had resurrected. "I had to throw all my weed overboard—and my backpack—when the Coast Guard came to rescue us. I forgot to take out my binoculars."

Katie pulled out a glass cylinder. "Oh, really? We heard about Jeremy taking you on the boat. But he left out the part about you throwing your backpack away."

While watching Katie make coffee, Tara described the frightening storm and her panic as the Coast Guard approached. "I nearly freaked out thinking they would put us in jail for possession. I thought that down South they might even throw away the key." She concluded with, "What a hoot that was."

Katie added a scoop of coffee grounds to the cylinder and poured in boiling water. After waiting thirty seconds, she inserted a screened piston and pressed the grounds to the bottom. Fresh coffee passed through the screens, leaving the grounds. Katie poured a big cup for Tara. "Would you like cream? Sugar?"

"A little sugar would be nice. Thank you. I'm surprised that you made this coffee nearly as fast as instant." She looked at the glass cylinder with curiosity.

"This is a French press," Katie explained as she poured hot water over tea bags for herself and Dave.

"Don't you drink coffee?" asked Tara.

"No, we'll have tea. *English* tea," Dave extended his jibe.

"The tea I served Jeremy was one hundred percent American-grown tea," Tara jibed back.

Katie placed a plate of cookies on the table. Ever friendly and having a heart to mother, she prompted Tara. "So what have you done since trying to steal our son?"

Tara added sugar from a dish Katie provided and tasted the scalding, fresh coffee. "Wow, that is good!" After another sip she started, "Oh, I drove straight to California after getting a new radiator in Biloxi. Saw a lot of sights, walked a lot of trails, mostly alone. Then I kicked around the country for a few years. I met some other men. Although Jeremy was naive, they were shallow. There's a difference.

"Anyway, when I learned my previous traveling companion, Bennie, would be released from prison, I drove to New Hampshire, picked him up, and brought him to California. But soon being with Bennie soured. He had gotten mean in prison. He'd picked up a taste for heroin in there, too. He used all the money we could collect getting high. I saw him suffer a couple of overdoses. I may have used some weed occasionally, but I've stayed away from that narcotic stuff.

"When he didn't have money for drugs, Bennie abused me. Once, after we had an argument about drugs and money, Bennie took my laptop and sent an email to my contacts. I only had a few, including Jeremy. Bennie told them that I was in rehabilitation for heroin addiction. Claiming to be my parents, he asked for money to help with the costs of the clinic.

"After that, I took the few dollars I had hidden from him—that's what had started the argument—and bought a twenty-five-dollar bicycle at Goodwill. Then I escaped in the middle of the night, leaving Bennie asleep in the van. Better leaving in one piece on a bike than getting beat up trying to take the van. I've been alone since.

"The bicycle brought me here. Redwood Hills is a laid-back and free-spirited place. I feel comfortable here. I camped out in the woods until I found the camper I live in now. The previous owner had skipped out owing three hundred dollars in space rent. This campground let me have the camper for the three hundred. I scraped together the money and bought it."

"How did you collect the three hundred dollars?" asked Dave without thinking ahead to possible responses.

"Basically, I begged for it." To answer Dave's look of incomprehension, Tara added, "You approach people in parking lots and ask for food or money for gas. Tell them some sort of story, maybe about being stranded and needing to get home. Most are in a hurry and just give you money. With older people, you can claim that you need money to clean up for a job interview. Reading people and knowing how to approach them can be like an entertaining game of wits. Still, collecting three hundred dollars took me almost a week down in Bodega Bay. The camper keeps me dry in bad weather."

"So, Tara, who do you think you want to be now?" Katie brought the conversation back to Dave's original question.

"I'm trying to figure that out. Maybe more permanent somehow."

On her way back to her camper after visiting another hour with Dave and Katie, Tara thought, *What a sweet old couple. I'll bet that they're living nice, quiet lives at their age. Probably never had a problem or major challenge.*

Katie answered her cell phone. "Hello."

"Katie, this is Denyse. Are you and Dave enjoying California?"

"Sort of." Katie proceeded to tell Denyse about the opioid investigation she and Dave had joined.

"Fair dinkum? And you found a dead body?"

"I'm afraid so."

"Well, I've got a problem of my own I wanted to talk to you about." Denyse first told Katie about Lena's situation with Trevor. She then described Sveta acting out and endangering herself. "Do you have any advice for Lena or for her sisters? Things are going from bad to worse here."

"Well, as for Lena and Trevor, they need to work out a mutually agreeable plan for their marriage, including ways to have fun together. That'll require learning how to communicate. You know about that from being married to my knuckleheaded son."

Denyse laughed. "Jeremy's not the only one who needed to learn a lot. Now what about the sisters?"

"Sorry, Denyse. If it was a marriage issue, I might be able to help. But teenage girls struggling to find themselves . . . I never had a daughter until Jeremy married you. You'd know more about teenage-girl issues than me, especially in Australia."

"Trouble with me understanding their concerns is I was pretty much what they call a straight arrow. From an early age, I felt responsible for myself and, until I left home for uni, also responsible for Trevor. Never acted out much myself. I was more like Lena than her younger sisters."

"Okay. Boys are nearly always important to girls. Try telling Lena's sisters about Evangeline searching for her true love."

"Who's Evangeline?"

"That's right. You're an Aussie. Of course you wouldn't know that American story. Forget her."

"Have you got anything else?" Denyse asked in desperation.

Katie thought for a minute as Denyse waited. "Then try telling the girls about Jeremy and Tara."

"Tara?"

"You know. The older woman Jeremy almost ran away with after high school. He nearly gave her his college fund, too."

No, I don't know, thought Denyse. But she answered, "Oh yeah."

"Believe it or not, Dave and I ran into Tara and have become friends with her here in California."

"Really?"

"Amazing coincidence, huh? She still thinks a lot of Jeremy."

"I'm not surprised."

Jeremy was watching a ball game on TV while eating a pizza when his phone rang. Juggling the pizza and trying to turn down the TV, he answered, "Hello."

"It's me again."

"Oh, Denyse. Hi, sweetheart. Did you talk to Mom?"

"Yes, your parents are involved in another investigation."

"You're kidding?"

"No. And this time there's a dead body." Denyse went on to outline the situation Katie had explained to her.

"Wow, Mom and Dad can't seem to stay away from trouble. Did Mom have any advice about Lena's sisters?"

"Maybe a little. Any luck on Old Yeller?"

"Not yet." Jeremy sighed.

"Well, keep trying. I asked the whole family to pray for you to find him." Denyse paused. "Jeremy, what's this I hear about an old flame of yours?"

Dorothy must have overhead Giselle's dinner invitation and told Mom and Dad, Jeremy thought. His laugh sounded guilty to Denyse.

"You know better than to worry, sweetheart. I turned Giselle's dinner invitation down."

Giselle? Dinner? thought Denyse. *How many old girlfriends does my husband have? I need to get back to Mobile.* But she simply said, "I'm glad you did."

Jeremy continued, "Of course I did. Giselle's just lonely for male company and needs some guidance after her divorce. But I didn't need to go out to dinner to give her financial advice. I did that at the office."

Silence from Denyse prompted Jeremy to ask again, "Well, what did Mom suggest saying to Lena's sisters?"

Denyse's voice sounded stern to Jeremy. "Katie told me to tell them about you and *Tara.*"

"That might work," Jeremy said, sounding clueless to Denyse. "Have you tried that yet?"

"Are you daft? I don't even know who Tara is. Why haven't you ever told me about this Tara person?"

"She was just my prom date. Telling you about her never came up, I guess. I stopped emailing with her and sending her money after we got engaged."

"You sent her money until we were engaged?"

"Only a little, occasionally."

"How much is a little?" Denyse pressed.

"Just a hundred dollars at a time."

"Your mum says you nearly gave her your college fund, too."

"Listen, Denyse. That was a long time ago. I didn't go traveling with Tara like she wanted or give her my college fund. That's because I decided to look for my true love, like Evangeline."

"Is she another old girlfriend?"

"No, no, she's a tragic heroine in a long poem by Longfellow."

"What is it with you Americans and this Evangeline person?"

"Mom loves that Cajun story. A young man, Gabriel, and a young woman, Evangeline, loved each other. On their wedding day, the British soldiers moved French-speaking colonists from Nova Scotia to Louisiana. Gabriel and Evangeline somehow got separated. Evangeline spent her lifetime searching for Gabriel and eventually found him in Philadelphia. They kissed and then both died. People buried them close to each other so they could be together forever."

"That doesn't sound like a happy ending."

"Never mind. What Mom means is that a deep, life-long love is worth waiting and searching for. I did. That person for me is you."

"Are you sure?"

"Of course! And I so wish you and Katelyn were here right now."

"Not as much as I wish you were here with us. But your experience with Tara sounds interesting."

"It *is* a good story."

"Then how about you finish telling me the whole story, so I can tell Sveta and Sandra? Sandra even asked about you."

"She asked about me?"

"Yes, she did."

Dave and Katie drove the loaner car to Redwood Hills' only funeral home and mortuary. They took a back seat in the small chapel. Harley Forbes' grieving parents stood to the side of an open casket. Quiet religious music played through hidden speakers. Harley's body had been shaved and groomed. The Parkers would not have recognized the man lying there as the corpse they had discovered three days earlier.

Various members of the community took turns leaving their seats to approach the parents and express sympathy. At a lull in the procession, Dave nudged Katie and pointed the way toward the parents—a middle-aged working-class couple with bewildered expressions.

"We deeply regret your loss," Dave spoke quietly to Harley's mother and father. He shook hands lightly with each.

"Thank you," responded the grief-stricken mother. "And how did you know Harley?"

Katie answered, "We're Dave and Katie Parker from Mobile, Alabama. We came to California on vacation and found your son in his car."

"Oh." Mrs. Forbes put her hand to her mouth. "Well, thank you for coming."

"Harley's death has deeply affected us both," said Dave. "With your permission, we'd like to call on you to learn more about Harley."

"Of course," answered Harley's father. "How about the day after tomorrow? You could come to our house in the morning about ten."

Dave nodded solemnly, turned, and led Katie back to their seats.

The funeral director guided Mr. and Mrs. Forbes to their seats. A local pastor stood to begin the service.

Chapter Seventeen

* * *

After the funeral service, Dave and Katie walked back to the car together. Katie said, "It's only eleven in the morning. What should we do with the rest of our day?"

"After finding the body and going to the hospital, we didn't really get to visit the redwoods and the park. We could try to get in a little bit of our intended vacation," Dave suggested.

"A great idea."

An hour later, the Parkers hiked in silence through the old-growth redwood forest. Trees as big as fourteen feet in diameter and nearly three hundred feet tall towered over them.

"This reminds me of that cathedral we visited at Cologne in Germany," Katie commented. "And do you remember the redwoods we saw planted on the North Island of New Zealand? Those five-foot-wide trees are just babies compared to these."

As they completed the trail loop and neared the visitor center, they saw a young woman wearing the uniform of a park ranger waiting at the trailhead.

Dave paused by her and asked, "How old are these trees?"

She responded with the enthusiasm of a nature junkie. "Most of our trees are only six hundred to nine hundred years old. But some redwoods in California are over two thousand years old. Unfortunately, only three percent of the original redwoods remain. Redwood forests once extended from the Bay Area all the way up the coast and into Oregon. Logging took most of the old-growth trees."

"What allows redwoods to live so long?"

"The wood is resistant to insects, and without resins—like pines or firs contain—redwoods can survive all but the hottest fires. And they favor growing in valleys to collect moisture; the valleys also shield them from winds."

"How do redwoods propagate?"

"Well, they can grow from seeds. But not many seeds can take root through the thick ground covering of moss and sword ferns." The young woman pointed to a ring of large trees. "Most trees sprout from the stump of a predecessor. That circle of trees all came from the roots of a tree that died for some reason about four hundred years ago. It's called a 'family.'"

A class of school-age children approached. "Here's my tour group. I have to go," the ranger explained. "If you have more questions, they could help you at the visitor center."

"You've been a big help. Thanks," answered Dave as the young woman started greeting the children.

"I'm just glad California had the foresight to preserve several sections of old-growth trees. Of course, there was that gift shop offering turned bowls and all things redwood just at the border of the park," Katie said with a grimace.

"You bought a turned redwood bowl yourself," Dave returned.

"Well, redwoods grow fast. I'm sure they made that bowl from the secondary growth. Do you remember the big trees we saw before reaching the park?"

"Do you mean the ones four to six feet in diameter?"

"Yes, those trees are the secondary growth," Katie explained, glad for a chance to use her science-teacher background. "They started growing after the original tree had been cut in the 1820s and afterwards. That also makes clusters or families like the ranger explained."

Dave looked back at the arched branches a hundred feet or more above them. "Speaking of clusters, I see you accumulating more stuff like the bowl as we travel."

Katie shrugged. "Collecting along the way seems a natural part of traveling to me."

✳ ✳ ✳

Later that night, Katie heard pounding on the RV's door. She looked at the clock. Who would be looking for them at 10:38 p.m.?

"Katie, it's me, Tara," she heard through the door.

Katie went to open the door as Dave rolled over in the bed and faced the other direction. She found Tara pacing back and forth outside.

"Come on in, Tara. What keeps you up so late?"

"Actually, I don't keep hours like most people. But I came to see if you'd show me how to make coffee the way you do." Tara pointed at Katie's coffeemaker on the small counter next to the stove.

Tara's urgency puzzled her, but Katie smiled. "You want to make coffee using a French press?"

"Yes, the way you made it for me after dinner the other night."

"Come on in, honey. I'll make you a cup."

"I'd like to see how you make it again, but I don't need to drink any right now."

As Tara watched, Katie took the coffee grounds out of the tiny freezer compartment in the RV's refrigerator and got out the French press.

"Okay, if we were making fresh coffee, I'd put one or two scoops of grounds—depending on how strong you like it—in the bottom. Then I'd pour boiling water on the grounds, filling the cylinder to about two-thirds full. After about a half minute, I'd separate the grounds and coffee like this." Katie pushed the plunger down to the level the coffee grounds would be. "Then you pour the strained coffee into a cup. That's all there is to it."

"Where would I get one of these? A French press. Isn't that what you called it?"

"You can buy a French press at nearly any store selling home appliances. But I'll give you this one."

"Yours? Don't you need it?"

"No, we brought this old one along for Denyse and Jeremy. They're the only ones in our family who drink coffee. They came with us as far as Los Angeles."

"Denyse?"

"That's Jeremy's Australian wife. She's visiting her family in Melbourne now along with their daughter, Katelyn. Jeremy went back to Mobile to run the accounting firm."

"Oh, yeah. I remember now."

"Anyway, you're the only friend we have in California who drinks coffee." Katie extended the French press to Tara. "And you might as well take the ground coffee, too."

"Thank you, Katie." Tara's voice showed her surprise.

Katie couldn't help prying a little. "Why the sudden interest in coffee?"

"I've got a job. Sort of, anyway, at the bike shop. Tomorrow morning I'd like to . . ." Tara trailed off.

"Make a good impression on someone?" Katie filled in the silence with an insightful guess.

"Maybe, yes."

"Golly! That's been good coffee today," said Jeff during the last hour of business on Saturday afternoon. "Really strong but not bitter. When I make coffee that strong, it's always bitter."

"Glad you like it," answered Tara. "It's really easy to make." She watched Jeff turn over the OPEN sign to close the shop for the day.

"You sold three more bicycles today," Jeff marveled.

"It was a hoot."

"Tara, I'm pretty behind on the rent for this place, and payments for inventory are due. So the profits from your sales are already gone. But I think you deserve a bonus." Tara watched as Jeff wrote a check for a hundred dollars and handed it to her.

"Why didn't you just mark this off my debt for the road bike?"

"I'd like to keep you working here to pay off that bike for at least three more Saturdays. Besides, you must need some cash for living expenses."

Tara nodded without speaking. Then thinking about meals for the coming week, she reached out to take the check. "Thanks." To herself Tara realized, *Jeff is a good man. Maybe better than I could ever hope for.*

"Supper with us?" Jeff nodded toward the back part of the store. "I made Crock-Pot chili."

"Sure."

Jeff gestured for Tara to go ahead of him. "Right this way."

In Jeff and Sam's quarters, Tara hesitantly approached Sam, who sat in her playpen. "Hello, Sam. Do you remember me?"

Apparently, the little girl did because she extended her arms to be picked up.

Jeff stirred the chili and got out some bowls and spoons. He turned around to find Tara bouncing his daughter on her hip.

"You can put her in her highchair when you like. Stay with her, though. She'll start bawling if she feels alone and trapped there."

Tara eased Sam into the highchair and lowered the tray in front of her. She made funny faces to hold the toddler's attention until Jeff brought some sweetened microwave oatmeal with milk.

"Chili's too spicy for her," Jeff said. "Would you feed her the oatmeal while I make us a salad?"

Feeding oatmeal to a toddler turned out as messy as the pudding had a week earlier. Despite herself, Tara enjoyed trying to get the mushy food into the toddler. *I got most of it into her,* Tara congratulated herself. Jeff relieved her by placing a few miniature marshmallows on Sam's tray for dessert. The child babbled happily as she reached for the treat and looked back and forth between Jeff and Tara.

As they ate the chili, Jeff said, "Tara, Sam really likes you. Do you think you could come in and watch Sam and the shop on Tuesday afternoon? It could count against your bicycle debt. I have to go to the county registrar and courthouse. Sales tax reporting and business legalities are tying me into knots. I should be only an hour or two. But you never know."

Tara looked at the child happily chewing a marshmallow and watching her. "Well, let me see. I'll have to check my

171

schedule." She gazed into the air and comically feigned trying to remember her commitments for Tuesday. "Sure, why not?"

"Great! You might have to change her diaper. I haven't made much progress potty training her. Disposable diapers are under the sink."

Change a diaper? I don't know how to change a diaper, Tara realized.

"The older lady, Mrs. Swanson, at the bakery down the street knows Sam. Close the shop and take Sam there if you need help."

"Mrs. Swanson. Got it."

"Of course, if you feel threatened by anything, you should call the police," Jeff added.

"Sure, I could do that," Tara answered with some hesitation.

Jeff sensed reluctance in her voice. "What's the matter?"

"It's just that at the commune where I grew up, calling the cops would be the last thing anyone would ever do."

Jeff's mouth gaped open. His silence posed an unspoken question.

Tara shrugged. "Most of the adults living at the commune had been part of the antiwar protests during the sixties and seventies. They got some pretty rough treatment from the cops. Some had scars to prove it. All of them knew better than to carry any drugs to demonstrations where they might get arrested. But a few cops carried something to slip into a pocket and then 'discover.' So I grew up suspicious of the police.

"Even after the Vietnam War ended, county deputies in rural Wisconsin made hassling our compound part of their routine. Sometimes during the night, men would crash in, shouting and pointing guns. They brought barking dogs, too. That can affect a kid for a lifetime. I'm just uneasy around cops." Tara didn't add that her uneasiness around cops was exacerbated by her history of scamming people.

Jeff leaned forward in interest. "What were the police looking for during the raids?"

"The cops claimed drugs and always said they found some. I never knew that for certain considering the stories I'd heard about the arrests at the antiwar demonstrations. I do know the cops cited civil forfeiture and usually took all the money in the commune's common treasury—money we'd made by hard work raising vegetables and selling them at a farmer's market. When I was a teenager, I opened a bank account to protect my money from the police."

"How did you earn that money?"

Tara laughed. "I started giving tours of the hippie commune to tourists and told outrageous stories to get tips. That eventually got me expelled from the commune. The money I had kept in the bank allowed me to go to college." Tara enjoyed the memory for a moment. "But, Jeff, if Sam were to be in any danger, I'd put my head out the door and scream so loud that everyone in Redwood Hills would come, including every cop."

Jeff couldn't help but smile. "Alright, then."

Chapter Eighteen

* * *

Early the next morning, banging on the RV's door interrupted Dave and Katie's tea routine.

"Katie, I need more help," Tara said as soon as Dave opened the door.

Katie joined Dave at the door. "What is it, honey?"

Tara looked embarrassed. "Well, the place I'm working . . . the owner asked me to watch his little girl for maybe a whole afternoon. I don't know anything about taking care of a kid. She's cute and all, but what will I do with her? And I might have to change a diaper."

"How old is the child?" asked Katie.

"Not quite two, I think. She can walk around, and she talks a little."

"Disposable diapers?" Katie asked. When Tara nodded, she continued, "Changing diapers isn't hard. Just use baby wipes or a damp paper towel to clean her up, then make sure the sticky tabs that fasten in the front aren't too tight for her legs. But some children can start potty training at her age. Did you see a potty chair in the bathroom?"

"A topper for the regular toilet seat with a smaller hole, right? Yes, I did."

"Good. Then look for signs the child needs to go, like facial expressions and fidgeting, especially after she first wakes up from a nap. Then take off the diaper she's wearing and place her on the potty seat over the regular seat on the toilet. Try to make a game of it. Be patient. And if she succeeds, give her lots of praise."

"Okay. I could try that. But what would I do to occupy her otherwise?"

Katie didn't need to think long. "Making cookies is always fun for kids. At her age, she'll like playing with a little flour or snacking on chocolate chips in her highchair while she watches you bake."

"How could *I* possibly make cookies?"

"Come on in."

"They only have a small toaster oven with a little cooking space." Tara held out her hands to indicate the size of a shoe box.

"Even better. Baking the cookies one or two at a time will take longer. And the child can watch the cookies bake through the glass door. Just be careful she can't reach the oven and burn herself."

Katie started laying out the ingredients for cookies. "Chocolate chip cookies are easy. And kids love them. Keeping kids attention makes them happy."

Tara watched intently and made notes on the back of a paper bag from the local grocery store she had in her pocket.

Katie took out the ingredients: flour, sugar, eggs, and butter. She stole a few of Dave's M&Ms to serve as chocolate chips. Being herself, she could not help probing a bit. "Where is the child's mother?"

"She died shortly after giving birth. An internal hemorrhage."

"And her father?"

"Jeff owns the bicycle shop downtown. That's where I've been on Saturdays."

Katie continued her questions as she mixed the cookie dough. "What's this young man's background?"

Tara, concentrating on the cookie making, spoke freely. "He tried to become a professional cyclist. Never quite made it. So he became a bike mechanic. He and his wife opened the bike shop to give their baby a stable environment."

"Sounds like they both are lucky to have met you."

"Maybe."

Jeremy picked up the ringing phone. "Hello."

"Hi, Jeremy."

"Hey, Dad. What's up?"

"Your mother and I have a surprise for you. We met a friend of yours."

"A friend of mine? Let me guess who. Tara?"

"How did you know?"

"Denyse asked me about her."

"Oh. Sorry about that."

"No problem. I told Denyse the whole story, including Tara being a great prom date. I emailed with Tara occasionally until Denyse and I got engaged. Where did you see Tara? Was she giving palm readings in California for five dollars?" Jeremy asked.

"No, but we did find her here in California. Well, your mother did. Tara is living at the same campground we do. Tara and your mother are becoming good friends."

"Tara and Mom? Friends?"

"Yeah. Your mother has started coaching her in relationships. Tara is apparently seriously taken by a young father and his daughter."

"Wow! I never would have guessed that getting relationship advice from Mom would be in Tara's future."

"But Jeremy, telling you that isn't the only reason I called. We've run into some trouble here." Dave briefly told his son about their experiences in Redwood Hills. "Can you come out here and help us with a little undercover work like you did in New Zealand?"

"Sure, Dad, I'll come. But I've got some problems here too."

"What's happened?"

"Well, do you remember that seminar on tax documentation you approved?"

"Yes, I do."

"Word of mouth publicized the free tax advice from Parker and Company. We've got nearly sixty businessmen registered. We had to move the venue to Calvary Baptist Church."

Dave decided to tease his son. "How are we going to get new clients if you teach them how to do their own taxes?"

Jeremy answered a bit defensively, "I think we'll get new clients. But even if we don't, it's the right thing to do. Doing the right thing is its own reward. You know, the Golden Rule."

Dave sighed. "You're right of course." Then he praised his son. "You're a better chip than I ever expected off my old block."

Jeremy laughed. "You're not that old. But Dad, I've also got another problem. I've lost Old Yeller."

"What? You've lost your mother's cat? How did that happen?"

"He seemed lonely by himself all day at your house. So I brought him home with me and let him go outside like you and Mom do. Then I fell asleep on the couch. After an hour or two, I went to let Old Yeller in, and he had disappeared. I'm doing everything I can to find him."

Dave groaned. "Don't tell your mother. No use giving her something else to worry about."

"Dad, do you want me to cancel the seminar and forget about finding Old Yeller? I could come help you then."

"No. Don't let the businessmen down. And do all you can to find Old Yeller. Your mother loves that cat. We'll manage here."

* * *

At nine o'clock the next morning, Jeremy stood before fifty-nine proprietors of presumably small businesses packed into the fellowship hall of Calvary Baptist Church. More than half of the business owners sitting ready at tables turned out to be females. The women of the church scurried among the attendees, serving coffee and baked goods.

Jeremy started by telling the group a bit about himself and made a self-deprecating joke about accountants. "A woman was told she only had six months to live. 'Goodness,' said the woman. 'What shall I do?' 'Marry an accountant,' suggested the doctor. 'Will that make me live longer?' asked the woman. 'No, but it will *seem* longer.'"

After a big laugh, he instructed, "Please turn to page three. The key to minimizing business taxes is proper record keeping. Never pay in cash. Run everything through your bank account. That gives you a legally solid record and makes calculating taxes a lot easier. What if you use credit cards for your business? Link them to your bankl. Both income and expenses . . ."

Three hours later, Jeremy tried to conclude, "I'd like to thank Calvary Baptist Church for their hospitality. And especially the ladies for their service. If Parker and Company Accounting can ever serve you, please call us."

A female voice shouted from the back, "The church has lunch ready for all those who can stay."

The crowd murmured appreciation. A woman stood up. "I'd like to say thanks for all of us to the church and to Mr.

Parker." A round of generous applause supported her. The businesswoman turned to those sitting around her. "I, for one, would like to hear about avoiding scams. Does anybody object if I ask Mr. Parker to talk about that while we eat lunch?" A general shaking of heads and a few verbal responses affirmed her. The woman looked back at Jeremy.

Another man called out, "I have some general questions about bookkeeping."

Jeremy looked at the room full of anticipatory faces. "Alright, then. Ladies of Calvary Baptist, if you'll start serving lunch, I'll start talking. Those who need to leave, please do so whenever you wish."

Jeremy was surprised to see Anthony approaching the front. "What's up?" he whispered to the teenager.

Rather than answer, Anthony took the microphone. "Before any of you do leave, we have one last announcement—a request really." Anthony hit a couple of keys on the laptop. The Christmas picture of Old Yeller filled the screen. "We're looking for senior Mr. and Mrs. Parker's cat. You'll find a flyer in the back of your handout. If your business is on the east shore, and you're willing, please post the flyer where your customers will see it." He handed the microphone back to Jeremy.

Jeremy nodded appreciation to Anthony. Motivated by the nighttime call from the scam artist about Old Yeller, he began with, "Some people are eager to take advantage of others. The most vulnerable are those in desperate circumstances . . ."

Two hours later Jeremy drew the program to a second close. "Thank you all for coming. And thanks again to Calvary Baptist for their hospitality."

The remaining businessmen and businesswomen clapped loudly and started to disperse. One distinguished-looking older man loitered as the younger businesspeople departed. The man then approached Jeremy. "That was quite a public service, Mr. Parker." He extended a hand.

"Thank you, sir." Jeremy shook the proffered hand.

"And I understand that only a few of these are Parker and Company's clients. You're coaching businesspeople to need your expertise less. That's an odd business plan."

"Yes, sir. We've adopted the Golden Rule as our motto."

"I heard that." The man nodded. "Where's your father, Dave?"

"Dad's in California on vacation and doing some pro-bono work for a small police force." He described a bit about his parents' opioid investigation in California.

The man listened intently then handed Jeremy a business card. "Have Dave call me when he gets home. We need to get reconnected."

"Yes, sir." Jeremy looked at the business card as the man walked away. He read, *Value Pharmacies President*. They had been Dave's biggest client before his temporary retirement.

"We have another day before meeting Harley's parents tomorrow. What do you say we lapse back into tourist mode?" suggested Dave.

"And we have a car to use," responded Katie. "Where would you like to go?"

"We've been to the rocky coastline. And we've seen the redwood trees. How about we visit part of California's wine country?"

Katie finished putting away the breakfast dishes she had washed. "Where is wine country?"

Dave started unfolding a map. "Napa Valley is the most famous area. But vineyards and wineries are also just to the east of where we are now."

"Why do you fool with that paper map? My cell phone can give us directions," offered Katie.

"A cell phone can help you find the place you want to go. An old-fashioned map can give you a larger perspective and help you decide where you want to go."

"But on my phone I can click on a location to see pictures, read reviews, visit websites, even look at menus . . ." Katie trailed off.

"I like to see the big picture. Know where I am."

"Okay, dinosaur."

* * *

"This is lovely," said Katie as they drove a narrow two-lane road winding through rolling countryside. Dark green oak trees dotted hills made beige with late-summer dried grass. To Dave and Katie's surprise, California live oaks spread their limbs across the road.

Dave pointed to a gray growth dangling from the branches. "Is that Spanish moss I see?"

"Couldn't be. This climate is too dry. Spanish moss needs high humidity to survive." Katie got out her cell phone and tapped in a query. "Lace lichen that looks like Spanish moss is what we're seeing. There's nothing else like lace lichen in America. Trees draped with lace lichen are called 'bearded oaks.' Lace lichen and Spanish moss do have one thing in common. Deer like to eat both."

"It does look like an old man's beard. I'm not surprised about the deer. They nibble at nearly everything."

Perfectly manicured vineyards and picturesque farms stretched on either side of the meandering Russian River. Gates announced the entrances to prestigious vineyards. Chateau-like houses sat among the lines of trellised vines. Some of the vineyards proclaimed themselves wineries and invited guests to stop and taste locally produced vintages.

Dave glanced up at the glaring sun in a hazy bluish-brown sky. "The air feels hotter and dryer here than back among the redwoods."

The science teacher in Katie reemerged. "That's because the redwoods thrive in the wetter places. Usually that's on a western slope where the clouds drop rain, and many days are shrouded in moist fog. Grapevines like a hotter, drier climate with plenty of sunlight to produce sugar. The sugar ferments to form the alcohol in wine."

They drove by a vineyard where sprinklers irrigated a hundred acres or more of vines. A rainbow formed in the mist. The unending rows of vines, mist, and rainbows combined to create a magical view. "I'd expect grapes to need a lot of water."

"A lot of water and a lot of sun. Volcanically enriched soil. California is perfect."

Chapter Nineteen

* * *

A weathered sign announced a roadside fruit and vegetable stand ahead. The sign promised FRESH, VINE-RIPENED, ORGANIC, SUSTAINABLE. Then another sign and finally the stand itself appeared on the side of the road ahead of them.

"Stop. I want to look," demanded Katie.

Dave pulled into a gravel parking lot. Under a low, barely inclined corrugated steel roof, vegetables and fruits waited in profusion. The Parkers saw scales scattered around for weighing and paper bags on every corner. Tables held almonds, pumpkins, pears, home-canned jellies, fresh and dried tree fruit, berries, avocados, and every type of vegetable. Dried pepper and garlic strands hung from the rafters. A cooler held locally produced cheese and other dairy products. A few other customers milled around making selections.

Dave discovered the section with ground fruits. "Look at all these types of melons. I've never seen some of them before."

"I'm looking at the grapes. I've never seen so many grape types in one place. Let's get some to eat." Katie examined at least ten varieties piled high in bunches on roughly framed wooden tables. Nearby, a robust teenage girl in coveralls wearing her hair in two long pigtails restocked enormous California peaches in a bin.

"How do you know which grapes are sweet?" Katie asked her.

"They're all sweet table grapes here. You can tell by their large size. Most wine grapes are pea sized." She waved her hand over the piles of grapes. "Try one of each kind to decide which one you like the best."

"I know this is an imposition," Dave said to the girl, "but would you mind if I took your picture next to the grapes?"

The girl smiled. "Of course not." She stepped close to Katie, who posed with a bunch of grapes in each hand.

Dave snapped the picture. "Thanks."

"No problem." The girl resumed piling peaches.

As Katie sampled the grapes, Dave returned to the girl, who had finished stacking the peaches and started unloading flats of apricots. "Are the foods sold here locally produced?"

"Virtually all of it," the girl answered as she continued to work. "This market is actually a co-op of California farmers. Different families specialize in various fruits and vegetables. A few also specialize in growing organic produce. My family raises melons and cantaloupes. We're traditional farmers—that is, we do use inorganic fertilizer and a little pesticide."

"Who raised these delicious grapes?" asked Katie while licking the juice off her fingers.

"Several families raise varieties of the table grapes. They also supply organic grapes to health-conscious grocery outlets down in the city."

"Doesn't everybody in this area raise grapes for wine?" Dave asked.

"In the Russian River Valley, mostly yes. An acre of good irrigated land capable of growing premium grapes should produce three to five tons—worth about five thousand dollars—of juice grapes most years. That's enough for maybe four thousand bottles of wine. Depending on the weather and scarcity, peak grape prices can bring ten times that. But not all the land has the right minerals and sun exposure to produce premium grapes."

Dave thought, *Fifty thousand dollars for California grapes grown in one summer on one acre? Maybe that's the real meaning of the Golden State.*

The girl continued, "There are two types of growers. Some—like my family—only have a few acres of wine-quality land. We lease our best acres to a big operation and grow other produce on the rest. Then there are the major vineyards with hundreds or thousands of prime drip-irrigated acres, probably with a labeled winery. Some are large extended-family businesses. But a lot of them are owned by bankers and internet millionaires. Their vineyard is a hobby, a getaway location for them, and maybe a business investment. They hire local farmers to raise the grapes and make the wine. My brothers work for bigger farms."

"I love the crunch this table grape has," said Katie. She held up a different variety. "And this one is as sweet as southern iced tea. I'll get some of both. And I'll take one of these honeydew melons."

The girl smiled and handed Katie a biodegradable paper bag. "I raised that melon. You can check out at the entrance."

As they drove, Katie ate grapes and passed a few at a time to Dave. In the broader river valley, the road straightened, and the vineyards stretched before them like cornfields in Illinois. She pointed out a winery sign that offered a free tour and tasting.

"Let's stop."

"I pictured a winery as old-fashioned wooden barrels and dusty bottles," commented Dave once inside. He stared at stainless-steel tanks connected by clean steel piping and filtration systems. Nearby, bright florescent lights illuminated a laboratory crowded with spotless testing equipment.

Katie studied a pamphlet the winery had provided. "Wine making has become a high-technology enterprise. Ninety percent of wine made in the United States is from California or uses grape juice purchased in California. To make consistent wines for a recognized label, they must monitor sugar content—called dosage—and acidity. Although yeast occurs naturally on grapes, most wineries sterilize the grape juice and introduce a proprietary yeast."

"There's still a lot of art involved, I'll bet."

"And science," she returned.

"Undoubtedly." Dave studied a display describing the process of wine making. "A European agreement of wine producers determined that only wines produced with high carbon dioxide in a certain region of France could be labeled 'champagne.' But US wines that were approved for use of the word 'champagne' before 2006, including certain wines made in California, can be called 'California Champagne.'"

A short walk under an arbor covered with laden grapevines ended in a wine shop. Several opened bottles offered samples. Katie tried four labels produced by the vineyard and winery they had visited.

"You're not supposed to swallow when tasting," Dave advised her. "And you should cleanse your palate with a sip of water between each vintage."

"Spit the wine out? Gross. And I'm not that sophisticated a taster. I like the grapes better anyway. Let's stop on the way back to Redwood Hills and get some more fresh fruit."

* * *

Denyse sat at Lena's kitchen table with Sveta and Sandra. "You've heard about my husband, Jeremy, right? How his parents found Lena when she was homeless with a baby? Then Jeremy helped rescue Trevor from some gangsters."

Sveta feigned a yawn. "Lena told us that whole boring story."

Denyse took a deep breath and pressed on. "Well, Jeremy once fell in love with a footloose and irresponsible older woman named Tara. She invited him to drop any future plans and travel across America with her in a van. Tara wanted a good time but didn't really love Jeremy. He decided to wait for his true love—a prize woman to marry and live a lifetime with."

"So you think of yourself as a prize?" Sveta interrupted.

"Yes, I was a prize. And I had waited for a man worth waiting for."

"I'm a prize too," Sveta insisted.

"Then make sure you save your prize self for the right man."

Sveta rolled her eyes. "More of that fairy tale." She looked at Sandra. "Has she fooled you too now?"

Sandra leaned forward and spoke earnestly. "Listen to Denyse, Sveta. She wants what's best for you and me. So does Lena. Our sister has been through as much or more than us. Her hardships made her a little crazy about doing everything right and trying to avoid such bad situations. Our experiences have turned all of us, except Denyse, a little crazy. So stop being so cheeky."

Sveta shook her head and stormed off.

"Thanks for supporting me, Sandra," said Denyse. "But I'm a little crazy, too."

Sandra shrugged. "Da. Everybody is crazy in some way."

The following day Dave and Katie followed Devin Conrad to Harley's home located in an unpretentious housing development. The Forbeses welcomed them graciously. After Katie expressed sympathy and regret, Harley's mother commented on the uniformed deputy accompanying them.

"Why are the police with you?"

Harley's father didn't wait for an answer. "Why aren't you out looking for whoever is responsible for our son's death?" he demanded of Devin.

Devin stood passively without replying.

Dave answered for Devin, "Actually, we *are* here in part trying to find those responsible for Harley's death."

"What do you mean?" asked Mrs. Forbes. "Are you undercover cops?"

Dave shook his head. "No, we're not the police. We're more like consultants to the sheriff's office. Could we sit down together?"

"Of course. Let's go into the living room." Harley's mother led the way and directed Dave and Katie to a couch and Devin to an easy chair. "Would you like something to eat? People from our church brought so much food." She and her husband sat down in straight-back chairs that had been brought in from the dining room for well-wishers.

"No thank you," Dave answered. "Could you tell us about Harley?"

Mrs. Forbes looked at her husband, who tilted his head toward the Parkers as an indication for her to speak for them both. "Well, he was always a nice boy. Never gave us any trouble. Harley wasn't a great student or anything. But he got a good job as an insurance claims adjuster. He always had plenty of money."

"We understand Harley lived at home," commented Dave.

Harley's father grimaced. "Of course he did. Here he had a full refrigerator, no rent, and free laundry service." The Forbses glared at each other for a few seconds.

Probably a prior source of contention between these two, thought Dave. "Did you know Harley's friends?" he asked.

Harley's mother resumed talking. "Not so much. He never brought anybody here to our house once he graduated from high school. We knew Harley drank some with his friends. And he stayed out late. We had hoped he'd find a nice girl to settle him down."

Katie leaned forward. "As you probably know, Harley died of a drug overdose. A powerful anesthetic called fentanyl. But someone told us that he wasn't an addict. Do you know how he might have come in possession of the drugs?"

Harley's father spoke again. "Had to be that girl. The one the paper said was found with him. Missy somebody."

"Possibly," returned Katie. "But we haven't found any evidence of that yet. Would you mind if we went through Harley's things? Maybe we can find a clue that would lead us to whoever was responsible for your son's death."

Both parents looked hopeful. Mrs. Forbes suggested, "You could look through his room. We haven't touched anything in there. In fact, we never went in there much at all." She stood up. "Harley's room is just down the hall."

Dave and Katie followed her to find a messy bedroom with an unmade twin-sized bed. Clothes lay in random piles on the floor. Pin-up pictures of scantily clad women covered the walls. Dirty dishes remained waiting to be returned to the kitchen. A computer with game discs stacked alongside sat idle on a table. Papers cluttered an old desk.

Dave turned to Harley's parents. "This will take us a while. Deputy Conrad is here to make certain we don't remove anything without your permission." Devin, who had also followed to the bedroom, nodded.

"Okay, then," said Harley's mother. "Call us if you need anything."

After the parents left, Dave asked Devin, "Do you have an official search procedure?"

"I'm a patrolman, not a detective. You two go ahead."

Careful not to disturb anything, Dave examined the papers. Katie started opening drawers and poking through the contents. A drawer in the desk intended for file folders instead held a zippered athletic bag. Inside the bag she found a plastic ziplock bag with about fifty pills plus a dozen partially filled plastic prescription bottles. She waved Dave and Devin over to see the cache. "We'd better call Sheriff Billingsly."

Chapter Twenty

* * *

Sheriff Billingsly arrived in eighteen minutes. Katie showed him the untouched drugs. After looking in the desk drawer, he said, "That makes this a crime scene. Conrad and I will need to take over the search."

"Do you mind if I examine the contents of the bag?" Dave asked.

The sheriff produced a pair of plastic gloves. "Put these on first."

With the gloves on, Dave removed several of the bottles. The bottle labels indicated that all had been issued by a local pharmacy, Wine Country Pharmaceuticals. Dr. Peter Lomax had prescribed the moderate-strength painkillers to various patients.

Before Dave and Katie left the bedroom, Sheriff Billingsly stopped them. "Looks like Harley was distributing. Did you pick up any signals his parents might be complicit?"

"No, I doubt the Forbeses had any clue about what Harley did. They willingly let us look through his room," answered Dave.

"I think they are genuinely naive and confused," Katie added. "They told us Harley had a job as an insurance adjuster."

Sheriff Billingsly shook his head. "He didn't have any job we could discover. You're probably right about the parents. Denial keeps a lot of folks ignorant of their kids' activities."

Holding Katelyn's hand, Denyse led her daughter in a park down a paved path shaded by London plane trees. "Americans call these trees sycamores, darling," she told her little girl.

A few dry leaves fell in a chilly breeze, the month of July being midwinter Down Under. A sweet, spicy smell from nearby eucalyptus trees permeated the air. A group of plumpish gray and pink parrot-like birds landed near where Denyse had taken Katelyn. Katelyn stared at them.

"Those are galahs," Denyse explained. "Australians consider them dumb. Calling somebody a 'galah' here is an insult."

Knowing Katelyn's growing love of wildlife, Denyse pointed to a bluish-gray bird. "See that fellow in the gum tree, or as Americans say, 'eucalyptus'? He's hoping a lizard will come by. They're about his favorite food. That's a kookaburra. They're related to the kingfisher we saw in America. If you listen, you'll hear kookaburras calling almost everywhere." Denyse mimicked an *ack, ack, ack* sound.

In another area of the park, several kangaroos dozed in the warm sunlight. Katelyn started to go closer. Denyse held her back. "They call a group of kangaroos a mob. And wild ones like this aren't safe, darling."

"Why aren't they safe?" asked Katelyn.

"See those hind legs? They can kick you. And they will, especially if they think you're endangering their joeys."

"What's a joey?"

"That's a baby kangaroo. The mother carries it in a pouch on her stomach until it gets big enough to take care of itself. Do you remember when we petted a koala that clung to a post in the sanctuary?"

"Yes. It was sleeping and had rough fur."

"That's right. Koalas are safe animals and won't hurt you. They're also marsupials like the kangaroo. A young koala lives about seven months in the mother's pouch and is called a joey, just like kangaroo babies."

Dave and Katie found Wine Country Pharmaceuticals on the main street of Redwood Hills. They asked to speak to the pharmacist. A somewhat corpulent man of about fifty emerged from the pharmacy office. He wore a light blue smock.

"I'm Cecil Harbanger, the pharmacist and owner here. How can I help you?"

"Thank you for taking a few minutes with us, Mr. Harbanger. I'm Dave Parker, and this is my wife, Katie." The pharmacist did not extend a hand to shake.

Dave continued, "We found Harley Forbes' body a few days ago. You've probably heard that Harley died of a drug overdose. We became curious about how kids like him got lethal quantities of drugs."

The pharmacist nodded and shrugged his shoulders. "I certainly wouldn't know how Mr. Forbes got the drugs.

Probably on the black market. All we do is fill orders legally prescribed by licensed physicians. And fentanyl prescriptions are given only as an anesthetic or in terminal cases." Harbanger's voice indicated irritation. "Now I'm really quite busy," he concluded the conversation as he walked away.

Outside the pharmacy, Dave said, "That didn't go very far. He certainly seemed wary, though."

"How did Cecil Harbanger know Harley died of fentanyl?" Katie asked.

"Good question. Let's try Doctor Lomax next."

Katie Googled Dr. Peter Lomax on her phone and located his office in Redwood Hills. After driving to the office, Dave asked the receptionist if Dr. Lomax might have a few minutes to talk with them about opioid prescriptions. She directed them to the waiting area and bustled to the back of the clinic. The receptionist returned only a few minutes later and reported that Dr. Lomax couldn't possibly see them, even for a few minutes.

"If you'll get a warrant based on what we found at Harley's house and collect Harbanger's sales records, I can look for patterns and compare quantities to national norms," said Dave in Sheriff Billingsly's office.

The sheriff leaned back in his swivel chair. "That would make me happier than a bear in a bakery. But Wine Country Pharmaceuticals is by far the biggest pharmacy in Redwood

Hills. You'd expect to see their name on most of the labels. What you found at the Forbeses' won't get us a warrant."

"But Harbanger knew that Harley died from fentanyl," Katie insisted.

"Could be just a guess from an expert in prescription drugs. Doesn't prove anything."

"Dr. Peter Lomax prescribed all of the pills we found at Harley's. He refused to talk with us. But what about examining his records?" asked Dave.

Sheriff Billingsly laughed. "Raid a doctor's office? That would make national headlines. Not only do you have no more probable cause than you did with the pharmacist, but the doctor can also claim patient confidentiality. Sorry."

As they left the sheriff's office, Katie suggested, "I think it's time we investigate Dr. Lomax and pharmacist Harbanger a bit more thoroughly."

After seemingly endless red tape at the courthouse, Jeff went straight home to check on his daughter. He found Tara in the bike shop showroom dangling a stuffed raven toy over Sam, who was sitting happily on a rug Tara had pulled from the living quarters. Tara made deep-throated croaks as she pretended the bird was swooping down. The little girl smiled, laughed, and reached after the toy.

"Looks like you two are doing fine."

Tara, her face flush with joy, looked up. "You're back."

"I'm sorry for taking so long. The line stretched out the door. I had to stand in line to get forms, fill them in, stand in line to turn them in, then start again at the end of the line when I had to redo one. Do I smell cookies?" He picked up Sam, who continued looking at the toy in Tara's hands.

"Sam and I made chocolate-chip cookies in your toaster oven." Tara handed the bird toy to Sam. She picked up and held out a plate of thick, chewy cookies. "I filled out four work orders and sold one bike. I think the smell of cookies helped catch the attention of people passing by. But you mostly have road bikes and cater to racers and distance bikers. I think you could improve sales by adding bikes targeting more casual riders."

Jeff nodded thoughtfully. "Maybe we *could* expand our inventory with the proceeds of the bikes you've sold. I'll include some variety when I restock this week."

"And we made a macaroni-and-cheese dish for your supper," Tara added.

"You two have been busy." Jeff put Sam down to enjoy a cookie himself. He marveled when his little girl tottered toward Tara.

Tara picked Sam up and tickled her. "Keeping kids' attention makes them happy," she quoted Katie.

"Did you change her diaper?"

"Didn't need to. I sat Sam on the toilet, and she peed."

Jeff froze in surprise. "Are you kidding? Sam's potty trained?"

Tara laughed. "No. I wouldn't say that. I got lucky with the timing. But one success is a start."

Jeff nodded appreciatively. "I'm starved. Let's try your macaroni and cheese."

While eating, Jeff struggled with asking Tara something. "I don't know how to . . . I know it's a lot to ask . . . I understand if you can't . . ."

"Sure, I've robbed lots of banks before." When Jeff merely smiled, Tara retracted. "I was just kidding." She put another spoonful of macaroni and cheese on the tray in front of Sam and smiled when the little girl reached for a handful. Tara looked at Jeff. "What are you trying to ask me, fella?"

"I've been offered a substitute job as a mechanic for a professional bike race, Tour of Napa, next weekend. The scheduled mechanic has the flu. I can make as much money in a few days as the shop usually makes in a month. Before you came, that is." Jeff took a deep breath. "Could you stay here next weekend and take care of Sam? I would pay you, of course."

Tara looked at Sam, who had creamy cheese all over her face. "Why not?"

* * *

"You're back," said Sheriff Billingsly from the seat behind his desk a day later.

"We are. Katie and I have been making some local inquiries," explained Dave. "It appears that both pharmacist

Harbanger and Dr. Lomax are living far above their means. Three years ago, Harbanger purchased a vineyard and estate in the valley east of here. He paid about four-and-a-half million dollars. And Lomax has built a tremendous mansion overlooking the Pacific Ocean. Similar places go for about six million."

"Doctors and pharmacy owners make a lot of money," Sherriff Billingsly replied. "And who knows what they might have inherited? Or won in a lottery? I'd bet my life against a Danish that no judge will give us a warrant based on your assumption of overspending."

Dave tried to not let his frustration show. "Then what can we do?"

The sheriff looked thoughtful. "You got Missy Clark to tell you a lot more than I got from her. How about contacting some other overdose victims? Or in some cases, the next of kin of the victims."

* * *

Back in the loaner car, Dave and Katie looked at each other.

"This investigation is downright frustrating," Katie started. "Is Sheriff Billingsly with us or against us?"

Dave threw up his hands in an I-don't-know gesture. "We need a tension breaker. Why don't you say something funny?"

"What I'm thinking right now you wouldn't find funny."

"Not bad, sweetheart. Let me take you for ice cream. Let's try that lavender-honey favorite downtown."

Chapter Twenty-One

* * *

Tara sat on the small couch in Dave and Katie's RV. Katie summarized, "So the cookies were such a big hit that the bike shop owner, Jeff, has asked you to keep his daughter, Sam, for a weekend? He'll be earning much-needed money working as a mechanic at a bike race?"

"That's right. But I still don't know anything about taking care of a kid."

"Sounds like you did alright."

"I managed for a few hours. Please tell me what to do for two nights and three days. Judging by Jeremy, you were good parents."

Dave looked over the newspaper he was reading. "We weren't always good parents. We nearly let our only son run away with a footloose older woman. No offense, Tara."

"None taken." Tara laughed. "But how do you take care of a toddler?"

Katie started, "Well, with kids her age, you have to establish a routine: meals, activities, bedtime. They're already discovering so many new things in their lives, a routine provides security."

"Okay, a routine."

"You can't leave most kids that age alone for long, either. Unattended, they'll find the wrong thing to put in their mouth or pull something over to hurt themselves. Some get separation anxiety, too."

"Don't leave Sam unattended. Got it."

"When do we get to meet Jeff?" asked Katie.

Tara remained silent.

"Sorry, Tara," Dave broke in again. "Once you baked cookies with Katie, you became a quasi daughter."

Katie gave a stern look at her husband. Dave quickly returned the newspaper to cover his face. Katie admitted, "Maybe I do have some motherly instincts looking for a place to rest. But I'm not trying to be *your* mother, Tara."

"Too bad, maybe. I see now how you were a good parent to Jeremy. Well, both of you, really. I never thought I'd say this, but I feel like maybe I'm missing something by not being a wife and mother," Tara answered.

"You're still young, honey. What are you, twenty-five?"

"Thanks. But I'm thirty-one. And living in a crappy trailer without a guy, much less a child."

"Thirty-one is still young. I was thirty-six before I had Jeremy. But Dave and I felt left out for years when all our friends managed to have kids and we didn't." Katie sat without speaking for a few seconds. "Does caring for Samantha make you want to be a mother?"

"I think so. And to have a family. How did you learn how to be a mother?"

"I learned from my mother, from books, and by making mistakes. Nurturing children brings the best out of most women: unselfishness, self-sacrifice, patience, forgiveness, and," Katie smiled, "long-suffering."

Dave spoke again, "That's the same for fathers."

"I can see those qualities in Jeff," said Tara.

Katie pried a little deeper. "Do you think Jeff likes you?"

"He likes what I do. He thinks I'm smart and capable. And I think he needs me. But I've been around a lot of men. Jeff doesn't look at me the same way most of them do."

"Sounds like maybe Jeff respects you. He could be more interested in you as a person than just what he might get from you. That's the right foundation for a long-term relationship. The sexual attraction is the easy part."

"This is really strange territory we've entered."

"Yes, honey, it is. But don't be put off because Jeff needs you. The strongest relationships are between two people who realize that they need each other. Then they're grateful for each other."

Tara grimaced. "I've been around some pretty dysfunctional men. They needed me. Are you saying I should have stuck with them?"

Katie spoke more firmly than her normal friendly tone. "Absolutely not, Tara! Some women with misguided intentions marry to rescue a man from himself. That never ends well. Needing *each other* is an entirely different matter."

"Okay then, how did you and Dave need each other?"

Katie smiled. "I needed Dave's emotional stability and a man I could respect. He needed me to bring fun into his overly serious life." She reached out to flick Dave's newspaper. "Isn't that right, dinosaur?"

"You do need emotional stability," Dave agreed.

Tara sat watching the little girl nap. She had given Sam lunch and read her a story about a young bear making friends with other animals in the forest. Before Tara finished the story, Sam had fallen asleep on the couch in the bicycle shop's living quarters Tara experienced odd feelings—joy and contentment. Almost like a drug, except totally natural! *This is the result of nurturing someone besides myself,* she realized.

Tara reflected on her own parents. Children in the commune had been cared for as a group. After about age fourteen they mostly reared themselves as individuals—members of the commune. *Unlimited freedom isn't necessarily optimal for children or their parents.*

A feeling of longing swept over Tara. But she shook it off quickly. *Jeff will be back in just two days. This situation is only temporary,* she told herself. *My parents didn't coddle kids. And I turned out okay. Or did I? I wasn't ever smothered but I also didn't experience much stability.*

Sam stirred. "Are you awake?" Tara asked. "Let's visit the toilet then maybe watch some *Sesame Street* on TV."

* * *

Dave and Katie found the previous overdose victims all reluctant to talk.

"I guess saving Missy's life encouraged her to talk to us," Katie speculated.

"The kids won't rat out their sources by telling us where they got the pills," said Dave. "Maybe we can learn something by talking to their parents or other relatives."

From the families, Dave and Katie heard a litany of sad stories. A high-school football player with a knee injury had become addicted to opioid painkillers and progressed to heroin. A gymnast battling a twisted ankle while trying to make the Olympic team had stolen pills from her convalescent grandmother. One kid had been unable to ignore a dare. Other adult victims had sought relief from emotional trauma: grieving a lost love, facing insecurity from unemployment, dealing with a financial reversal, contemplating a life with no apparent future.

Dave and Katie found nothing concrete, no consistent patterns, to report to Sheriff Billingsly. He had sad news to tell them as well. "The former football player you tried to get to talk died last night. Maybe fentanyl."

Dave and Katie sat before the sheriff's desk in despair. Katie's chin sank to her chest above her crossed arms. "His

parents hoped for our help when we met him. We failed them."
She looked up. "Approaching addicts who have an interest in
protecting their sources isn't getting us anywhere. Maybe we
should try in the other direction."

"What other direction?" asked the sheriff.

"Let's contact those whose prescriptions are finding their
way to the victims. Could we look at the containers we
discovered at Harley's house?"

"Devin Conrad and I listed all those prescriptions and the
patients' names." Sheriff Billingsly stood and opened a file
cabinet. He spent a minute searching through documents, then
pulled out a sheet of paper. After making a copy, he handed
the list to Katie. "It's worth a try."

"We traced down as many of the patients as we could find,"
Dave told the sheriff a few days later. "All are old and suffering
various severe ailments. Many suffer chronic pain, frequently
from cancer. Some are now deceased. A few are cared for at
home, but most of them live, or did, at Redwood Hills Loving
Care's facility. That's a nursing home in town."

"I know what that is," returned the sheriff.

"None of the patients have any idea how many drugs they
receive or how much is charged to their Medicare."

"That's typical of end-of-life care at nursing homes," said
Sheriff Billingsly.

"But listen to this," Dave insisted. "Public records show Cecil Harbanger and Dr. Peter Lomax as co-owners of Redwood Hills Loving Care."

An expression of surprise and alarm momentarily crossed Sheriff Billingsly's face. But he shook his head. "That still doesn't prove anything. I can't get a warrant."

* * *

Jeff returned from working the bike race to find Tara watching Sam in the highchair trying to eat yogurt with a teaspoon. Tara turned her head to look at him.

"Welcome home."

"You've got Sam feeding herself with a spoon?"

"Mostly. We made using the spoon into a game. I miss feeding her, though." Tara took Sam out of the highchair and began cleaning yogurt from her hands and face.

Jeff sat down at the table where they ate their meals, tired, but exhilarated. "Thanks, Tara, for taking care of Sam. I'm sorry the race expanded to four nights and five days. The organizers couldn't control the weather."

"That's okay, Sam and I had fun together." Tara didn't mention the eighteen phone calls she'd made to Katie for advice. "And I sold that recumbent bike you added to the inventory just last week. A local man with back trouble paid three thousand five hundred dollars."

Jeff stood amazed. "Three thousand five hundred?"

Tara nodded. "That was on the price tag. And an older lady asked for a single-speed straight drive, like she had as a girl. I ordered one for her online from a discount store, assembled it, and doubled the price."

Jeff then looked at his daughter, who had started playing with Tara's braided hair. "You've done marvelously. I've never seen Sam so content, so comfortable."

Tara repeated Katie's words, "Well, with kids her age you have to establish a routine: meals, activities, bedtime. They're already discovering so many new things in their lives, a routine provides security."

"How do you know these things?"

"I've picked up a thing or two about children." Tara put Sam into her playpen. "Did the race meet your expectations?"

"Better. They even paid me for the idle days. We earned more money than I've managed at the shop in any month since Sam was born—before you came, that is." Jeff continued talking using well-rehearsed words. "I had some time to think during the race suspension. You and I need to discuss something."

"Okay." Tara broke off bits of a homemade cookie and handed them one at a time to Sam.

"As a bike racer, I was subject to random drug tests," said Jeff. "And my wife, Megan, strongly opposed any drugs stronger than aspirin. Her brother had overdosed on heroin and died at twenty-one."

"I've always stayed away from addictive drugs, if that's what you're working around to," Tara responded. "But full disclosure, I have used a little weed in the past."

Jeff smiled. "Who in California hasn't? But do you have any drugs now, including marijuana? Are you still using, even occasionally?"

"No and no," Tara assured him. To herself, she admitted, *I've been too poor to buy marijuana.*

"That's good. Because I'm about to make a proposal, and I wouldn't want anybody dependent on any drug around Sam on an ongoing basis."

Tara nodded agreement. Her heart pounded in anticipation of a proposal that could change her life. Acting experience enabled her to speak with nonchalance. "What sort of proposal?"

"Thanks to you, Sam's and my financial situation looks a lot better. Tara, would you start working here full time? With your help, I could make a decent living for Sam. As she gets older, she'll need a better place to live than this." He gestured to their sparse living quarters. "She can't live in a bicycle shop once she starts school. Sam deserves a house and a home."

Tara hid her disappointment. *Is that all I am, an employee?* She stood motionless, considering the other implications. She remembered her own deprived childhood, looked at Sam, and thought, *This child should have a better home.* Then she questioned herself, *Me with a full-time job? Can I hold down a job? Do I even remember my Social Security number?*

"Well, I live here in Redwood Hills to spend a lot of time outdoors whenever the weather is nice. A full-time job would make that sorta hard."

Jeff nodded. "I remember you telling me that now. What if we were to consider you full time with flexible hours? Minimum wage plus a five percent commission on all you sell. Anytime you want time off for a hike or bike trip, all you'll need to do is let me know."

"We could try that."

Chapter Twenty-Two

* * *

"Let me drive you home," Jeff insisted. "It's foggy outside and nearly dark."

Jeff watched Tara as she looked out the shop windows at the low-hanging clouds. Surely a three-mile bike ride on a narrow highway in these conditions wouldn't appeal to her. Low visibility could prevent drivers from seeing her as well. Finally she responded with, "Okay. But I have to warn you that the place where I live isn't very nice."

Jeff pointed to the rear of the shop. "You've seen where I live."

Tara laughed. "You've got a point."

Tara held an umbrella for Jeff, who carried Sam to his late-model car. While Tara buckled Sam into her car seat, Jeff put Tara's bike onto a bumper-mounted bike rack. Tara then directed Jeff to the campground. As he turned in, Tara asked, "Would you please stop a minute? Meet some friends of mine while you're here. They'd be hurt if I didn't introduce you." She pointed to an RV. "Warning, though. They're hopelessly old-fashioned. And they act like 1960s TV parents."

Katie opened the RV door before they had even knocked. "Come in out of the dripping trees."

Jeff followed Tara up the steps and into the RV. He saw a tall, distinguished, gray-headed man and a perky, welcoming woman with salt-and-pepper hair. Both looked typical of many retirees visiting California. *Simple tourists*, he thought.

Inside, Tara spoke first. "Hope it's okay to just stop by."

"Anytime, Tara," Katie responded.

"Jeff, I'd like you to meet my camper neighbors, Dave and Katie Parker." To the Parkers she said, "This is Jeff Moynihan from where I work."

Dave smiled and stepped forward to shake Jeff's hand. "Glad to meet you, Jeff."

Katie made a similar greeting then focused on Sam. "Hello, honey."

The little girl hid her face on her father's shoulder. "She's a bit shy," said Jeff.

"Most girls her age *are* shy. I have a granddaughter who's nearly five. They're so cute at Sam's age."

Jeff noticed the woman's slight Southern accent. "Where are you from?"

"We're from Mobile, Alabama," Dave answered.

"Have you had supper?" asked Katie. "I just made a lasagna. We were going to offer Tara some when she came home."

"So that's how you knew we were at the door. You don't always watch out the windows for me, do you?" Tara teased.

Jeff had to admit he hadn't eaten. And an irresistible smell of the pasta dish—tomatoes, hamburger, and cheese—permeated the RV. He saw Katie start to set out plates on the RV's dining table.

Katie looked back at Tara and smiled. "You'll stay, won't you, Tara?"

Tara was right—they do seem old-fashioned, Jeff told himself. *Will they ask my intentions about Tara? What are my intentions?* He didn't know himself. *Tara is special. Too good for me, maybe. But am I ready for another relationship?*

After a brief grace led by Dave, Jeff started to eat. "What are you two doing in California?"

Dave answered truthfully, "We came here for a vacation." He didn't mention the opioid investigation that had kept them in Redwood Hills.

"How do you find California?"

Katie answered, "Because we hear so much about the big cities on the West Coast, we're surprised at how many Californians value small-town life. And Californians demonstrate tremendous freedom of expression, usually tending toward the eclectic."

"And in this area, they drink wine like we drink iced tea down South," Dave added.

"I don't drink wine," said Tara.

Jeff looked at her. "You don't drink wine? What about other alcohol?"

"None. I'm not against others drinking alcohol. I just don't want to myself."

"Me neither."

"You two seem to have a lot in common," said Katie.

Jeff avoided her implication by asking Dave, "So, what's your profession back in Mobile?"

"I'm an accountant."

Jeff's ears perked up. "I'm sure this is imposing, but could I ask a question about bookkeeping? I own a bicycle shop downtown. The paperwork and records are driving me crazy."

"Please, go ahead," said Katie. "My husband loves to talk accounting. Just don't ask him any history questions for all our sakes."

Lena found Sandra in the living room looking over literature for various universities and the curriculums they offered. "You're thinking about more education? Isn't twelve years of public school enough? Nobody in our family has had as much."

Sandra looked up. "Denyse said that a university education could help me get a good job. Maybe I'll get to be a teacher, like her. I'm good in math." Her eyes returned to the literature.

Should I tell her that we can't afford university classes? Lena asked herself. *No. God can provide a way. And Denyse has given Sandra some hope.* She saw a pleasant expression on Sandra's face as she eagerly scanned the pages. *At least Sandra isn't with Sveta, wherever she might be.*

"Sandra, do you know where your sister is?"

"No. We had an argument during our meeting with Denyse. Sveta is mad at me for siding with Denyse."

Lena sighed. "Today is Sveta's day to take care of Maria. Denyse picked up Vlady to visit Mama and Poppa and play with Katelyn. If you would help me by taking care of Maria for a few hours, then I could go out for a hamburger with Trevor."

Despite difficulty taking her eyes off the university materials, Sandra immediately laid them aside. "Food, then bath, then nap, right? After two hours of sleep, entertain Maria with toys?"

Lena smiled as Sandra went to the kitchen to prepare food for the baby. She walked down the hall and knocked on Trevor's door.

"Hey, in there. Would you take me to McDonald's?"

The door immediately opened. Trevor stepped out, smiling. "Recreate our first date, huh?"

Lena mimicked her first words to her then-future husband. "Da, I mean, yes."

Katie poured tea for herself and Dave the next morning. "So what do we do after Sheriff Billingsly's latest refusal yesterday?"

Dave added lemon and packaged sweetener to his cup. "We did the best we could here. Let's pull up stakes and hit the road again. We can drive west and visit Yosemite."

Katie sipped her tea. "I hate to give up. Girls like Missy are being victimized."

Dave finished his first cup and extended it for a refill. "I feel the same way. But we're at a dead end. Don't you want to see Half Dome?"

Katie, although feeling deep regret, nodded in affirmationy. "Where to after that?"

"Let's take a northern route home, I-70 through Colorado."

"Could we stop in Vail? I've heard it's beautiful even in summer."

The couple continued discussing their itinerary for traveling back to Alabama.

Katie noticed that Dave seemed very relaxed. He sighed and said, "Everything will be okay." He nodded slowly to himself, then added, "That tea is making me feel good. I'll have another cup."

"Sure, we've got a toilet right on board. Drink all you like."

Katie sipped her first cup of tea while Dave downed his third. She noticed him rubbing his arm. "Are you itching?"

"Yeah, I haven't been near any poison oak, though."

"Maybe you're allergic to something."

"All I've had is thee."

"Do you mean tea?"

"Uhhm, yeah, thee."

"Dave, are you okay?"

"I'm . . . I'm . . . okay."

"Look at me, Dave!" Katie demanded.

Dave slowly turned his head. He blinked several times. "Amm feelin' a bit sleep . . ." His head nodded forward. Dave caught himself. "I feel . . . fine." He reached for more tea and knocked over the cup. "Cloud pass over, darkly."

Katie grabbed Dave's chin, lifted it, and looked in his eyes. The pupils seemed enormous; the corneas narrow. He began to slump in his chair. His lips moved, but he didn't speak. She noticed a bluish tinge to his fingertips.

Katie grabbed her cell phone and dialed 911. "What's your emergency?"

"My husband is having a stroke or something."

"Your location?"

"Holiday Home Park Campground on Highway 116 in Redwood Hills."

"What are your husband's symptoms?"

Katie glanced at Dave. He appeared asleep with his head on the RV's dining table.

"He's fallen asleep. His skin is a bit blue. His eyes looked funny."

"You mean he's unconscious?"

"Maybe."

"Get him up, if you can. Walk him around. If he stops breathing, administer CPR."

Katie put down the phone and tried to pull Dave up. She couldn't manage his weight and let him slip to the floor.

"I can't get him to his feet," she told the 911 operator.

"Can you get someone to help?" the operator directed.

Without answering, Katie dropped the phone, darted out the RV's door, and ran in stocking feet to Tara's camper.

"Tara! Tara! I need help!" Katie yelled while banging on the door.

Chapter Twenty-Three

* * *

The door immediately swung open, hitting the camper side with a thud. Tara stood with a look of alarm. "What is it, Katie?"

"Dave—"

Tara didn't wait for any more details but ran to Dave and Katie's RV. Katie followed and entered to see Tara check Dave's breathing and lift an eyelid. After a quick look, Tara rubbed her knuckles roughly over Dave's upper lip.

"Whaaaa," Dave responded and turned his head to escape the pain.

"Help me get him up," Tara ordered Katie. Tara pulled Dave to his feet with Katie helping to steady them both.

"Walk!" Tara shouted into Dave's ear. He took two steps then started to slump again. Tara repeated her knuckle rub on his lip.

"Ahhh!" Dave feebly tried to brush Tara's hand away. He labored to breathe.

"Walk!" she demanded again.

"What's happening?" Katie asked.

"Looks like a drug overdose. I've seen this before. Back at the commune. My old boyfriend." Tara had to use the knuckle rub again. "Have you called 911?"

Katie remembered the phone and picked it up. The 911 operator had remained on the line.

"Help is on the way," the operator promised. "Is your husband still breathing?"

Tara leaned over to shout into the phone. "He needs naloxone." She put her mouth near Dave's ear and demanded, "Take slow, deep breaths!"

"Understood," the operator came back. "I'll advise the paramedics to have naloxone ready."

Katie heard a distant siren. With Katie's help, Tara continued commanding Dave to breathe deeply and walk around the RV. She put his arm over her neck to help support him. Whenever he hesitated, she administered the lip pain.

An EMT vehicle screamed into the RV park. Katie ran outside to wave them over. The same two paramedics who had responded to the call about Harley and Missy exited. "Where's the victim?" asked the woman. Katie pointed to her RV's door.

Both emergency responders hurried inside. The woman carried a nasal spray canister. After a couple of cursory checks, she applied the naloxone to each of Dave's nostrils. Within a minute, Dave started to breathe easier. "Nice work keeping him up," the male paramedic said to Tara.

"We need to take him to the hospital as a precaution," the woman said. "But he should recover." She helped Dave lie down on a gurney.

"Are you his wife?" the male paramedic asked Katie.

"Yes, I am."

"You can ride in the ambulance, then. Buckle yourself in."

Without thinking, Katie climbed into the vehicle after Dave. She noticed a police car pulling into the RV campground as the ambulance left for the hospital.

Tara watched the ambulance pull away. She saw Katie's phone lying on the ground where she had dropped it. *She didn't take her purse or ID either,* Tara thought. She picked up the cell phone and collected Katie's purse from inside the RV, walked to her bicycle, and started pumping eighteen miles to the hospital. *Should be okay to leave the RV. The police are here.*

* * *

Denyse sat patiently with Dingo watching a Rugby League game on the TV. Dingo mostly talked over the action, recalling his own exploits on the turf. The phone rang. Since Beatrice had taken Vlady and Katelyn to play in the sand near the bay and the game held Dingo's attention, Denyse rose and picked up the phone. "Hello."

"Denyse, this is Sandra. Lena went somewhere with Trevor—"

"Oh, good," Denyse interrupted. "They both need some time together."

Sandra ignored Denyse's comment. "We've got a problem."

"Is the baby okay?"

"Not about the baby. A friend from our school called to tell us that Sveta is going to a beach party with some older men. She overheard some of them talking about getting Sveta unconscious drunk. Then they would take her into one of the storage sheds on the beach and . . ." Sandra left the threat unspoken.

"Did your friend say where the party is?"

Sandra quoted the friend as hearing Shell Beach, a location on the eastern side of Melbourne Bay and the frequent scene of unmonitored gatherings.

"I know where that is. Now, do you remember where Lena and Trevor went?"

"I heard Trevor say something about a hamburger and recreating their first date."

"I know where that is, too."

"What are you going to do?"

"I'm going to take Dad and Trevor and go get Sveta."

Two days after the financial seminar at Calvary Baptist, Jeremy's cell phone rang with a message from an unknown caller. Suspicious of another scam call, Jeremy answered carefully, "Hello."

"Is this the number of the people looking for a yellow cat?" the caller asked.

Jeremy could not disguise his eagerness. "Yes! We're looking for a yellow cat. Do you have him?"

"No, sorry. But I saw a cat that looked like him in our backyard. Later I notice his picture in the window of the bakery I patronize. The owner said she had picked the flyer up at a tax seminar."

"Where do you live?" The address represented an area several miles outside the vicinity where Jeremy had posted the LOST CAT bulletins. After recording the address, Jeremy continued, "Please give me your number. You'll get a reward if we find Old Yeller."

"Oh, no reward is needed. I love cats. And my baker said that you're a really nice person."

"Thanks."

* * *

Dingo was watching a goal-line stand late in the keenly contested rugby match. Denyse came into the room and turned off the TV.

"Dad, get your shoes."

"What's on?"

"Some men have taken Sveta to a drinking party at Shell Beach. We're going to go get her. I'll write a note to Mum telling her where we are."

While Denyse wrote a note in the kitchen, Dingo thought, *We might need a bit of extra muscle.* He picked up the phone. "Hogan, I need your help, mate."

* * *

Jeremy's voice had grown hoarse from shouting for Old Yeller in the caller's neighborhood. Lights in the houses started to go out as the residents prepared for a night of sleep. Several locals had identified the photo of Old Yeller Jeremy showed.

"I saw a stray cat that looked like that. Maybe two days ago," one resident claimed.

Jeremy remembered Dorothy's words about the cat not necessarily responding to his voice. *I've got to keep looking.*

* * *

Trevor and Lena lingered over chocolate shakes at McDonald's. Lena listened and contributed ideas as Trevor described the plot of his next novel.

Commanding words surprised both. "Trevor, you need to come with me right now."

They turned to see Denyse beckoning. "What is it?" asked Lena.

"Something I need Trevor for. Trevor, I'll explain in the car. Lena, you go home and stay there. Sandra will tell you where we're going."

Chapter Twenty-Four

* * *

Katie sat alone in the hospital's emergency room waiting area.

A doctor came out to ask, "Are you with the older male overdose case? A Mr. Parker?" he added after looking at his clipboard.

"Yes, is Dave okay?"

"He should be fine. The paramedics treated him before the full effect of the drug set in. If you're ready, we'll be able to release him to you in a couple of hours. You'll need to fill out some paperwork first."

Katie realized for the first time she didn't have any ID, insurance cards, or credit cards. "Sure. But I came so quickly in the ambulance I didn't bring any identification."

"Perhaps you could get somebody to bring your documents to you," the doctor said before being called away to another emergency.

Katie searched her memory. She and Dave didn't have any friends in Redwood Hills, except Tara. But she didn't have a car or even a phone to call. Katie felt more alone and helpless than she ever had.

She heard a voice from behind her. "Katie!" Turning, she saw Tara.

Tara held out Katie's phone and purse. "I thought you would need these."

"How did you get here?"

"Same way I get everywhere. My bike."

Katie went to fill out the paperwork while Tara waited. Once finished, she rejoined Tara and they waited together. After a few moments of silence, Katie spoke softly and slowly as if she were forming the words one at a time. "I've never really thought about Dave dying. I mean, with my cancer history, I always thought I'd die first." Katie glanced at Tara, who remained silent.

"I know that husbands don't come with a warranty. But what would I do without him? Where would I go?" Katie's words trailed off.

Tara put her arm around Katie. "Dave is going to be alright. No need to think about that right now." She gave Katie a long, firm hug.

"You're a good girl, Tara. And you may very well have saved Dave's life."

Tara sat speechless.

Katie was surprised. "What's the matter, honey?"

"Nobody ever called me 'good' before."

* * *

The mid-winter sun had set by the time Denyse parked Beatrice's car with Dingo and Trevor. Nearly a dozen other cars lined the side of a road that paralleled the eastern shoreline of Melbourne Bay. She was surprised to see Hogan waiting for them by the narrow trail that led from the road to the water's edge.

"Are you attending this party?" Denyse asked him.

A lisp in Hogan's speech indicated he had been drinking. "Depends on what you mean by attendin'. My mate, Dingo, called me to help out."

Denyse gave a harsh look at Dingo, who simply shrugged. "Let me do the talking," Denyse told the three men with her. "Remember, all we want is Sveta. No troubles, ya hear?"

"Why don't you stay here, sis?" Trevor suggested. "You're pregnant. We'll get Sveta." He indicated himself, Dingo, and Hogan.

Denyse reflexively touched her slightly extended stomach. "Thanks, Trevor. But I have three men here to take care of me." She made eye contact with Dingo, Trevor, and then Hogan one at a time. "Let's go."

Loud music guided them along a sandy path winding down a steep bluff to a narrow beach. They found a dozen or more men drinking heavily in the light of several battery-powered LED lanterns. Wolf whistles followed Denyse as she moved through the crowd, followed by Dingo and Hogan. Trevor

233

trailed somewhat behind. A circle of men surrounding something drew her attention. Standing on her tiptoes to look over the men's shoulders, she saw Sveta being supported by two men while a third held a plastic cup to her mouth.

"Drink up, dearie," the man with the cup said. "Show us you're a mature woman." A beach storage shed stood open nearby with a pallet on the floor.

"Stop!" Denyse's command made all the heads turn toward her. "I've come for that girl."

"And just who the 'ell do you think you are?" the man with the cup demanded. "This woman came to our party of her own free will."

"She's too drunk to have any free will."

"Sheila here swallowed our booze with her own lips."

Denyse tried to push through the male watchers to reach Sveta. Several men stood firm shoulder-to-shoulder, forming a barrier. "I'm taking that girl," she asserted. Dingo stepped up to stand behind his daughter, followed by Hogan, who wobbled slightly. Trevor hung back.

"You're crashing our party. Now bugger off," one of the men forming the barrier demanded.

"I'm taking Sveta home," Denyse reasserted.

"You and who else? You and these two bogans?"

"Who are you callin' a bogan?" Hogan's voice boomed from behind Denyse.

"Sorry, I should have called you a galah."

Hogan stepped forward and delivered a quick punch to the speaker's nose. The man's nose gushed blood. "Now who's the galah?" Hogan roared.

Dingo grabbed Hogan from behind and tried to pull him back. The big man thrashed around, trying to free himself from Dingo's grasp. Denyse stepped in to prevent further blows and defuse the situation. The man who'd been struck by Hogan, intoxicated and dazed by the blow to his nose, swung wildly back at Hogan and connected with Denyse on her cheek bone, knocking her to the ground.

They all heard a wild shriek. "That's my sister! And she's pregnant!" Trevor charged into the group of men, flailing his fists and kicking in every direction.

After Dave's discharge at the hospital late that afternoon, Katie called a taxi and tried to think of a way to transport Tara and her bike back to the RV park.

Tara just shook her head. "It's no problem, really. I'll just ride my bike back."

Katie thanked her again and promised to see her later. She helped Dave into the taxi and directed the driver back to the RV park in Redwood Hills.

"What happened?" Dave asked once they had reentered the RV.

She turned to look at her husband. "Dave, the hospital says you overdosed on drugs."

"Overdosed? How would I have gotten any drugs?"

"I don't know. Why don't you lie down?"

Dave refused to be put to bed. "I feel fine." He tenderly touched his upper lip. "Why is my lip so sore?"

"You nearly died, Dave!"

Dave sat down in the easy chair opposite the RV's couch. "But I didn't die. And how does that explain my lip?"

Katie ignored his question. "When you were in the hospital, I started thinking about what my life would be like without you. Up to then I had always thought I'd die before you."

"Me left on my own is not a pretty thought either," Dave quipped, trying to lighten Katie's mood.

Katie smirked. "True. But the thought of me on *my* own isn't much better."

"We've had more years together than most people ever get. And they've been good years. We learned how to work as a team, loved each other well, raised a wonderful son, and had a lot of fun," Dave encouraged Katie.

"I guess our lives have been better than most, and I *am* thankful. If it all ended today, I'd have no reason to complain. But how can we maximize the time we still have left? However long that might be."

"Well, one thing we could do better is to realize we have no promise of future days, but we do have each day. Then we need to stop long enough to enjoy every moment we share, to be fully present every day. Like we're doing right now. Moments are fleeting. Memories are forever."

"My dinosaur. You always know how to give my heart joy. A new commitment to not let another day pass without being engaged with each other and the adventures before us. I like the sound of that."

"Me too."

"Would you like some tea?" offered Katie.

"I could use some," returned Dave. He stood and opened the refrigerator. "Where's my lemon juice?"

A rapping at the RV's door captured their attention. Opening the door, Katie found Sheriff Billingsly waiting in the twilight. Deputy Conrad stood a few steps behind him.

"The hospital reported your emergency," explained Billingsly. "Is Mr. Parker okay?"

"I'm fine!" Dave assured them from inside.

"Y'all come on in," Katie invited the two police officers. Dave rose to meet them and shook hands with each man.

The RV's sitting area seemed crowded with three standing men and Katie. "Won't you sit down?" Katie offered. "Can I get you something to drink?"

"We're actually here on official business," Sheriff Billingsly answered. "We follow up after every overdose report."

Dave sat back down. "I understand. We have no idea how I could have gotten any drugs. The strongest drug we carry is aspirin. I think maybe I had an allergic reaction to something I ate."

"What known allergies do you have?"

"None before now."

"Uh-huh," the sheriff nodded. "Do you mind if we look around?"

"Of course not," Katie answered. "What are you looking for?"

Without answering, Sheriff Billingsly pulled out a pair of plastic gloves. Deputy Conrad stood ready. The sheriff started visually scanning the interior of the RV.

"I can help if you'll tell me what to look for," offered Katie.

"Please just sit down, Mrs. Parker. This is our job."

Dave and Katie exchanged a long look. Dave shrugged and pointed to the RV's couch.

Katie sat down. From where she sat, she watched the sheriff check some drawers in the RV's kitchen, then turn his back to open the small refrigerator. After a few seconds, he turned around with something in his hand.

The sheriff returned to the RV's sitting area. "What is this?" He held the corner of a Ziplock bag in his gloved hand.

Inside, Katie saw a few tablespoons of a white powder. "I don't know. Could it be a deodorizer left from a previous renter?"

The sheriff extended the bag to Deputy Conrad. "Log this in, date the record, and we'll both sign it. Careful, the bag could have latent fingerprints."

The sheriff turned to Dave and Katie. He pulled a card out of his uniform shirt pocket. "You have the right to remain silent. Anything you say can and will be used against you in a court of law. You have the right to an attorney. If you cannot afford an attorney, one will be provided for you. Do you understand the rights I have just read to you?"

* * *

Old Yeller could be anywhere, Jeremy told himself on Sunday morning after walking streets, searching, and calling for three consecutive evenings and all day on Saturday. He imagined the joy of seeing an orange hunk of fur hiding under some shrubbery. Tantalizingly, a few people claimed to have seen the cat, or thought they had, most frequently in car headlights. The purported sightings covered nearly a square mile of housing developments and strips of woods. *Finding Old Yeller is hopeless. I might as well just tell Mom that he's gone.*

Today is Sunday, he realized. He couldn't face another day of heartbreaking disappointment. *Maybe going to church would help.*

An hour later Jeremy sat in a pew waiting for the worship service to start. *No sense delaying,* he told himself and bowed his head. *Thank you, God, that someone may have seen Old Yeller. I don't want to break Mom's heart by losing her cat. I sure could use a clue in finding him.*

Jeremy felt a vibration in the pew as the organ music began. The odor of a sweet, musky perfume reached his nose. Something brushed his leg. He looked up to find Giselle sitting next to him.

"Hello, Jeremy," he heard her whisper.

"Giselle, I haven't seen you here in years," he whispered back.

She leaned close to speak into his ear. "I haven't been here since I was, like, a teenager. Because I'm moving back to the area, I thought I should, you know, reconnect. I'm happy to have found a friend here."

Jeremy could feel her breath against his cheek. He heard the music director announce, "Hymn two hundred ninety-eight." Jeremy reached for the hymnal and stood. Giselle stood with him and pulled the hymnal toward her so that they shared. Sitting again at the hymn's conclusion, Giselle shifted her seat slightly so that their hips remained lightly touching.

Any thoughts of a lost cat evaporated from Jeremy's head. Throughout the church service he fought and lost a battle to not think about the sweet kisses he and Giselle had once shared.

"OMG, I hardly recognize anyone here," Giselle said after the pastor's benediction. "None of the kids I knew are here. Even the pastor is different. I'm so glad to have run into you."

This is church. You're supposed to be friendly to visitors, Jeremy told himself. "Yeah, things have changed. Our old youth leader, Walter, is a pastor in Birmingham now." He could not help noticing Giselle's slender neck exposed by her blond hair piled on her head. Dark red lipstick contrasted with her light complexion. *What a glamorous woman.*

"I had forgotten about Walter. And he had that skinny young wife with a thick Georgia accent." Giselle held onto

Jeremy's arm as they exited the church. "We had some fun times back then—before we tried to grow up too fast."

"Yes, we did," Jeremy admitted.

"Could I catch a ride with you, Jeremy?" asked Giselle on the sidewalk in front of the church.

"Didn't you come in a car?"

"I did. But one of those lights in the instrument panel had started blinking. I'll need to get somebody to look at it. Fat chance on a Sunday."

"I guess so. Where to?"

"I'll show you the way."

A few minutes later, Giselle pointed to the oyster-shell parking lot of a well-known seafood restaurant. "Here."

"I thought I was taking you home," said Jeremy.

"Oh, you are. But I owe you a lunch for giving me such good financial advice. And I still have a few questions about IRAs and stuff."

Chapter Twenty-Five

* * *

Several men on the beach struck back at Trevor, hitting him repeatedly. Dingo released Hogan and started grabbing men by their shirts with his left hand, pulling each forward and smashing them on the nose with his right. Each man so hit went down. Hogan followed Dingo into the melee, targeting one man at a time with his huge fists.

The men started to back away from Dingo and Hogan. Several crawled away. Trevor used the gap to rush the men facing them. He shouted curses and received three blows for every one he landed. Dingo and Hogan stepped forward, grimly striking the men who pummeled Trevor.

Behind them, Denyse, although addled, struggled to her feet. "Get Sveta," she shouted.

Dingo knocked down the man who had held the liquor to Sveta's mouth. The two men who had supported the girl on either side fled from him and Hogan. No longer supported,

Sveta slumped to the ground, unconscious. Dingo picked Sveta up, cradled her in his arms, and carried her to Denyse.

"Take her to the car," Denyse ordered.

Hogan fought a rear guard while following Dingo and Denyse. Looking back, Denyse saw Trevor kicking ineffectively at several men while on the ground. Three stood around him landing solid kicks.

Denyse grabbed Hogan by the arm and shouted in his ear, "Bring Trevor."

Hogan returned to the fight without Dingo. He fended off blows but managed to grab Trevor by the collar. He dragged Trevor, who continued kicking at his opponents. Once clear of the men, Hogan reached under Trevor's armpits and lifted him to his feet. Together they followed Dingo and Denyse up the sandy path of the cliff.

Sirens and flashing blue lights announced the arrival of authorities at the top of the cliff. Several uniformed policemen exited three squad cars. A police sergeant approached them.

"We got a call from a Lena Larkin about a possible assault on an underage woman at Shell Beach."

"We're her family. We came here to rescue her," explained Denyse.

"Is this the reported victim?" The sergeant shined a flashlight on Sveta's face in Dingo's arms.

"Yes, this is Svetlana Travnikov. She's fifteen years old and his sister-in-law." Denyse pointed at Trevor. "I'm his sister and this is our father." She indicated Dingo.

The sergeant shined the light on Trevor, who was bleeding and staggering. Then he put the light on Denyse and saw her right eye swelling shut. "Has there been a fight?"

"Fair dinkum, mate. And a right brisk one. We showed those party boys what for," Hogan answered.

"Alright, you're all under arrest. Except for the victim." The sergeant re-illuminated Sveta and spoke into his portable radio. "We'll need an ambulance for an inert female at Shell Beach. Send additional units for multiple arrests." Turning to Denyse and the others he ordered, "Lay Ms. Travnikov on the ground. Then all of you, put your hands palm down on the car." To the other patrolmen he said, "Round up all the belligerents down by the water. Don't let any cars leave."

* * *

"Yes, I understand my rights," Dave answered Sheriff Billingsly's question.

Katie started, "Why are you telling us—"

"The sheriff cut Katie off. "Just yes or no, ma'am."

"Yes."

The sheriff put away the card. "With these rights in mind, do you wish to speak to me?"

Dave shrugged. "Sure. We have nothing to hide. Maybe you can help us get to the bottom of this."

The sheriff stared at Dave. "Mr. Parker, the on-the-scene paramedics reported that you responded positively to naloxone. That can only occur when opioids are in your system. The hospital confirms the presence of fentanyl in your blood. Where did you get the drugs, Mr. Parker?"

Dave shook his head. "I don't have any idea where any drugs could have come from."

The sheriff looked at Katie. "Me neither," she volunteered.

"Mr. Parker, we found an unknown powder that appears to be some sort of drug in your RV. Finding fingerprints on the bag from you or Mrs. Parker is likely. Furthermore, the coroner reported that a combination of alcohol and fentanyl killed Harley Forbes. The same paramedics found you with Harley's body." The sheriff looked back and forth between Dave and Katie. "Maybe this isn't a simple vacation you're on. Are you dealing drugs, Mr. Parker?"

Dave shook his head. "*No.* I'm not dealing drugs. I have no idea what's going on. Are we under arrest?"

"Should you be under arrest?"

"What for?"

"Drug dealing. Homicide, if we link the drugs found in your refrigerator with those in Harley Forbes' system." The sheriff let that soak in. He turned to Katie. "Mrs. Parker, you're involved in this as well." He contemplated the two of them. "These are serious charges. Police work on TV is accurate in one aspect. Whichever of you turns state's evidence on the other will get a much lighter sentence."

"We have nothing to say. And we would like an attorney," Dave demanded.

The sheriff looked at Katie. "Ma'am?"

Katie looked at Dave, who shook his head. "Yes. I mean no. I say the same as my husband."

The sheriff nodded. "Mr. and Mrs. Parker, you are under arrest for suspicion of drug possession with intent to distribute and possibly involuntary homicide. I'll need to put you in handcuffs and transport you to the station." He turned to Deputy Conrad. "Cuff them, Devin, and hold them in the squad car while I complete the search."

"We withdraw our assent to the search," said Dave.

"Too late. Our discovery gives us clear evidence of probable cause now."

The deputy lifted the bag by a corner and smirked. "The dealers always think a refrigerator keeps their store fresher."

While the deputy escorted Dave and Katie in cuffs to the squad car, the sheriff went into the RV's bathroom. There he removed something and placed it in a ziplock bag.

Never had Katie felt so humiliated. After being handcuffed and transported to Redwood Hills' extension office of the county sheriff's department, she had been thoroughly searched by a female deputy, photographed holding a number, and fingerprinted. Residual black ink from being fingerprinted remained on her fingers. Perhaps the most degrading was the impersonal way the deputies had treated her—just another suspect, a likely perpetrator.

Then came the coup de grace. A female deputy escorted her to a holding cell. Not a cage of iron bars as depicted in so many film dramas, but a sterile-looking, well-lit room within white cinder-block walls. The deputy closed a solid door with a large wire-reinforced window behind her. Katie heard the click of a solid lock.

Katie was the only inmate in the compartment. She sat down on one of several wall-mounted steel plates covered by a cotton-filled pad. A small white pillow and thin folded coverlet on the plate identified that as her bed for the night. She saw a concrete floor sloping to a six-inch drain in the center, glaring fluorescent lights recessed in the ceiling, and a stainless-steel toilet and sink combination barely shielded from the window. An overhead vent brought air into the enclosure.

Through the window she saw Dave being similarly escorted by a male deputy to a presumably identical holding cell down the hall. He appeared to be in a daze. Katie rushed to the door's window, trying to get his attention and send him a reassuring smile. But he looked neither to the right nor left and didn't notice her. A few seconds later, she heard the click of a door lock down the hall indicating he had also been locked in. The deputy returning past the door glanced at her watching through the window but made no sign of acknowledgement.

Katie returned to her seat. *I can't believe Sheriff Billingsly turned on us so quickly. And where is he now? His office is right in this building. Why doesn't he at least come by?*

A voice coming through an aperture in the door interrupted her thoughts. "It's suppertime. You have any dietary restrictions, Mrs. Parker?" a female deputy asked.

"Not that I know of. But I'm not hungry anyway."

"Well, I advise you to eat and drink something. A Big Mac, supersized fries, and a coke, okay? Or would you rather have the chicken nuggets or a fish sandwich?"

"McDonald's?" Katie thought. From movies, she would have expected a tray of runny, gross food shoved under the door. "The hamburger and fries will be fine. Thanks!"

"You're welcome. Your only time being arrested, I'll bet?"

"Yes."

"Don't worry. I'm on duty tonight. My name's Wanda. I'll take good care of you and Mr. Parker. I'll be back with supper in a jiffy. A lawyer will be here to see you early in the morning."

Katie's own thoughts surprised her in the serious situation. *What would Jeremy think if he could see his mother in jail? Denyse? The Fogles? The Larkins? Will my example send Katelyn down a path of crime?* A sense of shame kept her worrying about fantastic consequences all night.

"Call for you, Jeremy," Dorothy reported. "A Ms. Asher in California. She claims to be your parents' attorney."

"Their attorney?" Jeremy picked up the phone in his office. He heard, "Mr. Parker, I represent David and Katherine

Parker in the state of California. They gave me your number for the arrangement of bail."

"Bail? What for?"

"Possession with intent to distribute narcotics. Bail is likely to be fifty thousand dollars each. Can you provide a hundred thousand dollars?"

Jeremy was flabbergasted. How could his parents be in jail? His mind went in a hundred directions at once, then he realized the attorney was still waiting for him to answer her question. "I can't. But the firm owned by my father can."

"Alright, here's the bailiff's number. You'll need to make arrangements with him to assure the means for your parents to be released."

"Of course."

Jeremy's phone rang at 2:00 a.m. to wake him from a fitful sleep. He had lain awake until 1:30 worrying about his parents in jail.

"Hello," he answered, expecting to hear his father or his mother's voice.

"Denyse is in jail," wailed Beatrice. Jeremy could hear her crying between the words.

"Why would anyone put my wife in jail?"

"There was a fight. They went to get Lena's sister, Sveta. Dingo and Trevor are in jail too, along with that mate of Dingo's, Hogan."

"Where's Katelyn?"

"I've got Katelyn, Vlady, and Maria at our old house in Melbourne. Lena and her sister Sandra have gone to visit Sveta at the hospital."

"Sveta is in the hospital?"

"Didn't I just say so?" Uncharacteristically Beatrice's voice revealed irritation.

"How's Denyse?"

"She's in the bloody jail. That's how she is. My darling daughter. Always the good girl. But the police didn't think her face was bad enough to take her to the hospital."

"What's wrong with Denyse's face?"

"I haven't seen her. And she's been separated from the men. I'm just repeating what Lena said after the police called about Sveta being taken to the hospital."

"Do you want me to come to Australia early tomorrow morning?" asked Jeremy.

"No, no, luv. There's nothing you can do right now."

"Well what do you want *me* to do?"

"Get ahold of your father. He'll know what we should all do. I've been trying to call Dave and Katie's number all day. Nobody answers."

Jeremy decided not to tell Beatrice that his parents had also been incarcerated. "I'll try to reach Mom and Dad for you."

"Thanks heaps."

"And you call me as soon as you hear anything else about Denyse."

"I promise."

251

Anthony could hear gunfire down the street from where he was housesitting Herschel's home in south Mobile. Almost nightly, gunfire erupted somewhere in the area where they both lived. Rarely did anyone report any shooters. He crept in the dark to peek around the curtains out the window. A late-model car rolled slowly down the street. Anthony saw a flash from a car window, followed by what felt like a blow to his chest. His hand reached to feel where something had struck him. His fingers felt a hot, sticky fluid—his blood. He coughed up more blood and had trouble filling his lungs with air. He stumbled to the house phone and dialed 911. He choked out, "I've been shot. Please help me."

Chapter Twenty-Six

* * *

Jeremy's phone rang again—this time at 4:30 a.m. He hadn't slept since the previous call from Beatrice. Fumbling to answer and expecting his wife, Jeremy answered, "Denyse?"

"This isn't Denyse. This is Anthony's mother, Rosie Marshall. He's been taken to the hospital. He's been shot. My son has been shot!"

"Is he okay?"

"No, he's not okay. Nobody is okay when they're shot. Anthony is in surgery now. I'm calling you because the police are here at my house. They want to know why Anthony was in Herschel Johnson's house."

"Let me talk to the police," Jeremy told Rosie. He heard voices in the background as Rosie summoned a policeman.

He waited until he heard a deep male voice say "Hello."

"Hello, officer. This is Jeremy Parker. I'm a junior partner at Parker and Company Accounting."

He heard a warm voice. "This is Sergeant Vance. I know who you are, Jeremy."

"Oh, hi, Mr. Vance. Herschel Johnson and Anthony Marshall both work at Parker and Company. Anthony was housesitting for Herschel while the Johnson family went on vacation."

Sergeant Vance's voice returned to an official tone. "Do you know where Mr. Johnson is now?"

"Herschel is at Disney World with his family."

"Do you have a contact number for him?"

"Yes, sir." Jeremy gave the officer Herschel's cell phone number. After that, he asked, "Can you tell me what happened?"

Without answering, the officer asked, "Do you know any reason anyone would want to assault either Mr. Marshall or Mr. Johnson?"

"No, nobody would . . ." Jeremy stopped. "Well, they both helped abort what almost turned into a racial riot last year."

"Could anyone confirm that besides you?"

"Caleb Fogle. Principal Fogle of Central High School."

"Thank you, Mr. Parker. We'll contact you later, when we need more information."

Anthony's mother returned to the phone. "Jeremy, I need to see my son. Can you drive me to the hospital?"

"Yes, ma'am. I'll be right over to pick you up."

The next morning in the Sonoma County Courthouse, Dave and Katie sat with a court-appointed attorney—a harried, middle-aged, local woman.

"Stand up," their public defender whispered.

A tired-looking older judge studied papers before him. He looked over glasses perched on the end of his nose at the Parkers. "You're accused of possession of illegal narcotics with intent to distribute. How do you plead?"

"Answer not guilty," whispered the state-appointed attorney.

"Not guilty."

"Not guilty."

A young male assistant district attorney stood. "Your Honor, the suspects are non-resident. And the charges are serious. Enough fentanyl to kill several people was found in their possession. Furthermore, the hospital reports a recent overdose of fentanyl by Mr. Parker himself. Just eight days ago the Parkers reported a fentanyl fatality, perhaps their customer. A charge of negligent homicide is pending. The state asks for remand without bail."

The judge took off his glasses. "The negligent homicide charge hasn't been filed yet?"

"No, Your Honor."

"And there's no direct evidence of distribution?"

"Not yet, Your Honor."

"Then all we really have before the court is possession?"

Dave and Katie's lawyer spoke to the court for the first time. "That's correct, Your Honor. And the Parkers are upstanding

255

citizens from Mobile, Alabama. Mr. Parker is the senior partner in an accounting firm bearing his name."

The judge spoke to the attorney. "You call all your clients 'upstanding,' Ms. Asher. Where are the suspects residing?"

"They're in an RV in Redwood Hills, Your Honor."

He took a long look at Dave and Katie before speaking again. "Ms. Asher, are your clients prepared to post bail?"

"Yes, Your Honor. Their accounting firm is ready to wire bail from Alabama and has demonstrated the means."

"Mr. and Mrs. Parker, will you give me your word to remain in Redwood Hills and to post the bail?"

Nudged by the attorney, Dave and Katie each answered, "Yes, sir."

"Okay, fifty thousand dollars bail for each. Mr. and Mrs. Parker, you can leave the court. But you keep your word to me. If you try to leave town, I'll have the sheriff put out an APB on you quicker than a bear can eat a donut. The state troopers will have you back here in handcuffs before you realize what happened."

"Yes, sir."

"Your Honor, we haven't actually received the bail yet," the assistant district attorney objected.

"This couple isn't going anywhere."

A few hours later while sitting with Rosie Marshall at the hospital, Jeremy recognized the number of the incoming call. "Hello, Mom."

He was surprised by his father's voice. "Hi, Jeremy. Thanks for arranging our bail."

"Yeah, Dad. You guys must have gotten in deep this time. What's this all about?"

Jeremy listened to Dave's recounting of their arrest and arraignment, including their inability to leave Redwood Hills. Dave finished with, "We need some help here, son. Can you come?"

"Sure, Dad. I'll get on the first flight. But we've got real problems here, too."

"What's the matter?"

"Anthony got shot last night while housesitting for Herschel. I'm at the hospital with his mother. The Johnsons are cutting their Florida vacation short. But they're not returning to Mobile yet, in case someone had deliberately targeted them. Anthony's mother needs me. The police are using me as the best source of information on both families."

"How's Anthony?"

"Under sedation right now. The bullet nicked one of his lungs."

"Never mind, son. You stay in Mobile where you're needed. We'll see if Denyse can come."

"I doubt if she can come," Jeremy answered without revealing his wife's legal problems. "Why don't you try Tara?"

"Ask Tara to help us?"

"Why not? It sounds like Mom has adopted her as a quasi daughter. She's got plenty of spunk. And Tara's an actress. She majored in theater at college."

"Tara went to college?"

"Yeah, Dad. There was always more about Tara than you and Mom got to see."

"We saw quite a bit of her, actually."

Jeremy laughed. "Yes, you did. But she could be exactly who you need now."

"Maybe you're right."

"Oh, Dad. There's something else I need to tell you."

"What's that?"

"I'm afraid I still haven't found Old Yeller. But I've got a good lead on his possible location."

Dave spoke carefully, lest Katie hear more bad news. "Okay, you can tell us about that later."

Dave rung off. He told Katie about Anthony and concluded with, "I told Jeremy to stay in Mobile."

"I heard. What was that about Tara?"

"Jeremy suggests asking her to help."

"I'd be more comfortable with Denyse. I'll call her. She's family."

"All rise for Honorable Judge Wilma Peabody."

Denyse, Dingo, Trevor, and Hogan stood behind the defendant's table in Australian inferior court. Denyse had a black eye above the cheek where she had been hit. Trevor looked like a herd of cattle had stampeded over him. Dingo and Hogan appeared unscathed by the fight except for some bruised knuckles. On the other side of the courtroom, the police sergeant who had arrested them also stood. In the courtroom, Beatrice, Lena, and Sveta stood. Sandra had stayed home to care for the children.

"You may be seated," said Judge Peabody. "I understand this is about the latest physical altercation involving the famous Dingo Larkin."

"Yes, Your Honor," answered the sergeant. "He's the shortest male." Dingo smiled a bit and nodded his head respectfully. "The woman and younger man are his daughter and son. The big man is an associate."

"State your full legal names for the record," the judge ordered.

"Graham Larkin."

"Denyse Larkin Parker."

"Trevor Larkin."

"Hogan."

"Mr. Hogan, we need your full name for the record."

"Do I have to, ma'am?"

"Yes, or be jailed for contempt of court."

"Ambrose Hogan."

His fellow defendants all looked at him in surprise. Hogan returned an embarrassed shrug.

"Where are their alleged opponents?" the judge asked the sergeant.

"We're holding fifteen of them on attempted assault charges, Your Honor. A female classmate of the victim heard some of those suspects say they would get the victim dead drunk and then have sex with her. Apparently, the four standing before you arrived in time to prevent the assault. But a public brawl occurred."

"And you verified the female victim to be underage?"

"Yes, Your Honor. The girl, Svetlana Travnikov, is a Ukrainian national with a resident visa in Australia. Her passport shows her to be fifteen years old." The sergeant pointed to where Sveta sat beside Lena.

"Then I determine the rescue justified. But the defendants should have delayed the assault and waited for the police rather than instigate a fight. I fine them each three hundred dollars."

Dingo and the others looked at each other, smiling. Clapping came from those who observed.

The judge continued, "After paying your fine, you may go." The judge paused. "Except for Mr. Trevor Larkin. Records show that he is under strict probation, which prohibits public fighting whatever the cause. Mr. Trevor Larkin is remanded to custody for transfer to prison in New Zealand."

A chorus of voices protested. The judge quieted them. "There's an ironclad legal agreement in place with New Zealand. Unless I undermine our working relationship with the Kiwis in all matters, my hands are tied."

Chapter Twenty-Seven

* * *

Katie heard Beatrice answer the phone. "'Ellow." Her voice sounded subdued.

"Good day to you too, Beatrice. Can I speak to Denyse, please?"

"Oh, Katie. Happy to hear your voice. Hope you and Dave are well. Denyse is with Dingo trying to see the judge."

"What's going on? Is Dingo in trouble?"

"Not Dingo, luv. Trevor. They say he has to go back to New Zealand and prison."

Katie could hear Beatrice start sobbing into the phone. "What happened?"

"Trevor got into a fight after a bloke punched Denyse. She has a black eye like Dave did. They were trying to rescue Lena's younger sister, Sveta."

"Why did Lena's sister need rescuing?"

"Because she's a daft girl. That's why." Beatrice's sobs kept her from continuing.

"That's okay, Beatrice," said Katie. "I'll talk to Denyse later. It sounds like she has her hands full."

"I think she's hoping that you and Dave could come down here and help her."

"Beatrice, I'm afraid we can't come right away. But could you ask Denyse to call us to explain, please? Maybe we can do something to help her from here."

Beatrice's tears subsided. "Thank you, luv. And I'm sorry about your cat."

"Old Yeller?"

"That's the one. Denyse asked Lena and the rest of us to pray that Jeremy would find him. I know how having a lost pet can hurt."

"Yes, it can," Katie responded. "I've got to go now, Beatrice. Have Denyse call me."

Katie put down the phone. "Denyse can't come. Trevor is in trouble again."

"What now with Trevor?"

"Beatrice wasn't clear. Something about Denyse being in a fight and Trevor going to prison."

"What?"

Katie only responded by shaking her head. Some tears started to trickle down her cheeks.

Dave put his hand on her shoulder. "Are you afraid for Trevor?"

Katie nodded. "Yes. But also, Jeremy's lost Old Yeller."

"Beatrice told you about Old Yeller?"

Katie sat down on the little couch. "You knew and didn't tell me?"

Dave nodded. "Jeremy told me. But I didn't think you needed any more bad news."

"You're right about that. But I feel so helpless. We've been in jail and are facing charges. Anthony has been shot. Trevor's on his way back to prison. Denyse is hurt. And I'm crying about a cat."

"Jeremy is trying to find Old Yeller."

"I know. But he's lost somewhere all alone, hungry, and frightened. We're stuck here and can't help anyone we love. What are we going to do?"

A rapping started on the RV's door. Dave opened the door to find Tara with a big smile on her face.

"I'm glad to see you're better, Dave. You gave us quite a scare," she said.

Dave motioned for her to enter and pushed the door wider.

Once inside, Tara instantly saw Katie's tears and sensed the Parkers' mood of despair. "If this isn't a good time, I could come back."

"No, honey. We need a friend to talk to right now," Katie answered while blotting her eyes.

"Katie told me about how you kept me alive until the paramedics arrived," said Dave. "And you brought the identification Katie needed to the hospital, too. Thank you, Tara."

"No problem," Tara responded then sat down next to Katie on the couch. "You have Dave back now. No need for more tears."

Katie started to pour out everything. She included jumbled references to their experiences in Minnesota, New Zealand, and Mobile. Occasionally Dave interrupted to add some clarification. Even with Dave's clarification, Tara couldn't follow everything. After a half hour of talking, Katie started to slow the description of her litany of troubles.

Tara leaned back and looked afresh at Dave and Katie. "Wow. There's a lot more to you two than I realized. I've never experienced anything that heavy. And I'm about as irresponsible as anyone could be. Nobody has ever tried to kill me, though. Although you probably thought about killing me when I tried to steal Jeremy."

Tara's humor and equanimity made Dave and Katie laugh. Encouraged, Tara asked, "And you're here in Redwood Hills investigating drug dealers? But you're not the police?"

"We *are* investigating a *local* opioid crisis. And we're consulting for the police, but we aren't law enforcement ourselves." Dave noticed that Tara appeared relieved at their disclaimer.

"And all this had been going on while you taught me how to bake cookies and take care of Sam?"

Katie and Dave both nodded.

Tara thought a minute. "Have you considered that someone might have tried to poison you?"

"Poison me?"

"How else do you think you might have ingested the fentanyl?" asked Tara.

"I have no idea. The only thing I had that morning was some hot tea."

Katie nodded and added, "I had the same tea. It didn't affect me."

"Do you both drink tea the same way?"

"Dave puts lemon in his tea," answered Katie. "Wait a minute! Just before the sheriff came and arrested us, Dave discovered his lemon juice missing."

Tara leaned forward. "Then who knew Dave uses lemon in his tea?"

"Sheriff Billingsly did. But how would he have removed the evidence of poisoning from our refrigerator?"

Tara gasped. "Just as you left in the ambulance, a squad car pulled into the campground. As I took off on my bike to carry your purse and cell phone to the hospital, I remember thinking that your RV would be safe unlocked with the police present. The sheriff could have removed the poisoned bottle and planted the drugs after I left."

"Sheriff Billingsly has also obstructed our investigation by refusing to get warrants," Katie thought out loud.

"From my experience and what you've said, I wouldn't trust the local police to exonerate you. Some of them planted drugs on demonstrators from the commune where I grew up."

Dave spoke somberly, "Unless we want to be railroaded into prison, we need to find some evidence and go to the state troopers."

Tara gave her wry smile. "Is there any way I could help?"

"Maybe you can. Jeremy told us that you're quite an actress," answered Dave.

"I used to be adequate. And I know a bit about the drug culture."

"Would you be willing to do some role playing for us? We need you to pose as somebody looking for drugs. Help us find where the opiates are coming from. Especially the fentanyl."

"This is real, not some TV show, isn't it?"

Dave and Katie nodded again.

Tara looked back and forth between Dave and Katie's desperate faces. "Why not? This could be a hoot. A hoot for a good cause."

Lena smelled lavender as she entered the bathroom where Sandra was bathing Maria in an inch of warm soapy water. "Have you seen Sveta?"

Sandra lifted Maria from the tub. "She's in her bed. She feels ashamed for what's happened. And she's worried about Trevor."

Lena went to the room that had once been Trevor's. She opened the door and found Sveta brooding in the bottom bunk with all the lights out.

"Come on, Sveta, you need to eat. We can all make something fun for supper. How about pierogi? Remember the times when we made something special to surprise Mama and Poppa after they worked hard all day?"

"Mama and Poppa aren't coming."

"No, they're not coming. But remember the fun we girls had? Making the noodle dough, chopping up and wrapping the fillings, boiling the pierogis, then frying chopped onions to top them?"

Sveta rolled over, turning her back to Lena. "I don't feel like having any fun."

Lena started to react but decided against it and walked away.

Sveta lay in the dark. The door opened again. "Sveta, you need to join the family." The emphatic voice came from Sandra.

"I didn't ask anyone to help me."

"No, but you needed help. We all do sometimes. Now our sister Lena is facing losing her husband. She needs our help to do something that will give her some joy."

"If everybody had left me alone, then Trevor wouldn't be in jail."

"We've all had hard times, Sveta. None harder than Lena. How would you being gang-raped have made your life any better? Do you think that having our baby sister treated so would have made our lives better?"

"No."

"Now listen to me, Sveta. Despite all we've been through, we've found a family, the Larkins, that cares about us. Three men fought to protect you. Denyse is injured for you and looks like hell. Trevor, who has been good to Lena and us, may go to prison. Now it's time for you to stop thinking about just yourself and be part of a family."

When silence answered her, Sandra closed the door and left Sveta in the dark.

A few minutes later Sveta entered the kitchen where Lena had lined up flour, raw potatoes, hamburger meat, cheese, and sauerkraut for the pierogi. "What can I do?"

Lena smiled at her younger sister. "First peel the potatoes."

Chapter Twenty-Eight

* * *

"Missy, phone call for you," called Darla.

"Who is it?" Missy yelled back.

"A girl, Suzy Hunter. She says you two were school friends before she moved away in tenth grade. She's moving back to Redwood Hills."

I don't remember any friend named Suzy Hunter, thought Missy. But she trudged to where her mother held the house's landline.

Darla held her palm over the receiver. "This could be good for you, Missy. Re-establish some friendships from before . . . you know." Darla handed Missy the phone and turned to leave.

"Whatever." Missy took the phone. "Hello."

"This is Suzy. Do you remember me?" said a cheerful voice.

"No."

"Well, I'll bet you remember another friend of mine. His name was Harley Forbes."

Missy froze. She looked to determine if her mother could possibly hear. "How do you know Harley?"

"Harley used to provide stuff for me. Now I've run out and need to find a new supplier."

"You and me both."

The voice speaking to Missy said, "Let's you and I meet to talk about our mutual interests."

"My mother won't let me out of her sight."

"Ask her to pick up the extension," the voice instructed. "Let me talk to her."

"Mom, Suzy wants to speak to you too."

"Hello," said Darla into the upstairs phone.

A chirpy voice spoke to her. "This is so totally neat that Missy is at home this summer. I need to reconnect with her and some of the other girls. Mrs. Solsen, could Missy join me at the Dairy Queen? We would, like, split an ice cream sundae and catch up like we used to."

"Maybe, Suzy. You and Missy would be there alone, right? She's sort of grounded right now."

"Just me. I'm hoping to get all the girls together, eventually. Maybe we could have a sleepover at your house or something."

"Okay," said Darla. "When did you have in mind meeting at the Dairy Queen?"

"How about right now? I'll wave when I see you."

* * *

Anthony opened his eyes and blinked. The room seemed to be out of focus.

A voice said, "He's still sedated but waking up. Try speaking to him."

"Anthony, baby. Can you hear me?"

"Mama?"

"He knows me," Rosie rejoiced.

"I'm here too, Anthony," spoke Sherri.

Anthony recognized the voice of his girlfriend. Gradually his eyes made her clear. "Where am I, Sherri?"

His mother answered, "You're in the hospital, baby. You've been in surgery. Do you remember being shot and dialing 911? One of your lungs nearly filled with blood after the bullet hit you. The doctors have patched you up."

"How will we pay the bill, Mama?"

A male voice spoke. "Don't worry, Anthony. Herschel's home insurance and medical insurance carried by Parker and Company will settle with the hospital."

Anthony shifted his focus. He saw Jeremy standing slightly behind Rosie.

"Who did this to—" he tried to ask.

Rosie interrupted him, "The police don't know who shot you yet, baby. But the doctor says you're going to be alright."

*   *   *

"Have you found Old Yeller yet?" Denyse asked Jeremy over the phone.

Jeremy posed his own question rather than answering. "Are you hurt, sweetheart? Beatrice said something about a fight and your face."

"I've got a black eye on one side. But the swelling has gone down. I can see fine through that eye again." Denyse repeated her question, "Have you got the cat?"

"The baby is okay, too?" Jeremy persisted.

"Yes. The baby and Katelyn are both fine. What about Old Yeller?"

Jeremy sighed in relief. "No, I haven't found him. I've got a decent lead on the area he might be in. I wanted to ask Mom or Dad to come home. He might respond to one of their voices. But they've got their own troubles and can't leave California."

"Don't we all have problems? Trevor is back in jail. The judge says that because he violated probation in Melbourne, he'll have to go back to New Zealand to serve his ten-year sentence."

"Troubles all over," said Jeremy. "Anthony is going to recover, though."

"What happened to Anthony?"

"He got shot while housesitting for Herschel. That's why I couldn't go when Dad asked me to fly to California to help them out of their mess. They've been in jail themselves; did you know?"

"Dave and Katie in jail? What for?"

"Suspicion of drug trafficking. I posted fifty thousand dollars bail for each of them. Well, the firm did."

"What are your parents going to do?"

"They've asked Tara to help. She was my prom date—"

"I remember."

"She's an actress—"

"I'm not surprised." Denyse sighed. Everything felt so out of control. "Well, one good thing about all this trouble is that the Larkin family has learned to pull together. Lena and her sisters have invited us all over for a special Ukrainian meal tonight."

Seated at a table facing the plate-glass windows, Katie and Tara watched the parking lot of a Dairy Queen. "That's them," said Katie when a BMW driven by Darla pulled into the parking lot. Missy rode in the passenger seat.

Tara had dressed in faddish teenage clothes, wore wide sunglasses, donned purple lipstick, and put her hair into a loose ponytail. She left the restaurant and walked up to the BMW's passenger-side window as if she knew Missy.

"Thank you, Mrs. Solsen, for letting my best friend in all Redwood Hills come. We'll, like, be just inside catching up." She opened the door for Missy and hugged her once she had stepped out of the car.

When Darla made signs of parking and accompanying Missy, Tara added, "Thanks for giving us some girl time to talk, Mrs. Solsen. I'm never one to use seven words when nineteen will do. Maybe you could pick her up in an hour? I want Missy to tell me who's doing what and ask about a couple of boys I knew. You know. Are they seeing anyone?"

"Of course," answered Darla. "I'll be back in an hour. And we'll have that slumber party once you've gotten re-established."

Tara returned a girlish grin. "You guys are totally awesome."

Tara linked her arm with Missy and walked her into the Dairy Queen.

"I'll have to hand it to you," Missy whispered. "You got me away from my mother."

"Aren't you a little old to be grounded?" Tara whispered back.

"Legally, yes. But you don't know my mother. Once I snuck off trying to find drugs and returned in a cold rain to find all the house doors deadbolted. I sat alone on the porch all night. I had no other place to go. When my mother opened the door the next morning, she assured me that there would be no money, no transportation, not even a dry place to sleep, unless I obeyed her."

Inside the restaurant, Tara unlinked arms and approached the counter. "My situation wasn't much better until I took responsibility to find what I needed for myself."

"What's your real name?" Missy asked.

"Tara." She pointed to the menu on the wall. "We should make this look good. Can I buy you a sundae?"

"Whatever."

Seated at a table with two sundaes before them, Tara began, "Cutting through the bullshit, I'm looking for Harley's supplier."

Missy sat, her ice cream untouched. "Why should I help you?"

"Because you need something just like I do. I took my last dose yesterday. Once before, I ran out for a week and nearly died. I was saying to people, 'Take this baseball bat and try to knock me out.' Then, once I found some stuff, I came to my senses and realized that the pills won't kill me, as long as I don't do more than I can handle. But right now, I can't concentrate on anything. I've got growing anxiety and insomnia. The pills can bring me back to normal."

"I feel exactly the same way," said Missy.

Tara dug into her ice cream. "When I do manage to get to sleep, I have drug dreams."

"You too? I get depressed when I wake up and find out the dream wasn't real."

"I'm the same. That's why we need to do something to help ourselves. Harley made a stupid mistake. I won't. Harley's supplier is likely looking for a new distributor. I aim to take Harley's place. Unlike you, I also need a source of income."

Chapter Twenty-Nine

* * *

"What's in it for me if I help you?" Missy asked Tara.

"Ten percent of the profits paid in merchandise for connecting me. More if you want to become a full partner."

"Me a drug dealer? I don't think so."

"How did you pay Harley?" Tara asked between spoonfuls of ice cream. When Missy sat silently, Tara suggested, "Favors?"

Missy nodded but didn't speak.

"Harley have you provide favors for others?" probed Tara.

Missy nodded again.

"Would you rather be my partner or a whore?" asked Tara.

"Your partner," Missy admitted.

Tara pointed at Missy's melting sundae with her spoon. "Are you going to eat that?"

When Missy shook her head, Tara exchanged her empty bowl for the full one. "Then, tell me what you know about Harley's sources."

"Harley started buying pills from kids who stole them. Then he made some sort of deal with a local pharmacist. The pharmacist could provide prescriptions to certain names. Harley could cite the name like a password and get the pills."

"Cecil Harbanger, the pharmacist?"

Missy nodded again. "I think so."

"What were the names Harley provided?"

"Walker. Altman. Yost. He remembered them by 'WAY.' Those were the names I saw. Harley told me the pills cost two hundred dollars per order. He sold them for more than double that."

"Okay. If that pans out, then you're entitled to ten percent for six months."

"Wait, you didn't say anything about only six months. What will I do after that?"

Tara finished Missy's ice cream. "Well, I don't want any 'favors.' But you can be a partner by bringing new customers." Tara looked out the window and nodded toward the parking lot. "That's your mother, I think. She's early. Tell her the ice cream was good."

"When do I get something?"

"I told you on the phone that I'm out. I'll need to connect with Harbanger for both of us. Then I'll find some way for you and 'Suzy' to get together. Maybe come to your house."

Tara led Missy to Darla's BMW. She spoke in her chirpy voice. "Thanks, Mrs. Solsen. Missy, my feelings about you-know-who are just between us girls, okay?"

Missy made an awkward attempt to play along. "He's cute enough for anyone. If you don't try for him, I will."

"What did you find out?" Katie took off the hat and sunglasses she'd been wearing while sitting with a laptop at a back table in the Dairy Queen.

"Harbanger, like you and Dave suspected. I had to feed her a total line of lies to get her to trust me. But I may have the key to open the door," answered Tara.

"What's the key?"

"WAY. Walker, Altman, and Yost."

Australian news media couldn't resist the juicy story. All the TV stations, newspapers, and other media featured the report of Dingo Larkin involved in a public brawl, rescuing an underage girl in peril. They presented Trevor as a rising author and consultant to the police. An innocent-looking school picture of Sveta garnered sympathy for her rescuers.

Local politicians grabbed news coverage by demanding another hearing. Judge Peabody yielded to public pressure and scheduled another hearing. A crowd of witnesses assembled to testify on Trevor's behalf. Reporters hovered to cover the story.

Lena started the proceeding by making a tearful appeal. She told about Trevor rescuing her in New Zealand.

Hogan took the stand. "I started the fight, Your Honor. The lad is straight-up. He tricked me and my mates fair and square at poker. Later he returned our money even when he didn't have to 'cause he wanted to make things right."

Dingo begged, "I was a terrible father to the boy. Send me to prison in my son's place."

Beatrice confirmed Dingo's confession about poor parenting before insisting, "But Dingo's changed." She cried in the docket.

Denyse pointed out the good Trevor's books had done alerting readers to possible scams and hustles.

Sveta took the stand. "If I hadn't been so stupid, nothing bad would have happened."

Judge Peabody listened patiently to every witness. "Anyone else?"

"Me please, Your Honor." Mr. Broadmoor, Trevor's former public-school principal, stood and came out of the watchers to testify. "Trevor started as a scoundrel but is now a credit to our college."

To everybody's surprise, the police sergeant who had originally arrested them and represented the prosecution asked to speak to the court. "Mr. Trevor Larkin came to the station and gave a talk about identifying con artists. Her Majesty's police recommend letting him go."

Trevor himself took the stand. Overwhelmed by all the support, he could hardly speak. "I lost my head when I saw my sister struck. She's pregnant." All could see Denyse's extended stomach and black eye.

After everybody spoke who wished to, the judge shook her head. "You've convinced me that Mr. Larkin represents an asset, not a threat, to our community. But nobody has presented any legal basis for setting aside the binding agreement with New Zealand. Not even our prime minister could change that."

* * *

"You know me, Mr. Harbanger," whispered Tara at the order window of Wine Country Pharmaceuticals. "I work part time at the bicycle shop on Main Street. I sold you a bike for your nephew."

"I've also seen you on the sidewalk," returned the pharmacist with a bit of a leer. "That's why I came into the shop."

"Well, I'm glad you liked what you saw," Tara pretended to flirt back. "But I'm not here to talk about bicycles. I believe we had a mutual friend. Harley Forbes used me to deliver medicines to customers named Walker, Altman, and Yost."

Harbanger visibly pulled back. "How do you know those names?"

"I was Harley's partner. You could say I delivered for the delivery man. I know the customers better than Harley did. I'm ready to take Forbes' place. Only I won't do anything so dumb as he did."

The pharmacist instinctively glanced each way. "Same terms as with Forbes?"

"Harley told me he paid you three hundred dollars a prescription," Tara lied.

Harbanger paused a few seconds. Tara could almost see him calculating the long-term benefit of increasing the price from two to three hundred.

"Yeah, that's right."

"Then I'll take three prescriptions to start." Tara counted out nine one-hundred-dollar bills that Dave had given her. "Walker, Altman, Yost."

Katie and Tara sat in an interrogation room at the state troopers' offices in Santa Rosa. The state investigator sitting across from them listened with a grim face.

"So here's what you're telling me? You . . ." he pointed at Tara then looked at his notes, ". . . Ms. Grabowski purchased opioid painkillers without prescriptions at a pharmacy in Redwood Hills? And you are an employee at Freedom Road Bicycle Shop in the same town."

Tara hid her fear of the law enforcement officer and nodded.

"You say that you were assisting Ms. Parker," he indicated Katie, "in some sort of civilian investigation?"

Both Tara and Katie nodded.

"Furthermore, Ms. Grabowski, you have no mailing address and no ID other than an expired Wisconsin driver's license and a library card?"

"Sorry," answered Tara.

"Now, Ms. Parker. You and your husband, Mr. David Parker, have been indicted here in Sonoma County for possession of illegal narcotics? And you suspect the local sheriff's authority of complicity in a drug operation. But Sheriff Billingsly had originally co-opted you into an investigation?"

"That's correct," answered Katie. "Maybe Billingsly wanted to see how exposed they were. We think he may have tried to poison my husband and frame us when we got close to the truth."

"Where is Mr. Parker now?"

"He's in Redwood Hills. Judge Tatum ordered us to not leave town. We thought that half of us remaining would fulfill that requirement. And I only left to come to this police facility. I'm sort of in police custody now."

"Have you got anything to convince me that you're not making this all up?"

"Well," said Katie, "we're in here willingly turning in illegally sold prescription drugs."

"That *is* something," the investigator admitted.

"We're hoping that you'll obtain warrants for the records of the pharmacy and Dr. Lomax's practice."

"I'm afraid that these drugs were purchased illegally by your own admission. No judge would accept illegally obtained evidence to justify warrants for medical records. That's a path to getting an entire investigation thrown out of court on appeal."

Tara and Katie looked at each other. "Isn't there something you can do?" pleaded Katie.

"The legal complexities of this are above my pay grade. But the two of you please wait here while I check out your stories."

Chapter Thirty

* * *

An aide interrupted Judge Peabody with a note and whispered in her ear. The judge read the note then spoke to all assembled.

"Hold your places. Court is still in session. I'll be back in a few minutes."

"All rise," the bailiff said. Everybody stood up as the judge hurried to her chambers.

A low murmur of voices filled the courtroom in the judge's absence. A few minutes stretched into thirty, forty-five, an hour. Those remaining in the courtroom fidgeted in anxiety as the minutes continued to tick off.

"All rise for Honorable Judge Wilma Peabody."

Everybody stood again.

"Please be seated," Judge Peabody told all present.

"I've received a call from a Lieutenant Malcolm Fraser in New Zealand. Our counterparts in New Zealand have made an exception. Mr. Trevor Larkin, you will be free to go. In view of the circumstances and your record of public service, the Kiwis will ask their courts to suspend your sentence there. Until that judgment is rendered, you must continue to observe the conditions laid out in the original probation agreement."

The courtroom erupted in cheers and applause. Dingo and Hogan roughly pounded Trevor and each other on the back.

Judge Peabody shouted and hit a gavel to restore order. "Mr. Larkin, the Kiwis have one request. In view of their leniency, I order it. Mr. Larkin, you will travel to New Zealand at their expense, give a series of lectures on identifying con artists, and autograph your novels. You are free to go."

* * *

Jeff picked up the ringing phone. "Freedom Road Bike Shop."

"This is Sergeant Gomez Hernandez of the California State Troopers. Is there a . . ." he paused to pronounce the name ". . . Tara Grabowski employed by that enterprise?"

"Why, yes. What's the trouble, officer?"

Without answering Jeff's question, the state policeman continued, "Have you seen Ms. Grabowski purchasing or using prescription opiate pharmaceuticals for any non-medical purpose?"

"No, I haven't. Is Tara, I mean Ms. Grabowski, in some sort of trouble?"

"Are you aware of any medical reason Ms. Grabowski would have such pills in her possession?"

"Certainly not. What's this all about?"

"Sorry, I can't comment on an ongoing investigation."

"An investigation?"

"That's all the questions I have. Thank you for your time."

"You're welcome."

Jeff hung up after hearing the click-off on the other end of the line. *What is Tara up to? How well do I really know her? Maybe not as well as I thought.*

* * *

An impromptu celebration convened at Trevor and Lena's home. Beatrice had stopped at a bakery and purchased several pavlovas and other treats. Lena put on the teakettle. Hogan brought two bottles of beer for himself and two more for Dingo. Katelyn and Vlady ran around enjoying the hubbub.

"Does anybody know what happened for the New Zealand police to intervene?" Dingo shouted over the commotion.

"I just called Jeremy to tell him the news. He says Dave called Malcolm Fraser in New Zealand from California after he had talked to me," Denyse shouted back.

"Bully for Dave!"

Hogan began teasing Trevor about his lack of martial skills.

"The lad's got heart, though," Dingo defended his son.

Trevor pointed to his own battered face. "Why don't you two look like me?"

"Good on ya for your spirit, lad. But ya can't take on more than one man at a time," Dingo explained. "You tried to fight five at once."

"How do you take on only one man?" Trevor asked.

"You circle."

"Circle?"

"Here, let me show you. Suppose I'm fightin' you and Hogan. You move so that one man stays between you and his mate." Dingo demonstrated by stepping so that Hogan stood between him and Trevor. "Now, you try to reach me," he told Trevor.

Whichever way Trevor tried to get around Hogan, Dingo circled so that Hogan remained between him and Trevor. "See, that way you only fight one bloke at a time. Once you've knocked the first one down, his mate will look at him, then you can take care of the second one." Dingo slow motioned a roundhouse blow to Hogan's jaw. Hogan pretended to collapse to the floor. Trevor instinctively glanced down at him. Dingo reached out to tap Trevor open handed on the cheek. Hogan nodded in approval.

"Stop, Poppa!" Lena demanded. "Don't you be teaching Trevor to fight."

"I won't be fighting," Trevor promised his wife. "But as a writer, I might need to describe fights."

Lena rolled her eyes and moved to serve more tea.

"Dad, what do you do if someone tries to tackle you in a fight?"

"You lift your knee into his face. See, like this." Dingo and Hogan began role-playing various fight moves to educate Trevor.

Most of the women clustered around Sandra. She showed them her university literature.

"What will you study, luv?" asked Beatrice.

"I think engineering. There are a lot of good jobs for engineers. And math is my best subject. I'll find the money to go to uni somehow."

"Dingo and I will help you go to uni, luv. We have money."

"Would you? Then could I call you and Dingo Mama and Poppa like Lena does?"

"Certainly, luv."

Denyse noticed Sveta seated apart, taking no part in the communal joy. She went to sit down by the girl. "Sveta, you did well to testify for Trevor today. Thank you."

"I was the cause of it all." She looked at Sandra excitedly talking about career opportunities. "I'm glad Sandra has a future." A tear ran down Sveta's cheek.

"You can have a future, too, honey. Just don't try to grow up too fast."

"All I have are good looks. I have to take advantage of that while I'm still young."

"Don't underestimate yourself, Sveta. You're a Travnikov. You've already endured a lot. Channel that strength to survive into making something of your life beyond physical appearance."

"How?"

"Well, Sandra is going to uni. That would be a good goal for you, too."

"Do you think I could?"

"We can find a way together, honey." As Denyse gave Sveta a hug she thought, *I have now become Katie.*

* * *

An hour later the investigator returned to where Katie and Tara waited. "I'm confiscating the drugs, which you admitted are illegal. But we won't detain either of you. You can go."

"What have you done?" asked Katie.

"I can't give you information on police business. But I *will* warn you about meddling in police affairs. We could even arrest you for interference in a police investigation. And Ms. Parker, you stay in Redwood Hills like Judge Tatum ordered."

* * *

Tara reported for work at 9:00 a.m. the following morning. "How was business yesterday? Did that older couple I talked to come back for the tandem bike?"

Jeff gave a curt reply. "Yes. The Coopers bought the tandem."

Tara detected harshness in his tone. "What's the matter?"

"The state police called yesterday. They asked about you and drugs. The officer said you were under investigation."

"What?"

"Tara, did you buy any prescription painkillers recently?"

"Yes, but—"

Jeff cut her off. "Do you have an injury or a prescription?"

"No, but—"

"Tara, I can't have you here anymore—around Sam."

"Jeff, I was helping Dave and Katie."

"If their need is legitimate, the Parkers can get their own pills."

"You don't understand. I was—"

"Let's not make this any harder than necessary. Please just go."

Tara felt anger at the false accusation. "Alright, fine." Without another word, she turned and left the shop.

On her road bike, Tara pedaled without thinking about the direction she was traveling. *Jeff's just been using me to sell bikes and babysit for him anyway. I'm better off without him or any man.* Then she remembered Sam holding up her little arms to be picked up. Tears of sadness blurred her eyes.

Chapter Thirty-One

* * *

Caleb Fogle was looking forward to one of his wife's suppers. *Maybe we'll have spaghetti tonight,* he hoped. He approached his car—the last in the parking lot at Central High School.

"Got a minute, Principal Fogle?"

The sudden words startled Caleb. He saw a large black man in his mid-twenties step from behind a tree. Despite being black himself, Caleb felt a surge of fear. "What is this about?"

"It isn't right, what happened," the man said.

Caleb stepped closer to look at the young man. On examination, Caleb recognized him. "Tyrone, I haven't seen you since the night we argued here in front of the school. What have you been up to, son?"

"Been stayin' low. Got some threats."

"What sort of threats?"

"Some blame me for not attacking the racists. Others say I nearly caused a race war."

"I'll admit you scared the hell out of me."

Tyrone shrugged. "Sorry, Mr. Fogle. I was just doing what I thought I should, to be a man and stand up for right. And I was angry because my life hadn't turned out well. So maybe I wasn't thinking so clear in the situation."

"What did you mean when you said, 'It isn't right, what happened'?" asked Caleb.

"They shot that kid, Anthony. He was makin' something of himself."

"Did someone target Anthony?"

"No. They was just showing some street muscle. Shooting up a rival gang's neighborhood. They didn't even know Anthony was in that house."

"Do you know who they are?"

Tyrone stepped forward and extended a slip of paper. "This is the car's license tag. The police find this car, it'll lead them to the gun that shot Anthony."

"Why are you telling me, son?"

"If someone sees me talkin' to you, they won't think nothin'. But if someone sees me talkin' to the cops, I'm a dead man."

Caleb nodded understanding. Tyrone turned to go. Caleb challenged him, "Wait, son. Are you making something of *yourself* like Anthony is trying to do?"

"Me? What can I do? I'm not like Anthony."

"You've got something Anthony doesn't, Tyrone."

"What's that?"

"You're a born leader, son. That's why the other players elected you captain of our football team."

"What kind of future does that lead to? Sure, I played a little ball at South Alabama. But wasn't good enough for the pros. An' there's no good jobs for somebody who didn't graduate."

"Ever hear about the US army? The army needs leaders like you."

"Yeah, I've thought about the army. It'd get me away from here. But they won't have me."

"Why not?"

"I been arrested coupla times."

"Any felony convictions?"

"No."

"I'd go with you to the recruiting office, Tyrone. I'd vouch for you."

"Who do you think they'd listen to—you or the police?"

"They'd listen to Harmon Floyd."

"Mobile's police chief? The one who stood down the racist militia? He doesn't even know who I am."

"Harmon would learn who you are if I asked him to meet you. And he wants men like you to make something of themselves."

After a moment's indecision, Tyrone answered. "Tell me what I should do to get into the army, Mr. Fogle."

"Come back here tomorrow morning, son. Together you and I will go meet Harmon. Maybe have lunch at the police station. Talk about football. Harmon once played for Central High like you. After meeting and talking, he'll know you a little when he talks to the recruiter."

"Yes, sir."

* * *

Jeff heard the bell over the shop's front door ring. Coming out of the workroom, he saw an older man. Jeff recognized him as Tara's would-be surrogate father, Dave Parker. *Is he here to threaten me?* Jeff asked himself.

The man started right away, "Could I talk to you a few minutes, please, son?"

"If this is about Tara—"

"Somewhat. But about Katie and me first."

"I'm pretty busy."

Dave looked around at the empty shop. "I can see that. This will only take a few minutes. And you'll want to hear this." Without waiting for an answer, Dave pointed at the shop's computer. "First, Google Dave and Katie Parker of Mobile, Alabama."

Humoring the man seemed the easy way out of a possibly awkward confrontation or worse. Plus no one else was in the shop. Jeff wished for a customer, even an idle shopper, in case he needed a witness. He entered *Dave and Katie Parker* into Google. To his surprise dozens of references came up. Jeff looked at Forensic Accountant Hero Down Under; Conman Convicted on Parker's testimony; Visitors to Minnesota Solve Decades-Old Mystery; Web of Corruption Unraveled.

Jeff looked back at Dave. Who was this guy? At Jeff's look, Dave continued, "Now Google the phone number of the FBI in Montgomery, Alabama. Call the number listed and ask for Agent Mark Witten. He's expecting your call."

Dave watched as Jeff made the call. Jeff's eyes grew wider as he listened. After five minutes of intense listening, Jeff said, "Thank you, sir," and placed the phone back on its receiver.

"I'm sorry, Mr. Parker. I didn't realize. Apparently, you and Ms. Parker are more than a sweet old couple."

"Please call me Dave. Katie and I *are* a sweet old couple. Well, Katie's sweet and I'm old. But who you really need to say sorry to is Tara."

Jeff had to ask, "Are you working on a case here in Redwood Hills?"

"Yes, we are. Sheriff Billingsly asked us to investigate. And Tara is helping us."

"What's the case about?"

"We're trying to find the source of illicit opiates here in Redwood Hills. Tara only posed as a buyer for us. She was a theater major in college, you know?"

"No, I didn't know that."

"Well, you need to go talk to Tara, son. You've made a big mistake."

Dave answered the ringing phone to hear Jeremy on the line. "Hello, Dad."

"Oh, hi, Jeremy. Had any luck finding Old Yeller yet?" Dave looked to see Katie rise to her feet from the RV's couch and approach him.

"I hope Mom can't hear you."

"She already knows about Old Yeller. In fact, she's standing right here looking a little perturbed."

"Give me the phone," demanded Katie and reached for it.

"How'd she find out?" asked Jeremy.

Dave turned away from Katie to keep the phone. "Beatrice told her, I think."

"Tell Mom I'm sorry. And the reason I've called is to ask you, at least one of you, to come home. People in an area south of Fairhope have spotted Old Yeller. But I can't find him. He might come to your voice or Mom's."

Dave gently fended off Katie, who tried to wrestle the phone from him. "Jeremy, we're under a court order to stay here. But your mother will be glad that someone has spotted her cat."

Finally, Katie simply shouted loud enough to be heard through the phone, "You've got a dog! Take Ripper to nose Old Yeller down."

Tara heard tapping at her camper door. "Come on in, Katie," she called.

"It's me, Jeff," came through the door.

Tara got up and opened the door. "Yes?" She could hear Sam whimpering in her seat from Jeff's car, parked directly in front of Tara's camper.

Jeff remained standing outside the camper. "I've made a big mistake, Tara."

"You certainly have."

"I'm sorry. I was wrong to not give you a chance to explain. I thought I knew you. I had trusted you and then felt betrayed. I don't handle the feeling of loss very well. Could you forgive me? I want us to go back to how things were before."

Tara folded her arms. "How were things before, Jeff? What was I to you? A bike seller? A babysitter? Anything else?"

Jeff fumbled for words, "Yes, you're a great employee and Sam adores you . . ."

"And?"

"I have feelings for you too . . ."

"What sort of feelings?"

"I don't know. Since my wife died . . ."

"What are we, Jeff?" Tara prodded him.

"We're two people who need each other. I need *you* anyway."

"How do you need me?"

"You're my friend. I like being around you. Talking to you."

"Do you find me attractive?"

"Oh, yeah. It's just that since Megan died . . ." Jeff struggled to express himself, then confessed with a rush. "I feel guilty being so attracted to a woman besides her."

So he does find me attractive, Tara acknowledged to herself. Yet she felt the conflict and angst within Jeff. She decided to make the situation easier for him. "Alright, I'll be back at the shop tomorrow morning." She stepped around him and headed toward the car where Sam remained strapped in and had started crying.

"Where are you going?"

"To soothe Sam. She's in distress." Tara lifted the child out of the car seat. Sam stopped crying.

Jeff ran his fingers through his hair. "I guess I became preoccupied and neglected her."

Tara smiled at him. "You're a wonderful father, Jeff. Let's see if Katie has some milk and a cookie we can give Sam."

Chapter Thirty-Two

* * *

Jeremy parked the car on a subdivision street where the most recent sighting of Old Yeller had occurred. He let Ripper out and held the picture of Old Yeller before the dog. Ripper's eyes never focused on the two-dimensional paper. He frisked around eager for an early evening walk.

Jeremy put the blanket he had collected from Old Yeller's heated sleeping box at his parents' house to Ripper's nose. "Smell this, boy." That interested Ripper, who inhaled and exhaled rapidly with his nose to the cloth. "Now, find Old Yeller."

Ripper started sniffing along the ground in a random manner but apparently didn't detect the cat.

Jeremy started walking up and down shady home-lined streets followed by Ripper with his nose to the ground. Occasionally Jeremy refreshed the dog's memory by holding Old Yeller's blanket before his nose.

After an hour of canvassing, suddenly Ripper paused. He swung his head back and forth, nose still to the ground, rapidly sniffing in and out. Then he turned perpendicular to the direction they had walked, his nose sweeping the ground ahead of him.

"Have you got something, boy?" Jeremy grabbed Ripper's collar and held the cat's blanket to his nose again. The dog sniffed and wriggled free to resume following a scent. *He's after something,* Jeremy encouraged himself and released Ripper.

Ripper started slowly and picked up speed. Jeremy found himself running to keep up. Across lawns and through shrubbery, he followed Ripper. Near some parked cars Ripper appeared to lose the trail. While Ripper nosed around, Jeremy looked at one of the cars. On the car's windshield, cat paw prints gave him hope. He used the blanket to refresh Ripper's memory again. To Jeremy's surprise, Ripper started running in a widening circle, his nose to the ground. Suddenly the dog stopped circling then accelerated away perpendicular to the circle. He had reacquired the scent.

Jeremy couldn't keep up with the running dog. He remembered movies with braying hounds straining at leashes while chasing a fugitive. *I should have brought a leash.* Fortunately, or unfortunately, a fence stopped Ripper.

Jeremy found Ripper with his paws against a chain-link fence surrounding someone's backyard. *Maybe the residents won't see us.* He picked up the squirming eighty-pound dog and dropped him over the fence. Ripper nosed the ground on the other side as Jeremy climbed the fence himself. Ripper picked up a scent and charged across the backyard. Jeremy followed past a startled lady watering some flower gardens.

"Sorry, ma'am, we're trailing a cat."

The fence stopped Ripper again on the other side of the yard. Again, Jeremy lifted his dog over. But by the time Jeremy crossed the fence, Ripper had disappeared. Jeremy stood panting. *Now I've lost the cat and the dog.*

"Ripper. Ripper. Come back, boy," Jeremy called as he returned to the street. Then he started jogging in the general direction Ripper had gone.

After a hundred yards, his ears picked up the faint sound of barking a block away. Jeremy recognized Ripper's deep *Ruff, ruff, ruff.* He started to sprint in the direction of the barking.

Around a corner he found Ripper—the black dog hard to see in the deepening twilight—with his paws against a live oak tree. Jeremy huffed up. Ripper paused a few seconds before resuming his bark. Jeremy pulled back on the dog's collar.

"Quiet, boy."

In the silence that followed, Jeremy heard *Rrrow* come from up in the tree. Still holding Ripper's collar, he tried to see into the branches from different angles in the near darkness. There. Something light. Something orange. Old Yeller.

The cat clung to a horizontal branch about twenty feet off the ground. *Rrrow.* Jeremy nearly collapsed in relief. "Here kitty, kitty, kitty. Come down, Old Yeller."

Rrrow.

A nearby voice startled Jeremy. "Is that your cat?" A late-middle-aged man, apparently the homeowner, had heard

Ripper and come outside to stand peering into the tree beside Jeremy.

Still out of breath, Jeremy gasped, "My parents' cat. I lost him nearly two weeks ago."

"Well, being lost and hungry unnerves any cat. Then the dog," the man pointed at Ripper, "scared him. See how the cat's tail is bristled out?"

"Well, how can I get him down?"

"The last I heard the fire department only rescues cats in children's books. And if your parents' cat has been lost, I wouldn't try leaving him up there all night. He'll be lost again tomorrow."

Jeremy looked at the homeowner. "What are you suggesting?"

"I'm not suggesting anything. But if you want that cat back, you'll need to climb up there and get him. And don't drop him. He might land on his feet but break a leg. If he doesn't break a leg, he'll likely run and be lost again."

"How do you know so much about cats?" Jeremy asked the man.

"My mother had cats. Lots of cats. As a teenager I pulled several cats out of trees for her. My wife has cats, too."

"How would I even get up there?" Jeremy asked.

"I'll loan you a ladder to get up to the lower branches," the homeowner offered and turned toward his garage. After a few minutes, he returned with an extension ladder. The man's teenaged daughter with a cat carrier followed him.

To Jeremy's relief, the ladder, when leaned against the tree truck, reached to just under the limb on which Old Yeller crouched. While his helper held Ripper by his collar, Jeremy climbed the ladder. Ripper started to bark again.

"Hush," the man told the dog and stroked his head. "You'll frighten the kitty." Ripper quieted.

Jeremy stood on a top rung and put his elbows over the limb before trying, "Here kitty, kitty, kitty. Come here, Old Yeller."

Rrrow. The cat didn't budge. But without the dog barking, Old Yeller's tail had de-bristled. *Rrrow, rrrow.*

To Jeremy, the cat's plaintive cry sounded hopeful. He pulled himself up to straddle the live oak branch. "Here kitty, kitty, kitty. Come on, Old Yeller."

Rrrow. The cat remained in place about eight feet away.

Jeremy started to edge out on the branch, watched carefully by Old Yeller. Fearful, the cat retreated further from the trunk while Jeremy talked. "You know me, Old Yeller. I'm here to take you home."

Rrrow, rrrow, rrrow.

Finally, Jeremy reached out to let Old Yeller sniff his hand. Then he gently stroked the cat's head. He inched a bit closer. Old Yeller waited to be rescued. Then Jeremy leaned over, reached out, and put both hands around old Yeller's body behind his front legs. He lifted the cat and pulled him to his chest. Old Yeller, deprived of the safety of the solid branch under his feet, twisted in Jeremy's grasp and sunk his claws into Jeremy's chest.

Despite the pain of claws in his flesh, Jeremy held on and stroked Old Yeller's head. The cat gradually relaxed enough for Jeremy to cradle him with his left arm. Jeremy used his right arm to work his way back to the tree trunk and start down the ladder. When his feet touched the ground, Jeremy wrapped both arms around Old Yeller, who—although tense—didn't struggle.

"Well done. Bring him inside the house before you loosen your grip," the homeowner suggested.

As Jeremy carried Old Yeller, the man led Ripper by his collar. The daughter opened the house's front door. Inside a closed room, lest Old Yeller escape, Jeremy forced him into the cat carrier. The cat offered no resistance.

The man slapped Jeremy lightly on the back. "Nice rescue, young fellow."

"Thank you for your help, sir. I'll bring the carrier back tomorrow."

* * *

Not until inside his parents' house with all the doors closed did Jeremy open the cat carrier to release Old Yeller. Assured by the odor of home, the cat walked out, looking around. Jeremy served him a can of Katie's tuna and provided clean water. The cat ate ravenously and lapped water for nearly a minute. Jeremy snapped a cell phone picture of Old Yeller eating then forwarded it to Katie and Denyse.

Ripper watched the cat eating with some jealousy. Jeremy opened a large can of beef stew for him. Emotionally and physically exhausted, Jeremy lay down on the bed in the guest room on top of Katie's white bedspread. In a moment, he had fallen asleep. Old Yeller joining him didn't wake Jeremy. Ripper jumping up on the bed to lie beside them both didn't bother man or cat.

Closing time at the bicycle shop on Sunday afternoon couldn't come quickly enough for Tara. Weather reports had promised Monday would be clear and even a bit chilly.

"Are you coming into the shop tomorrow?" Jeff asked as he turned over the OPEN/CLOSED sign to end the business day.

"I thought a day hike through the redwoods would be fun. I need to spend some time outside. I'm going to bed early tonight to get a good night's sleep."

Jeff first looked disappointed. Then he asked, "Would you mind if Sam and I tagged along?"

Tara retrieved her bike to start home. "What about the shop?"

"Business is always slow on Mondays. I thought I would stay closed and take a day off."

Tara stopped on the way out. "How would Sam keep up?"

Jeff grinned. "We'd have to take turns backpacking her."

Tara tried to hide her pleasure by shrugging. Then she gave him a welcoming smile. "Why not?"

"Pick you up at your camper about nine?"

"Sure."

Chapter Thirty-Three

* * *

Tara hadn't realized how heavy twenty-seven pounds of child could become on a long hike. She looked at Sam behind her in the backpack using a mirror Jeff had provided. The little girl seemed mesmerized looking at trees and flowers. Tara breathed deeply, enjoying the clean alpine air, and rejoiced in providing the experience for Sam.

"You doing okay?" Jeff called from the trail ahead. "Want me to take her for a while?"

Tara found herself reluctant to give up the toddler. "I'm good for another mile or so." She lifted her eyes to gaze at the towering canopy of green a hundred feet above their heads. She spoke softly to the little girl. "I know you won't remember this day, Sam. Your first day in the forest. But I'll remember." She concentrated on the trail at her feet to avoid tripping on rocks or roots while carrying the child.

Jeff's voice surprised her. "I think we'll both remember this day." Tara looked up to see him waiting in the path.

"We can help Sam remember." He pulled out his cell phone for a picture. "Turn sideways so I can get you both in the shot." After Tara had turned, he added, "Now smile. Not that cute whimsical smile you have. Show your teeth like you're happy."

He thinks my smile is cute.

"You seem to know a lot about backpacking," Jeff commented later while they ate the sandwiches and cookies Tara had brought. They had stopped for lunch alongside a rushing stream. "I've never done much hiking. But I like this. Being on a bike, you can't see things as well, like flowers."

"I *have* spent a lot of time on trails," Tara explained. "If you do more hiking, taking care of your feet is the most important thing. Keep your boots away from any fires, especially if they're wet. A dried-out boot can cause blisters the next day. And carry extra socks. I like to put on a clean, dry pair of socks each night. Keeps my feet warm in the sleeping bag. And then I put my boots on over them the next morning."

"What do you do if it rains?"

"I carry some big plastic bags, the kind they sell for raked leaves. When rain comes, I put my pack and sleeping bag in the plastic bag and seal it with a twist tie. Then, even if I get wet, my sleeping bag and spare clothes remain dry."

"Have you had much trouble with wild animals?" Jeff asked.

"Not a lot. Most of them try to avoid trouble. Except for chipmunks."

"Chipmunks?"

Tara laughed. "Yeah. In the mountains, chipmunks can ruin your backpack by gnawing holes when they're looking for food. If you must leave your pack unattended, like when you're swimming or collecting firewood, unzip the pockets so any chipmunks can help themselves without damaging your gear."

Jeff nodded appreciatively. "I've got a lot to learn."

"You won't be sorry for taking up hiking."

At the conclusion of the day-long hike, Jeff asked, "Would you be willing to change our shop schedule again this week?"

"How do you mean?"

"We could both work the store tomorrow and Wednesday. Then on Thursday we'd close again and take Sam to see the coastline and ocean. Might even spot a whale. There are some reports of sightings from the cliffs."

Tara gave Jeff a big teeth-showing smile. "I'd like that."

On that bright, sunny Thursday, Tara and Jeff took turns carrying Sam along a path on top of the bluff at the coastline. Below them, waves choked with kelp splashed against rocks. A breeze blew from the ocean occasionally carrying traces of spray and odors of barnacles exposed to air. Where a tiny creek flowed down from the hills, they descended to a cove and an isolated beach. Jeff lifted Sam out of the backpack. Tara carried her to let her play in the sand at the water's edge.

Tara sat down beside Jeff on a three-foot diameter driftwood log. "I had an idea after our hike the other day. Your shop's display floor has a little empty space, especially if you hung some racks from the ceiling. You could carry sporty-looking riding clothes, sunglasses, gloves, and helmets. You could also add bike gear—at least auxiliary mirrors, padded seats, and baskets."

Jeff nodded. "The profit from that recumbent bike alone could get that started."

Tara continued, "And a section of camping gear could attract a completely different set of customers to the shop. Your overhead costs wouldn't change."

Jeff shook his head. "That would probably work, but I don't have any money for name-brand camping equipment."

"You wouldn't have to start with new goods. Lots of perfectly good second-hand stuff is for sale at yard sales, flea markets, Goodwill, even on the internet. Without a steady income, I've learned how to get quality stuff cheap. I got a bike worth twenty-eight hundred from you for four fifty in labor."

Jeff couldn't help but laugh. "That you did. And I got sixteen thousand dollars in bike sales for four fifty."

Tara smiled and nodded in acknowledgment. "Okay. Both of us know how to get a deal."

"I think that once people learned what a camping and backpacking expert you are, Tara, they'd come into the shop for advice. What do you think a section of camping equipment would cost to start?"

"I'll bet we could begin with a thousand dollars. Discount stores sell incidentals like sierra cups, portable cook stoves, and water purifiers. You could get a trunk load of stuff there for two hundred dollars, display it well, and double the price. With the remainder, we could collect a lot of quality secondhand gear."

Jeff noticed that Tara had used the first-person plural, *we*. "With the bikes you've sold and the money I made as a mechanic, I could invest a thousand dollars."

"We could also set up local Bike and Hike Clubs for different ages. We'd want your shop to be the local hub of such activities. Affluent parents, like many who live in the area, would even pay for an expert to teach their kids biking or hiking—maybe guide them on an expedition."

Jeff started to get excited. "We could offer Bike Camp and Hike Camp." He looked at Tara with admiration.

She didn't notice and continued dreaming. "Once you establish a reputation as a source of equipment, I'll bet the name-brand gear manufacturers would loan you merchandise to sell on consignment. No up-front inventory cost for you."

"This week has been fun, Jeff. Thanks," said Tara when he stopped the car in front of her camper after having spent the day at the ocean. Sam slept exhausted in her car seat behind them.

Jeff nodded. "You're welcome. Thank you for taking us to the woods. And for making a day at the ocean so much fun. Plus, you've got great ideas for expanding business."

"I'm glad we took Sam. Her first major outings to see the forest and the ocean."

"She liked the sand the most."

"Yeah, but what a view for a sandbox!"

An awkward silence followed. Jeff started to lean over to where Tara was sitting. *Let him determine what type of kiss this will be,* she told herself.

But Katie accidently determined that there would be no kiss. Knocking on the driver's side window, Katie shouted through the glass, "I've got supper made. Can you come in?"

Jeff rolled down the window. "We wouldn't want to cause you any trouble."

"I've already made it. A Gulf Coast seafood boil. More than Dave and I can eat for a week. We've gotten some good news from home. Our son found our lost cat. We made a special dinner to celebrate."

Jeff looked at Tara. "I'll have to admit that I'm starved," she said.

"I am too," Jeff replied and opened the car door. "Let's bring Sam in but try not to wake her."

Tara held the door while Jeff carried sleeping Sam into the RV. Dave directed them to the RV's bedroom where they laid her, still sleeping, on the bed and covered her with a blanket Katie provided. From a pot Katie had simmering on the stove, odors of pungent Cajun spices summoned them. A large platter of steaming hot red potatoes, corn on the cob, sausage, and shrimp waited in the center of the small table.

"This is what we in the deep South call a 'seafood boil,'" Katie explained. "Sorry that I couldn't find any crayfish to include. Y'all just take a place and help yourselves, please. I'll mind Sam if she wakes up."

As Jeff and Tara seated themselves, Dave described the traditional way to serve a boil in the summer. "A plastic tablecloth is placed over a picnic table. The cook simply dumps the boiled food in the center."

"What would you like to drink? We have iced tea, coke, and water," Katie said.

As they ate, Jeff asked about the status of the drug charges.

"We're still looking for evidence strong enough and solid enough for the state troopers to get a warrant."

"Let me help," Jeff insisted. "I've lived in Redwood Hills longer than any of you. I'm part of the community. Nobody would suspect my involvement with you."

"Maybe," answered Dave. "We can't allow you to endanger yourself, though. You're responsible for Sam."

"Oh, and you think that I'm expendable," Tara teased him.

Dave smiled. "No one is expendable. But Katie and I do place a lot of importance on parental responsibility."

Tara turned to Jeff. "Dave and Katie's son, Jeremy, had a thing for me once. They raised a nice kid. I went to his high school prom with him. Introduced him to marijuana. But they've forgiven me for that. And despite my corrupting influence, Jeremy turned out well. He's married and a father now, like you."

Katie took over. "Then let's review our suspects. We've got Doctor Peter Lomax. What can you tell us about him, Jeff?"

"Well, Dr. Lomax is single again for the third time. Local rumor is that his former wives garnish most of his income through alimony. But he still managed to buy a mansion overlooking the ocean and drives a Ferrari. Some local women swoon over him. A private invitation to his mansion is coveted. Some local marriages broke up when the wives accepted the invitation. Whenever I've run across him, Lomax reeks of a sense of entitlement."

"What about the pharmacist, Cecil Harbanger?" asked Dave.

"He's married to a world-class social climber. She conducts lavish parties at the vineyard and winery they own east of here. A full-time manager runs their winery. Mrs. Harbanger only invites elites to her shindigs. Never ordinary folks. A lot of her guests come up from San Francisco. She also keeps a ritzy apartment there. She and Cecil attend a lot of socially connected fundraisers and galas down there. Seems pretty highbrow for a small-town pharmacist."

Jeff thought a minute before continuing. "Harbanger himself has a reputation for being somewhat of a leech. He's also a member of the San Francisco Bohemian Club."

"The Bohemian Club? What's that?" asked Dave.

Jeff spoke in a confidential tone. "They're an exclusive social club just for men. Writers and journalists founded the group in the 1870s. Nowadays the title 'Bohemian' is ironic in respect that the membership is mostly wealthy businessmen, corporate CEOs, and politicians, plus a few famous artists and musicians. Some say that the big decisions for the country are made by a few members of the Bohemian Club, not by Congress. Others think the world's economy is manipulated by them.

"The members have a clubhouse in San Francisco. But they also own over four square miles of redwoods in our region and keep it totally private. Called the Bohemian Grove, it's near here at Monte Rio. They have a men-only meeting there each summer with most guests arriving in private jets and limos. They claim that the discussions to build the atomic bomb in World War Two started there. I've heard they have a yearly ceremony burning the word 'Care' in effigy. Locals call them Bohos. I've never seen inside Bohemian Grove or know anyone who has."

"I've seen inside Bohemian Grove," offered Tara.

Chapter Thirty-Four

* * *

Jeff, Dave, and Katie turned their heads to stare at Tara in wonder at her claim.

She shrugged and started to explain. "The hippies I grew up among in Wisconsin believed the Bohemian Club represented the evil oligarchists of the world. A cabal of powerful men having secret meetings and deciding everything to their advantage. Starting wars to make profit. Manipulating economies for the benefit of an elite few. The stuff of a million rumors.

"Several summers the commune sent a delegation during the Bohemians' summer meeting. They encamped outside the Bohemian Grove's entrance. Along with protesters from across the country, they maintained a twenty-four-hour vigil, waving signs and sometimes getting arrested for blocking the gates. Our commune membership had sent the delegates away like warriors to battle and welcomed them home as heroes. I always resented our demonstrators for leaving the remainder of us back in Wisconsin with all the work—trying to raise enough vegetables to eat. When the 'heroes' came home, they helped consume the little food we'd managed to grow." After speaking, Tara sat remembering hard times—her eyes unfocused.

"But you said you'd seen inside. How did that happen?" Jeff prompted her.

"Oh, yeah. I had read that after some tumultuous years, the Bohemians improved their image by giving tours of the grove to a few select people, including some women. They contributed to local organizations like fire departments, started hiring some locals, spent money in area businesses, put on an annual benefit for women's shelters and the like. When I came to Redwood Hills, I found that the residents had pretty much accepted their Bohos and the demonstrations had trailed off.

"But I still wanted to see what the fuss had been all about. So one morning during their annual retreat, I rode my bike to a spot six or seven miles away. I put on some dark long-sleeved camouflage clothes I'd bought at a yard sale, tucked my hair under a baseball hat, and rubbed a little charcoal dust over my lower face to look like uncut stubble. Then I hiked into the grove from the other side of the mountain. After climbing a fence, I was inside. Most of the old-growth redwoods have been logged by the Bohemians, leaving only a small section of the original trees. Those remaining trees are immense and majestic—truly unspoiled. By sunset, I'd located a couple dozen rustic log cabins, a remote meeting hall, and a man-made lake tucked away in the forest. The facilities looked and felt like a summer camp for mostly middle-aged men. In the twilight I could see men walking and talking in twos or threes between the cabins, meeting hall, and various outdoor amphitheaters.

"After dark, I left the woods and crept around the camp, watching from the shadows; I saw a lot of beer drinking, some ribald skits and music performances, plus more than a few men urinating against trees. Once, I nearly got caught on a path when groups of men were approaching from both directions. I spread my legs, stood facing a tree, and moaned 'Ooooh' as if I were peeing. They all walked right by me."

Jeff, Dave, and Katie laughed. The actress came out of Tara as she warmed to her small audience and embellished her tale with gestures and expressions. "I tiptoed up to a cabin window to hear the captains of American enterprise planning, like a bunch of boy scouts, a prank on the intellectual contingent. Then I heard raucous cheering and laughter from one of the open-air amphitheaters. Sneaking over, I found maybe sixty men watching a racy and sexist film—not so much like boy scouts after all. With the leaders of the free world focused on the screen, I tiptoed to the concession table and helped myself to a big bag of popcorn and a cold Coke. It was a hoot."

As her listeners smiled at Tara's story and shook their heads in amazement, she continued, "Once most of the activity settled down, I began eavesdropping at cabin windows. High-flouting debate about all the world's problems—alcohol fueled—dominated some of the cabins. In other cabins, men played cards, smoked, and drank. From a few cabins, I heard snores like a dozen chainsaws operating. I read later that Walt Disney

321

got the idea for the snoring dwarfs in the film Snow White from trying to sleep in one of the cabins. I can believe it. And the Cremation of Care ceremony, that's just a symbolic setting aside of daily worries during the camp."

Tara looked around at her listeners. "I've no doubt that the Bohemian Club enables political and business networking. Maybe even some shady private dealing or insider trading. But an international cabal they are not. After everything quieted for the night, I turned on my flashlight and hiked out the way I had come."

"Why do you think some reacted so strongly against the Bohemian Club?" asked Katie.

"Well, they're undeniably chauvinistic and elitist. But also, I think that a lot of people just want a bogeyman to believe in—a Don Quixote windmill to tilt."

Once Tara remained silent, Jeff commented, "Okay, they're not an international cabal. Still, shady private dealing and insider connections seem to fit Harbanger."

Both Dave and Katie nodded. Dave broadened the discussion by asking Jeff, "Know anything about the sheriff?"

Jeff reacted in surprise. "You suspect Sheriff Billingsly?"

Tara nodded. "He hasn't acted on some of the information Dave and Katie uncovered. Then he supposedly found the drugs used to indict them. And who else knew they suspected Lomax and Harbanger?"

"Okay, then. Sheriff Billingsly seems to know everything that's going on in his town. A lot of people owe him favors."

"We've noticed that," said Katie. She looked at Jeff. "What do they owe Billingsly favors *for*?"

"I've no idea. Fixing parking tickets, maybe."

"Or looking the other way," contributed Tara.

"That would fit better," said Dave.

"So where do we go from here?" asked Jeff.

"Tara has already gotten some drugs without a prescription from Harbanger. We need something incontrovertible to enable the state troopers to get a warrant."

"Shall we try the cell phone trick we used in New Zealand?" Katie asked Dave.

"Might work. Jeff, are you willing to go undercover?"

Jeff hesitated. "I've never done anything like that. I'm not sure I can pull it off."

"I could go with you," Tara offered.

Katie smiled. "I'll happily watch Sam."

"I used to be a professional cyclist," Jeff told Dr. Lomax at the doctor's office. Jeff sat nearly naked under an examination robe. Tara stood nearby wearing skintight exercise clothes. Obvious to the doctor, neither of them could possibly be wired.

"Every cyclist needs a little painkiller to keep up the training regimen. I'm afraid I got used to the—"

Tara broke in. "He doesn't feel normal without a little something. Can't sleep. Worries constantly. And is irritable.

I'm afraid he's going to hurt our child during one of his moods. Can't you give him something, doctor?"

The physician sounded doubtful. "His symptoms aren't part of a recent injury."

"Okay, doc. We'll cut the crap. Both of us need something to function. We'll pay a premium."

"Cash?"

"Of course." Tara pulled from her pocket a stack of twenty-five hundred-dollar bills Dave had given her.

Lomax took the bills and pulled out a prescription pad. "Here's an open prescription for three months. Go to the pharmacist Cecil Harbanger. You'll need to pay him full price."

Tara took the paper. "Thanks, doc."

Jeff and Tara joined Dave and Katie back at the bike shop where Katie had been caring for Sam. "Did you record it?" asked Jeff.

"Yes . . . we . . . did," answered Dave. "Tara, that was clever to put the cell phone in the pants Jeff took off after you dialed our number."

"Yeah, I doubted Lomax would suspect a wire while Jeff wore that examination robe."

Katie relinquished Sam to Tara. "Now we've got Lomax taking cash for prescribing drugs without limits even though you admitted addiction beforehand. And then he sends you to

Harbanger. This should be enough to get the state troopers involved."

"Tara, you'll need to take this to the state troopers in Santa Rosa, lest Judge Tatum put us back in jail for violating a court order," said Dave.

"I'll go with her," offered Jeff. "Would you watch Sam again, Katie?"

"I'd be delighted."

Chapter Thirty-Five

* * *

"You're back," said Sergeant Hernandez. "Where is Mrs. Parker?"

"You told her to obey the court order to stay in Redwood Hills," answered Tara.

"Oh, yeah." The trooper made a silent sigh then looked at Jeff. "And you are . . ."

"Jeff Moynihan. You phoned me to ask about Tara's employment at Redwood Hills Bicycle Shop."

"That I did." Sergeant Hernandez looked at Tara again. "Now, let me guess. You're still meddling in police affairs?"

Tara bit back the retort that thundered in her head. She forced herself to speak respectfully. "Yes, sir. But we have people dying of overdoses in Redwood Hills. Please just listen to what we've got."

The overworked policeman nodded.

Jeff played the cell phone recording of Lomax. Tara handed over the open-ended yet signed prescription. "These are the serial numbers for twenty-five hundred-dollar bills we paid Dr. Lomax."

The officer perked up. "Can I have these?" he indicated the recording, prescription, and the list of serial numbers.

Tara looked at Jeff, who nodded. She handed all she had to Sergeant Hernandez. "Is this enough for a warrant?"

"Sorry, but I can't comment on that. Let me ask one other thing that the judge would ask. Why didn't you go to Sheriff Billingsly in Redwood Hills?"

"We think that he could be involved somehow," answered Tara. She recited the clues she had identified with Dave and Katie.

Sergeant Hernandez tried but failed to conceal a look of amusement. "Okay. We'll look into that as well."

"Dave Parker suggested that you subpoena the records of Loving Care Nursing Home. Dr. Lomax and Cecil Harbanger own it and the drug wholesaler to the pharmacy, too," added Jeff.

"Thank you for your help. Now you two go home and stay out of this! Don't talk about our meeting publicly."

LOCAL PHYSICIAN AND PHARMACY OFFICES RAIDED BY STATE TROOPERS, Redwood Hills' local newspaper proclaimed on the front page. RECORDS OF LOVING CARE NURSING HOME SUBPOENAED.

Dave, Katie, Tara, and Jeff crowded around the newspaper spread out on the front counter in the bicycle shop. "Says here that the records are being examined in Santa Rosa," commented Dave. "I wonder who they've got doing that?"

"I don't see anything mentioning Sheriff Billingsly," said Tara.

Katie's cell phone rang. The others heard her speaking. "Hello. Yes, David Parker is at this number. Okay, here he is." She handed the phone to Dave. "It's for you."

"This is Dave Parker." The others continued to examine the newspaper until they heard Dave speak again. "And you have copies of the records?" He waited another minute. "Okay, I'll come to your offices in Santa Rosa. I'll be there this afternoon."

They all stared at Dave as he shut off the phone and returned it to Katie. "That was an accounting firm in Santa Rosa. They've been contracted to examine the records collected by the state troopers. But they don't have a forensic accountant on their staff. Somebody recommended they hire me temporarily as a consultant. They've already asked Judge Tatum to relax the court order and allow me to go to Santa Rosa. He authorized it."

* * *

"Gross malfeasance has been easy to identify," Dave said to a young CPA in Santa Rosa, Sergeant Hernandez, and an assistant DA representing California. "Wine Country Pharmaceuticals received far more painkillers, including fentanyl, from multiple generic wholesalers than they have records to document distributing. The prescriptions link Cecil Harbanger to Dr. Peter Lomax. The pseudo-names Walker, Altman, and Yost led us to Loving Care Nursing Home. Their records show each patient received far more painkillers than any human could survive. Some deceased patients continued to receive painkillers. I'd bet that investigation would prove the nursing home attendants skimmed the pills or even falsified records. Somebody there will likely turn state's evidence if pressed. There's even the stack of blank prescription forms signed by Dr. Lomax found at the pharmacy. Serial numbers on the bills Tara gave to both Harbanger and Lomax for illicit prescriptions match cash found by the searches."

Sergeant Hernandez turned to the state's attorney. "What do you say?"

"I'll get the arrest warrants for Harbanger and Lomax."

"Working through this thoroughly and methodically could take weeks, maybe months," Dave warned. "You're likely to find others implicated. Especially when some start to plea bargain."

Tara dropped in on Katie at the RV. "Is Dave still in Santa Rosa?"

"Yes, the state is putting him up in a hotel for a few nights. Not that Dave will sleep much once he starts trailing money records. Judge Tatum didn't lift the court order on me. I'm still restricted to Redwood Hills."

"Then could I ask you a question?" Tara asked.

"Sure, honey."

Tara got right to the point. "Jeff has a religious streak. And he isn't the cohabiting type, especially with Sam watching. What if he asks me to marry him someday?"

Katie smiled. "Would that be so bad?"

"I wouldn't know how to be married. You and Dave are the only happily married couple I've ever known. I know how to hang out with men, but not be a family with them. Plus, how do I know if Jeff is my soul mate? Isn't that important?"

"I guess some people would say so. But Tara, let me tell you a little secret. Few people really find their soul mate until the second decade of marriage. A soul mate is a partner you do life with. That's why commitment is the most important thing to make a good marriage."

"I thought love was most important," Tara objected.

"True love is willing to sacrifice for the other person. Some people who may feel romantic love for each other don't have the commitment to sacrifice and live as a family. I'm talking about more than a commitment to stay married. A lot of couples who would not consider divorce are miserable in their relationships. What couples need is a commitment to having a *good* marriage, including loving sacrificially. That takes a lifetime of work from each of them. But a good marriage is worth the effort."

Tara paid close attention. "Okay. Then what else?"

"The second most important thing in marriage is having a common plan for your marriage."

"What sort of plan?"

Katie continued, "A contractor needs a blueprint to build a house. The problem is that newly married couples nearly always have different ideas about marriage. Their blueprints are different. Can you imagine two contractors working on the same house while using different blueprints?"

"Then maybe I have an advantage, since I don't have any idea what marriage is about," suggested Tara. "No blueprint."

Katie laughed. "You may think you don't. You'll likely find you do. Certainly, Jeff does."

"How was your blueprint different from Dave's?" asked Tara.

"My father turned over all of the money he made to my mother. Mom paid any outstanding bills first and then felt free to spend all the remaining money before the next paycheck. But on our honeymoon, Dave created a strict budget for us, including aggressive saving. He insisted on sticking to that budget even when we had plenty of money in the bank. I couldn't understand why we had to save for a new car rather than buy one on payments we could make with our combined salaries. We had plenty of arguments about money.

"Another issue was communication. The family I grew up in would argue about everything. That was our way to discuss things. Whenever Dave and I had a disagreement, he would completely clam up. Our dog communicated better."

Tara laughed, trying to imagine Dave and Katie at odds. "Where would we find a blueprint?"

"I can tell from the books in your camper that you like to read. We could give you some books providing a starting point to create your own marriage blueprint together."

"What about religion? Jeff is more religious than I am."

"Well, having children makes a lot of people want to take a closer look at religion. You should explore that aspect of life. At least check it out."

"I've always thought religion was just made-up stories. There's no evidence to support it like the things I've learned about nature."

"Do you think that you and us being here in the same remote campground was a coincidence? Our second meeting when you needed us? When we needed you?"

Tara sat stunned. "You mean that's evidence of God?"

Katie smiled and nodded. "Maybe yes—all the way back to you meeting Jeremy. You certainly became a turning point in his life. An answer to Dave's and my prayers."

"You think God used *me*?"

"Sounds like He did. To me that's more reasonable to believe than all these things just randomly happening." When Tara sat in silence, Katie added, "Tara, do you remember when you told us how your kindness for Jeremy made you feel?"

"Sure. I felt good sacrificing for someone else. Since you and Dave told me about the effect I had on Jeremy, I've felt like my life had some meaning. I felt the same helping Jeff and Sam."

"That's an important part of Christianity. You can do more good things for people, Tara. Putting others first is a big part of living as a Christian."

"Would being a Christian require going to church every week? Sending in money to TV preachers?"

Katie laughed again. "Only if you want to. Dave and I don't make it to church every single week, and we don't send money to TV preachers."

After a few moments of silence, Katie kidded, "You're not an angel, are you?"

"Certainly not." Tara had to smile.

"None of us are angels. Dave and I believe that Jesus was a real person who died on the cross to make up for the less-than-angel in all of us. He accepts us as we are, if we're willing. Jesus' resurrection after death proved that he was God's son and had the authority to say, 'I am the resurrection and the life. He who believes in me will live even though he dies.' How Jesus wants you to live is by putting others first. That's real love inside and outside a marriage."

"You mean I was a Christian when I did that for Jeremy? When I took care of Sam?"

"No. But you had a taste of living like one. Being a Christian is believing, then living. Maybe God had more to do with you meeting Jeremy and now Jeff and Sam than any of us had realized."

Chapter Thirty-Six

* * *

The bell over the door to the bike shop rang. Jeff left the bike he had been working on to attend to the potential customer. *Too bad Tara isn't here,* he thought. *But she's looking for second-hand camping gear and taking a hike.*

In the display room, Jeff found a man about his size and age. The man had greasy-looking, shoulder-length black hair. Rather than stylishly unshaven, his facial hair looked uncared for. He wore a T-shirt over dirty jeans and ragged tennis shoes. A racist swastika and a rebel flag adorned his two arms.

"Can I help you?" Jeff wiped his oily hands with a rag.

"Where's Tara?" the man asked.

"She's not here now. Could I show you something?"

"Naw, I'm not looking for a bike. I'm looking for Tara. I've been missing her. Saw her picture on the news. We used to travel together, until I got sent to the pen. She picked me up when I got out. I thought we were back on track. Then she split one night."

"Oh," answered Jeff.

"Do you know when Tara will be back?"

"In a day or two. She took my car into San Francisco then planned on going hiking."

"Yeah, Tara always liked getting out into nature." The man looked around the shop. "Nice place you've got."

"Thanks. Can I tell Tara you were looking for her? What's your name?"

"Tell her Bennie came for her. I'll make it up, whatever I did." He turned and headed toward the shop door. "See you later."

"Okay. I'll tell Tara you came by."

The next morning Tara arrived for work at the shop at 9:00. She parked Jeff's car and then backed through the shop's door carrying a quality second-hand backpack in each hand. "Wait until you see what I got for nearly nothing," she shouted toward the living quarters.

Jeff came into the display room. He saw one of the backpacks still had the sales tags attached. "Good morning. Did you have a nice hike?"

Tara threw back her head. "Glorious. I went to Point Reyes National Seashore. I love walking along a lonely beach. I had a chance to think about my future. Maybe after the shop closes, we could talk."

"Sure," answered Jeff. "By the way, a friend of yours came in looking for you. He said his name is Bennie."

Tara stood stunned. "Bennie came here? What did he want?"

"He wanted you. He said that he'd make up for whatever he did to make you leave. He didn't seem to know what that was, though."

Figures that Bennie wouldn't know, Tara said to herself. "What did Bennie tell you?"

"Only that you picked him up at the prison and you had traveled together."

"Listen, Jeff. I—" The shop's bell interrupted her.

A well-dressed man entered the shop with a teenage boy. "I'd like a mountain bike for my son," he said. "A good bike, one that can hold up in rough terrain."

"We have some exactly like that. Tara will be happy to help you," Jeff responded. To her he whispered, "We can talk more later," as he returned to the workroom.

"Okay," responded Tara with trepidation.

As Jeff walked to the work room, Tara began asking the boy questions about what types of terrain he expected to traverse and the kind of bike he wanted. She made a few jokes and built an easy rapport as they looked over the available bikes.

After selling an expensive mountain bike to the father for his son, Tara could not stop fretting. *What will I say to Jeff? Bennie was never exemplary, but prison turned him into a lowlife.* She hated that Jeff might judge her by Bennie. *But what else do I deserve? Living in a van with Bennie—and others worse than him. Begging and lying to survive. Putting my freedom ahead of everything and everybody else.*

The shop doorbell rang, interrupting her private angst. She heard, "Hellooo, Tara." Bennie stood before her. "I want you back, baby." Bennie extended his arms, attempting to appear engaging.

"What are you doing here, Bennie?"

"You and me belong together. Fun and freedom on the road. No guilt. No responsibility. The van's waiting." Bennie stepped forward to embrace Tara. She pushed him away.

"No, Bennie."

"What's the matter, doll?"

"I feel . . . I don't know . . . I'm different now."

Bennie looked around the shop for the second time. "Got yourself a sweet thing going here, huh?"

"This isn't a sweet thing, Bennie. This is real life. This is my job and responsibility, at least a little while longer. Go away, Bennie. And don't ever come back. I don't know what life I can expect, but it won't be like before. And it won't be with you."

"You come with me, or I'll make a call about your panhandling activities up and down the state."

"I guess then I'd have to tell the authorities about you violating your probation by using drugs."

Bennie reached for Tara. She stepped back. "Touch me and I'll scream so loud that police cars will come from all over Sonoma County."

"Yeah, I saw the story on TV. You're tight with the cops now. Your loss, bitch." Bennie opened the door and stalked away.

Silence remained after the door closed. Jeff surprised Tara by appearing and walking to the OPEN/CLOSED sign on the door. He turned it over, closing the shop. "I listened to you from the back. I'd have come out swinging if he'd tried to harm you. We need to talk right now."

"Listen, Jeff. I should have explained how I've lived for the last eight years. I know Bennie is a sleazeball. I—"

Jeff spoke over her. "I don't care, Tara. You're a terrific woman. I love you. Sam loves you, too. Do you love me? Love us?"

Tara remembered Jeremy expressing his love years before. Being honest with him had cost her the best man she'd ever met. Yet her own words came back to her: *the most decent thing I've ever done.*

Jeff stood still waiting for her answer. Tara pondered, *Katie said, 'True love is willing to sacrifice for the other person.' Do I love Jeff and Sam like that? Yes, I do,* Tara realized.

She looked Jeff in the eye. "I do love you, Jeff. And I love Sam, too."

"Do you love me enough to marry me? Love Sam enough to become her mother?"

"Get married? You want to marry *me?*" Despite her conversation with Katie, Tara's head reeled at the words being spoken, the commitment before her. *Am I willing to commit to making a good marriage, not just to staying married? Yes, I am. But what about Jeff once he gets to know me?*

"I'm afraid, Jeff. When you get to know me . . . if you knew all the dishonest things I've done."

"I said that I didn't care, Tara. I called you a terrific woman. I trust you. Can you trust me?" Jeff stood waiting.

I've never really trusted anyone, Tara realized. *I've had good reason not to. And where has that gotten you?* she asked herself. Tara swallowed before speaking. "Yes, I'll marry you and be Sam's mother."

"Alright, then." Jeff seemed to be at a loss for further words.

Tara prompted him, "Well, aren't we supposed to kiss or something?"

Jeff immediately approached her. "You bet."

Chapter Thirty-Seven

* * *

Dorothy looked up from the front desk at Parker and Company when someone came through the front door. The woman stood before her in a low-cut dress that looked like it had been shrink fitted onto her gym-conditioned body.

"Is Jeremy here?" Giselle asked.

"No. He's picking up Anthony from the hospital."

A look of disappointment crossed Giselle's face. "When do you think he'll be back?"

"Probably not today. Can one of our other accountants help you?"

"I wanted Jeremy. I have a bottle of wine to thank him for his advice. Why don't you give me his address? I'll take it to his house."

Dorothy shook her head. "Giving out home addresses is against our policy. You can leave the wine with me for Jeremy."

"No. I'll just come back tomorrow."

"You're wasting your time, girl," said Dorothy. "Jeremy has a wife and a child he loves. He's a lifetime-commitment type of man."

Giselle returned a sour look and left without speaking.

* * *

Katie sat admiring photos of Old Yeller safe at home and reading emails from Jeremy and Denyse. Dave stumbled out of the RV's bedroom in his normal early-morning stupor. She put her laptop aside and stood to hug her husband.

Despite sleepiness, he returned her embrace. "My, you're chipper this morning."

"I feel like we've survived a hurricane. The state troopers are pursuing the evidence from our opioid investigation, Old Yeller's home, Trevor's free, Lena's sisters are excited about their futures, and Anthony is awake and recovering. Mobile's police have even made an arrest in his shooting."

"That *is* a lot," Dave admitted.

"And listen to this. Tara stopped in late last night."

"I know. I heard you get up and answer the door. What did she want?"

"Just to give me some news. Tara and Jeff are getting married. She's over the moon."

"That's great. I'm happy for her and Jeff." Dave thought another minute. "Our job is done here. Let's go see our attorney this morning. With all that's been discovered, Judge Tatum would probably let us leave Redwood Hills."

Katie could hardly restrain her joy. "This adventure is over. We can resume our vacation."

Dave still tried to blink some sleep away. "My thoughts exactly. Let me go take a wake-up shower. Then we can see. We might be on the road again tonight."

* * *

Dave could hear Katie's teakettle whistling when he returned from the campground's communal shower. Katie had already enjoyed her first cup of the morning. The campground ravens croaking outside added to the sense of peace he felt.

"I just heard on the radio that the state troopers have arrested both Lomax and Harbanger based on the records the state troopers subpoenaed," Katie told him as he entered the RV.

"Any implication of Billingsly?" Dave put the damp towel and his bathroom items in the RV's tiny bathroom.

"Not yet."

Both the Parkers' heads turned when a squad car stopped alongside the RV. Through a window they watched Deputy Conrad emerge. Dave opened the RV's door and held it. "Good Morning, Devin. Come on in."

The uniformed deputy came up the steps into the RV.

"Can I offer you some tea this beautiful morning?" asked Katie.

"No, thank you." Devin took a deep breath. "I need you both to come with me."

Dave put some lemon and packaged sweetener into his tea. "What for?"

"Questioning."

"We've told the state troopers all we know. They told us to leave the investigation to them."

Devin fidgeted. "What I meant was, you're under arrest."

Dave looked up from his tea. "Under arrest? What's the charge?"

"Drug dealing and impeding a police investigation."

"Do you have an arrest warrant for that charge?"

"We arrested you before without a warrant," Devin persisted.

"That was when you had found drugs in our RV. That constituted immediate probable cause. Without that, you need an arrest warrant signed by a judge. And Judge Tatum has released us on bond." Both Parkers stared at Devin.

"Sheriff Billingsly has the arrest warrant. He ordered me to bring you in."

"Then let Sheriff Billingsly come and show us the court-approved arrest warrant," Dave spoke with concern. "Devin, this is highly irregular. You could lose your job for arresting us without a legal basis."

Devin pulled the taser off his police belt. "Do we have to do this the hard way? I'm arresting you and that woman Tara who's been helping you."

Katie looked at Dave with alarm. She saw a determined look on his face. She heard him say, "Deputy Conrad, you are exceeding your authority. Katie, call 911."

"Don't do that," Devin ordered. He pulled two pairs of handcuffs out. "Both of you turn around."

"I don't believe you're representing the law or legitimate authorities," Dave responded.

Katie's cell phone lay on the tiny dining table out of reach. "Let's all relax," she suggested. "Devin, have some tea with us." She poured boiling water into a mug over a teabag and stepped closer to Devin.

Devin advanced toward Dave with the taser extended. "I warned you."

Katie splashed the cup of scalding hot water into his face.

"Aaah!" Devin screamed and lunged forward, blindly trying to make a connection with the taser.

Dave dodged him and pushed him down from behind. "Run, Katie."

But Katie had already scampered down the RV's steps and was running toward Tara's camper. Dave followed her. Halfway to Tara's camper, Dave slowed and looked back. He saw Devin open the squad car and pull out a shotgun.

Tara lay on the bunk in her camper leafing through a magazine on weddings she had picked up at a late-night grocery store. Beside it rested a library book she had finished about the life of Jesus. *Jeff's acceptance of me despite my past with Bennie illustrates how Jesus forgives us,* she thought.

Without warning, her camper door banged opened. "Come with us, Tara," Katie demanded. "Right now!"

Tara recognized the urgency in Katie's voice and dropped the magazine. Looking toward Dave and Katie's RV, she saw a uniformed deputy loading a shotgun.

"Run, Tara!" Dave shouted.

Despite wearing flimsy flip-flops, Tara passed Dave and Katie running to the woods. She slowed to help Dave and Katie cross the tributary stream.

Behind them Devin shouted, "Stop or I'll shoot."

Once past the stream, all three of them darted into the woods.

Bang. A tremendous explosion of noise like a small cannon came from behind them. Buckshot pellets ripped through the foliage and impacted tree trunks.

Despite the dire situation, Tara found herself thinking, *This must be how a rabbit feels when shot at.*

Tara led the way, trying to put as many solid redwoods as possible between them and the muzzle of the shotgun.

Bang. Another shotgun blast chased them. But nearly all the pellets had been blocked by the trees. Deputy Conrad shouted in pent-up frustration and fury behind them, "How can anyone live in California on a deputy's salary? The kids like Missy Clark had everything handed to them. I had nothing. I was like dirt to their kind in high school. Harbanger is already asking for a deal to roll over on me. Do you know what happens to law enforcement officers in prison? You're going to pay for ruining the only chance I ever had."

Katie had trouble keeping up with her long-legged husband and bicycle-strong Tara. She paused, panting. "You two go on! He won't shoot me."

"He's already trying to shoot you," Tara insisted.

"Tara, you take Katie on and I'll try to ambush him," said Dave.

"With what?" Katie asked. "He's young, got a taser, and a gun. You've got nothing."

"I'm not leaving you," Dave insisted.

Tara shouted at Dave and Katie, "Are you two going to argue until he kills us all?"

"You go on, Tara. We'll talk to him," Katie suggested.

"I'll go on, alright. But not until you two have hidden. I'll let him see and chase me. You can double back and call for help once he's past you."

Tara pushed Dave and Katie behind a family of redwoods that had sprouted from one old stump. She heard Devin's footsteps coming toward them. She started to run. A strap on one of her flip-flops broke. She shook the flip-flops off and continued barefoot, following the carpet of ferns and needles. In a clearing, she paused long enough for Devin to see her.

"I've lost my shoes," she shouted as though Dave and Katie had run ahead of her. "You two run ahead and call for help."

Bang. Another shotgun blast tore through the undergrowth. Tara heard the buzz of pellets missing her head by inches. *I nearly cut that too close,* she realized. She ran like a frightened deer heedless of the path.

*　*　*

Dave and Katie peeked around a tree trunk to see Devin's back as he shot in Tara's direction then chased after her. "We can sneak back and call for help now," whispered Katie.

Together they hurried back toward the campground. At the stream, Dave simply picked Katie up and splashed through the water. On the campground side, he put her back on her own feet. "Get your phone and call 911."

Katie ran to retrieve her phone in the RV and dialed. She heard, "What's your emergency?"

"We're being chased by a policeman. He's shooting at us!"

"Then give yourself up."

"No, you don't understand. He's trying to kill us."

"Put down any weapons you have and lie on the ground."

"Send help to Holiday Home Park Campground," Katie demanded.

Dave had run to Devin's squad car. He sat on the driver's seat with his feet outside the car then leaned over to pick up and speak into the police radio microphone. "We need help," he pleaded to anybody who might hear.

A terse voice came back. "You are not authorized to use this radio. Put on a law enforcement officer."

"Anybody who can hear this, please respond to Holiday Home Campground. Every authority available please come. Someone is trying to kill us."

"You're not authorized to use a police radio, Mr. Parker."

The words startled Dave. He looked to his left to see Sheriff Billingsly in uniform standing close to the open driver's side door. "Put down the mic and get out of the car, Mr. Parker." The sheriff waved with his left hand. Dave noticed Billingsly's right hand holding his service revolver pointed to the ground.

Dave put the police radio microphone back on its holder with his right hand. He pulled himself out of the car with his left and brought up his right fist in a round-house blow to the sheriff's temple. Billingsly fell at the surprise haymaker. Dave stepped over him and ran for the RV. "Run, Katie!"

Her adrenalin already sky-high, Katie dropped the cell phone and bolted out the RV's door.

"This way," Dave yelled and ran toward the campground's entrance and the highway. Both expected to hear a pistol shot taken at them. No shot came.

From behind them, they heard the squad car speaker. "This is Mike Billingsly, Devin. Come back here to me. I'm with you in this and need your help. The Parkers are here. We'll take care of them together. Then you can deny any involvement. Without the Parkers, there's no corroborating evidence to implicate you."

Chapter Thirty-Eight

* * *

Tara heard the sheriff's broadcast from where she was playing a cat-and-mouse game to occupy Devin in the woods. She stopped running and hid behind a clump of enormous ferns. A hundred feet away, she saw Deputy Conrad pause to listen to the sheriff. Then he turned and sprinted toward the campground. She first felt dismay that they might still catch Dave and Katie. Then she felt pain. Looking down at her bare feet she saw blood from splinters and cuts. *I'm like a wounded animal leaving a blood trail.* For the first time in her life she prayed. *God, please save the Parkers.*

Then Tara gingerly limped through the woods toward a secluded section of the stream. She eased her bleeding and swollen feet into the cold water.

* * *

Dave and Katie ran down the highway toward town. Both jumped into the road and waved their arms over their heads when a state trooper car approached with lights flashing and siren blowing.

"Did you get the emergency call?" Dave asked when Sergeant Hernandez stopped.

"You made that call, right, Mr. Parker?" asked the trooper. To Dave and Katie's exhausted nods he added, "You're safe now. It's a good thing we were in the area following up on leads the first opioid arrests gave us."

Sergeant Hernandez waved on another state trooper car then said, "You can ride with me. Just stay in the car until you're told you can get out." He drove them back to the campground.

From the state patrol car, Dave and Katie saw Deputy Conrad lying on the ground with Sheriff Billingsly putting cuffs onto him. Billingsly then conferred with the two state troopers. The second trooper to arrive read Conrad his rights and took him into custody.

The Parkers heard Sergeant Hernandez ask Sheriff Billingsly, "So this is the one on your force who's dirty?"

"I suspected Conrad but didn't know for sure or have any evidence until now. He had a loaded shotgun in his hands. That's why I pretended to be part of the collusion and said that we cops would stick together. When I got close enough, I tasered him. I'm sad to say that we may also uncover a couple of others on my force looking the other way for payoffs."

"How did you get here, Mike?" asked Sergeant Hernandez.

"I was looking for Conrad in my private car and listening on the police radio. I just didn't anticipate him trying to assault the Parkers. Knowing that others could implicate him, he must have reacted and panicked when you arrested Lomax and Harbanger."

"Well, it looks like your crazy plan worked." Sergeant Hernandez started canvassing for witnesses among other residents of Holiday Home Park Campground who had gathered to watch the commotion.

Sheriff Billingsly approached the open window of the state trooper car where Dave and Katie were watching and listening. "Mr. and Mrs. Parker, I'm certain that a lot of this is confusing to you. You'll get all the details when Devin Conrad is arraigned. And I wouldn't say anything about . . ." the sheriff rubbed his swelling cheek where Dave had hit him. "It's illegal to strike an officer for any reason. But I don't blame you for misunderstanding my intentions. You're free to get out of the car now. Judge Tatum will sort all this out."

"Tara is still out there," said Dave after he and Katie had left the state trooper car.

Sheriff Billingsly waved toward the squad car Deputy Conrad had brought. "You can use the squad car speaker to give her the all clear. She'll likely respond to your voice."

A minute later they heard Tara's voice shouting from upstream, "Bring my boots."

* * *

353

Dave and Katie stood before Judge Tatum again. Ms. Asher, their state-appointed attorney, stood with them. Jeff and Tara with Sam stood on the other side of Ms. Asher. Sheriff Billingsly stood nearby along with Sergeant Hernandez. The young assistant DA who had previously objected to bail stood slightly behind his boss, the county DA.

"What a mess," the judge mumbled to himself. "And me only two months from retirement."

He looked at the papers before him and spoke first to the DA. "You say the warrants leading to the arrest of Dr. Lomax and Mr. Harbanger are solid."

"Yes, Your Honor. You authorized them. The warrant discovered blank prescription forms signed by Dr. Lomax at the pharmacy. A forensic accountant found clear evidence of illegal distribution of opioids by Mr. Harbanger."

"And that forensic accountant turned out to be Mr. Parker, who had been arraigned for illegal drug possession himself."

"The state didn't directly hire Mr. Parker, Your Honor. A local accounting firm didn't have forensic certification and took him on as a consultant. You lifted the court order and allowed him to go to Santa Rosa."

"That I did," the judge acknowledged. "And the hair samples taken from the RV's bathroom by Sheriff Billingsly have exonerated the Parkers from drug use. Furthermore, we have sworn testimony from the Parkers and Ms. Graboswki implicating attempted murder by a police officer, Deputy Devin Conrad."

"Yes, Your Honor. Conrad's attorney is currently negotiating a plea deal with our office for incarceration out of state. We hope that deal will reveal others who participated in the opioid distribution."

Judge Tatum then spoke to all of those present. "In my twenty-eight years on the bench, I've not seen a more convoluted case. Those of you in the legal profession are reprimanded for unorthodox procedures. I'm retiring soon and will let my successor sort it all out.

"However, some items do need to be attended to immediately. First, the Parkers. Mr. Parker, witnesses at Holiday Home Park Campground report that you struck a police officer, Sheriff Billingsly. And I can see his black eye clearly. Sheriff, what do you say to that?"

"The witnesses are mistaken, Your Honor. Mr. Parker noticed a wasp had landed on me and tried to remove it."

The judge stared at Sheriff Billingsly. "Lying to a judge can earn a contempt citation."

"It could, Your Honor. I ask the court to let this matter go."

Judge Tatum sighed and nodded. He looked at Dave and Katie. "The charges against you for illegal drug possession are dismissed based on the evidence and testimony of Sheriff Billingsly. You are held in contempt of court for Mrs. Parker leaving Redwood Hills to visit the state police in Santa Rosa against my orders. I sentence you to get into your RV and return to wherever you came from . . . ah, Alabama. You'll come back to California to testify if the DA needs you. Your bail will be refunded."

"Thank you, Your Honor," responded Dave.

"Ms. Grabowski and Mr. Moynihan: Although you've done a great public service this time, don't you two interfere in police affairs again."

"Yes, sir," Jeff and Tara answered in unison.

"Sheriff Billingsly, how many times have I warned you about your unorthodox methods of trading favors and using civilians in police investigations?"

"Several, Your Honor. But it won't happen again. I'm retiring the same time you do."

"That's good, Mike. Stay a few minutes after adjournment so we can talk about our fishing trip to Alaska. I only hope your replacement doesn't take on your methods. But neither of us will be around to deal with it."

"Absolutely, Your Honor."

"The rest of you, try not to cause my successor so many headaches. Court adjourned."

Dave and Katie waited outside the courtroom for Sheriff Billingsly, who had lingered inside to talk about Alaskan fishing with Judge Tatum. They confronted him when he emerged. "I thought we were helping you!" said Dave.

The sheriff smiled broadly. "Oh, you did help me. I thank you deeply, Dave and Katie." He looked at each individually as he spoke their names.

"You didn't give us much cooperation," Katie insisted.

"Who do you think told the state police to not arrest you for interfering in police business and circumventing the sheriff's office in Redwood Hills? You and that accomplice of yours, Tara. She's quite a gal. That boy Jeff will have his hands full with her. And who do you think recommended you to the accounting firm in Santa Rosa, then convinced Judge Tatum to let you go there?"

"Why did you ignore us at the jail?" asked Katie. "And when we had been trying to help you."

Billingsly laughed. "Officers of the law must be perceived as objective. You can't have them being openly chummy with someone about to be indicted. I did what was necessary to exonerate you behind the scenes. And I told Wanda to take good care of you."

Dave spoke again, "We appreciate you clearing us with the hair samples you took from our hairbrushes in the RV. But why didn't you bring this forward earlier?"

"I'm sorry for having to arrest you. But I found fentanyl in your refrigerator. As an officer of the law, I couldn't just ignore evidence, even if I suspected it to be bogus. My suspicion was why I collected the hair samples. And testing hair samples takes time."

"You could have expedited the tests."

"Would you have gone home to Alabama if cleared right away?"

Katie answered, "Probably."

The sheriff shrugged. "I apologize for endangering you. But I had kids dying here. Kids I had a sworn duty to protect. I had to face their grieving parents knowing that I had failed. Sometimes you have to take some risks that transcend law enforcement. And I also suspected somebody on my force had been compromised. Arresting you gave the collaborator hope that you'd take the blame he deserved."

"We thought you planted the drugs in our refrigerator."

"No. The refrigerator is one of the first places I always search. I suspected Conrad, because he expected me to look and find the drugs there."

Dave continued to press the law enforcement officer. "Why didn't you get the search warrants when we asked for them?"

"Marginal probable cause . . . and you were making progress. I needed you to keep digging until you got something solid enough to flush out all the culprits. I knew you were getting close when you linked Lomax and Harbanger to the nursing home. You helped pull in the state troopers, too."

Katie asked, "Why did you think we could help you in the first place?"

"I may be a backwoods sheriff. But I can use Google. You two have quite a track record of solving crimes. I could hardly believe my luck having you land in my lap. I can call police chiefs, too. Chief Harmon Floyd in Mobile had lots of good things to say about you. Even here, he's famous for going unarmed to disperse a mob of white supremacists."

Dave didn't mention that he and Katie had witnessed that occurrence, lest the sheriff think them among the racists. "You talked to Harmon? Do you know that he had made the

Oakland Raiders roster to play professional football before he got hurt?"

"Oh, yeah. And I remember him destroying the Auburn line when he played for the University of Alabama."

Dave sighed, "I remember that too."

Dave spent a moment contemplating the sheriff's unconventional ploys for a good purpose, then nodded in acknowledgment. He extended a hand. "Well, enjoy your retirement in two months."

Sheriff Billingsly firmly took Dave's hand to shake. "Call me Mike. And I'm not retiring."

"But you told the judge—" Katie started.

"Yes, I did. But I plan to change my mind after our fishing trip." The sheriff gave a hopeful smile. "Hey, if I need you again, do you suppose . . ."

Dave and Katie could not help but smile at the sheriff's guileful, manipulative ways. "Maybe," Dave answered for both himself and Katie.

Epilogue

*   *   *

Jeremy met Denyse and Katelyn at Mobile's airport. Jeremy and Denyse wrapped their arms around each other and held on. After a minute, Katelyn felt left out and started tugging on their sleeves. Jeremy released his wife and picked up his daughter. "Welcome home, sweetheart. Did you have a good time in Australia?"

Katelyn put her arms around Jeremy's neck and hugged. "I missed you."

"I'm so glad to be home," said Denyse. "That was anything but a vacation."

Jeremy nodded in acknowledgment. "You had a lot to face all by yourself. Next time I'll go to Oz with you."

"Same with you here. I'm not leaving you home alone again."

"You two need each other," said Katelyn.

"And we need you, sweetheart," answered Jeremy. "Ripper missed you, too."

* * *

Jeremy, Denyse, and Katelyn were waiting at Dave and Katie's house when they arrived in the RV. Katie stumbled out and complained, "Denver to Mobile non-stop."

Dave joined her as everybody exchanged hugs. "Yeah. But we spent nine days meandering between San Francisco and Denver. Would you rather have spent part of that time on the prairie?"

"Go on inside," Jeremy suggested. "Denyse and I will unload your bags."

Inside, Old Yeller came running to Katie's voice. She picked him up for a hug. *Rrrow.* "I'm glad to be home. Even the cat's had enough adventure for this summer."

Dave had carried Katelyn inside. He put her down to hold open the door for Denyse and Jeremy carrying their bags. Katie's voice came from the guest bedroom: "Jeremy, why are there black dog hairs on my good white bedspread?"

* * *

Six months later

Ever unconventional, Tara and Jeff held a reception in a local elementary school before their wedding ceremony. Along with his parents, Jeff's riding associates and fellow shop proprietors in Redwood Hills mingled and enjoyed the refreshments. A contingent of teenage Bike and Hike Club

362

members bunched together and jostled each other. The actual ceremony to be conducted by a local minister would be held among some redwood trees a few miles outside town.

Clean-shaven Jeff looked dapper and professional in a nearly new suit Tara had found at a Goodwill store in Silicon Valley. He explained their circumstances to the guests as they arrived. "Tara is like a rock star among backcountry enthusiasts. She's also an amazing entrepreneur. Our business is really taking off. Next week we're moving into a former car dealership on the edge of town. We'll have room for not only bikes, but all sorts of outdoor merchandise. And we'll have rooms for meetings—even a climbing wall. We've already turned the management offices into a home where we can live. Tara and I will take a honeymoon as soon as we can find some time."

Tara stood quietly next to him, leaning to the side slightly in order to balance Sam on her hip. Unaccustomed to such praise, she fidgeted a little. *Jeff honestly thinks I'm terrific,* she acknowledged to herself. At Jeff's insistence, Tara had found a wedding dress—a high-necked, full-length white dress with a plunging back. She had piled up her hair onto her head for the occasion, exposing an elegant neck. After getting ready earlier, she could hardly believe the sophisticated woman looking back at her from the mirror. *This is actually you. You're not playing a role,* she had told herself.

Sheriff Billingsly arrived to congratulate the happy couple. He pulled Tara away to speak to her. "The way you reached out to Missy Clark is pretty special. Darla Solsen tells me you talked Missy into going back into rehab. And you've convinced Missy that she hasn't completely ruined her life."

Tara nodded. "That was your idea, Mike. At first, Missy hated me for lying to her. Then she found out that I care about her and would listen to her without any judgment. I've made plenty of mistakes myself."

"Her mother thinks the rehab will stick this time because Missy has hope for a good life after. Nice work, Ms. Grabowski—soon to be Mrs. Moynihan." The sheriff looked at her with respect for a moment before asking, "Maybe sometimes you'd counsel some repeat offenders or do a little non-dangerous undercover work for me?"

Me trusting and working with the local police? She thought. *Well this one, maybe.* "Sure, Mike. Why not?" she answered and gave him a wry smile.

"I'll call you then, Tara. Thanks." Sheriff Billingsly squeezed her elbow gently and moved on to work the sizeable crowd.

Tara turned to find Dave and Katie waiting to greet her. "Which side of the redwood grove will be the bride's side?" joked Dave.

"Dave and Katie! You came all the way from Alabama?"

"Of course, honey," Katie answered. "Aren't you our quasi daughter? Can I watch Sam while you greet your guests?"

Tara passed her daughter to Katie. "Sure. And thank you for coming. I don't have many friends here. Living on the road the way I used to didn't foster making real friendships."

"You've got one more friend here than you realize." Dave pointed to the school's entrance. There Jeremy stood holding a cute five-year-old girl's hand and looking around the venue. Behind him Tara saw a tall, handsome young woman carrying a baby.

Dave caught Jeremy's eye and waved them over. Jeremy held out his arms to Tara for a hug. Unused to such conventions, Tara acted the part and returned a chaste hug.

"Good to see you again, Tara," said Jeremy. "Mom and Dad told us how you protected them. Thanks!"

Tara could not hold back a few tears. "Thank *you* for coming, Jeremy."

Jeremy turned to his wife and said, "Denyse, I'd like you to meet Tara. The woman who showed me how to become who I wanted to be regardless of what others might think. And the best prom date anybody ever had."

To Tara, Jeremy said, "This is my wife, Denyse; our daughter, Katelyn; and son, David."

"You're a beauty," Tara said to Denyse. "You're the true love Jeremy turned down my invitation to find."

Denyse handed Jeremy the baby and hugged Tara herself. "And from all I hear, you're a corker."

"A corker is a compliment in Aussie speak," Jeremy told Tara.

Tara admired Denyse's infant son. "I hope to get pregnant soon. Is childbirth as bad as I've heard?"

"Believe me, it's worth any amount of discomfort," Denyse answered.

Jeff saw strangers greeting Tara and joined them. Katie started explaining to Jeremy and Denyse about Tara and Jeff's roles in the opioid investigation.

Tara motioned to Dave and stepped away from the group. "Dave, my parents are rather free-spirited. They don't really believe in marriage. They call weddings bourgeois. Although Jeff and I invited them to attend our formal joining, they stayed in Wisconsin."

Dave shrugged. "I'm sorry, Tara."

Tara continued, "But today I'd like a bit of ceremony to remember. Would you be willing to stand in and give me away?"

"I'd be honored."

Author's Note

* * *

All the characters depicted in *Challenge in the Golden State* are purely fictional and from the imagination of the authors. Residents of Sonoma County in California might recognize Armstrong Redwoods State Natural Reserve. Our fictional town of Redwood Hills is very similar to the charming unincorporated community of Guerneville near the park. Not exactly Guerneville, though. Our Redwood Hills is a compilation of several towns including Calistoga in nearby Napa County. Otherwise, locations, science descriptions, and historical backgrounds are as accurate as space and most readers' attentions will allow.

Readers often ask us, "Are Dave and Katie the same as Drew and Kit?" No, we have deliberately tried to make our primary characters different from the authors. However, many of the places visited and experiences of Dave and Katie are described from our first-hand observations and personal experiences.

Although each cat and dog is unique, the behaviors of Old Yeller and Ripper are typical of most. Cats *are* difficult to get out of trees, and Labrador retrievers trail a scent in the manner described.

We first thought we had found a writer's dream source of villains when our research uncovered the mysterious Bohemian Club and their camp in the vicinity of our story. Some sources would denigrate them. Our research and a first-hand interview showed otherwise. We sincerely wish they had been more sinister.

Even before we published the novel *Jeremy's Challenge*—which introduces our colorful character Tara—reviewers and editors expressed interest in a future for her. At Kit's suggestion, Tara was incorporated as a major character in *Challenge in the Golden State*. Readers can meet a younger wit-living and irresponsible Tara as the world-wise con-artist threat to Dave and Katie's son, Jeremy, in *Jeremy's Challenge*.

What is a more than ordinary life?

Each person's life is unique and special. In that sense, there is no such thing as an ordinary life. However, many people yearn for lives more special: excitement, adventure, romance, purpose, character. Our site is dedicated to the premise that any life can be more than ordinary.

At **MoreThanOrdinaryLives.com** you will find:

- inspiring stories
- ideas and resources
- entertaining novels
- free downloads

https://morethanordinarylives.com/

Novels by Kit and Drew Coons

"Challenge for Two has characters that are more than colorful!! The settings from the downtown diner to the mansion are charming. It gave me so much pure reading pleasure. Looking forward to the next adventure with Dave and Katie."

Marnie Rasche

A series of difficult circumstances have forced Dave and Katie Parker into early retirement. Searching for new life and purpose, the Parkers take a wintertime job house sitting an old Victorian mansion. The picturesque river town in southeastern Minnesota is far from the climate and culture of their home near the Alabama Gulf Coast.

But dark secrets sleep in the mansion. A criminal network has ruthlessly intimidated the community since the timber baron era of the 19th century. Residents have been conditioned to look the other way.

The Parkers' questions about local history and clues they discover in the mansion bring an evil past to light and create division in the small community. While some fear the consequences of digging up the truth, others want freedom from crime and justice for victims. Faced with personal threats, the Parkers must decide how to respond for themselves and for the good of the community.

Dave and Katie Parker's only son, Jeremy, is getting married in Australia. Despite initial reservations, the Parkers discover that Denyse is perfect for Jeremy and that she's the daughter they've always wanted. But she brings with her a colorful and largely dysfunctional Aussie family. Again Dave and Katie are fish out of water as they try to relate to a boisterous clan in a culture very different from their home in south Alabama.

After the wedding, Denyse feels heartbroken that her younger brother, Trevor, did not attend. Details emerge that lead Denyse to believe her brother may be in trouble. Impressed by his parents' sleuthing experience in Minnesota, Jeremy volunteers them to locate Trevor. Their search leads them on an adventure through Australia and New Zealand.

Others are also searching for Trevor, with far more sinister intentions. With a talent for irresponsible chicanery inherited from his family, Trevor has left a trail of trouble in his wake.

"Adventure finds Dave and Katie even at home. Mobile and the Gulf Coast are the sultry setting for the couples' latest foray into a world of corruption, extortion, and racial tension. Thick southern charm and potential financial ruin swirl about them as they strive to serve those they love. A fast-paced and engaging story with colorful characters. A great read!" Leslie Mercer

Dave and Katie Parker regret that their only child Jeremy, his Australian wife Denyse, and their infant daughter live on the opposite side of the world. Unexpectedly, Jeremy calls to ask his father's help finding an accounting job in the US. The Parkers risk their financial security by purchasing full ownership of the struggling firm to make a place for Jeremy.

Denyse finds south Alabama fascinating compared to her native Australia. She quickly resumes her passion for teaching inner-city teenagers. Invited by Katie, other colorful guests arrive from Australia and Minnesota to experience Gulf Coast culture. Aided by their guests, Dave and Katie examine their faith after Katie receives discouraging news from her doctors.

Political, financial, and racial tensions have been building in Mobile. Dave and Katie are pulled into a crisis that requires them to rise to a new level of more than ordinary.

"This is the story you'll want your kids and grandkids to read. It's engaging, involves relationships between young men and women, and leads to using good judgement. Adults who have enjoyed the Dave and Katie novels will enjoy learning about their background and travails raising a son."

Who has the bigger challenge—a teenager growing up with old-fashioned parents or parents trying to raise a modern teenager? Before their other exploits, Dave and Katie Parker had the challenge of raising a son—a son with an adventurous spirit. At an early age, Jeremy perceives the ordinariness of his parents' lives and resolves that he can do better.

Disappointment, bullies, alluring girls, peer pressure, and surging hormones combine to challenge Jeremy. His questions—Who do I want to be? What will I do with my life?—remain unanswered. Amid rich deep-South and Cajun-influenced culture, Jeremy explores routes to a future different from the heritage he received. Jeremy's dilemma becomes more complicated as Dave and Katie experience personal problems of their own.

Into the uncertainty of Jeremy's world comes an irresponsible and beguiling older woman. Tara is a vagabond and a practiced con artist. To Jeremy, the street-smart and philosophical woman holds the secret to life. She offers him a path with her to a young man's dreams: adventure, passion, freedom. All Tara asks is that Jeremy bring his college fund with him.

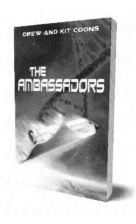

"The Ambassadors combines elements of science fiction and real-life genetics into a story that is smart, witty, and completely unique. Drew and Kit Coons navigate complex issues of humanity in a way that will leave you pondering the implications long after the book is over. If you're ready for a compelling adventure with humor, suspense, and protagonists you can really root for, don't miss out on this one!" Jayna Richardson

Two genetically engineered beings unexpectedly arrive on Earth. Unlike most extraterrestrials depicted in science fiction, the pair is attractive, personable, and telegenic–the perfect talk show guests. They have come to Earth as ambassadors bringing an offer of partnership in a confederation of civilizations. Technological advances are offered as part of the partnership. But humans must learn to cooperate among themselves to join.

Molly, a young reporter, and Paul, a NASA scientist, have each suffered personal tragedy and carry emotional baggage. They are asked to tutor the ambassadors in human ways and to guide them on a worldwide goodwill tour. Molly and Paul observe as the extraterrestrials commit faux pas while experiencing human culture. They struggle trying to define a romance and partnership while dealing with burdens of the past.

However, mankind finds implementing actual change difficult. Clashing value systems and conflicts among subgroups of humanity erupt. Inevitably, rather than face difficult choices, fearmongers in the media start to blame the messengers. Then an uncontrolled biological weapon previously created by a rogue country tips the world into chaos. Molly, Paul, and the others must face complex moral decisions about what being human means and the future of mankind.

Made in the USA
Columbia, SC
26 September 2020